THE ROAD TO THE RIVER

By the same author

THE ANTONOV PROJECT
BANNISTER'S CHART
THE CHALK CIRCLE
DEATH OF A SUPERTANKER
KLEBER'S CONVOY
THE MOONRAKER MUTINY
RUNNING WILD
THE SEA BREAK
SEA FEVER
SMOKE ISLAND
THE SOUKOUR DEADLINE
TOWARDS THE TAMARIND TREES
TWO HOURS TO DARKNESS
THE WHITE SCHOONER
YASHIMOTO'S LAST DIVE
THE ZHUKOV BRIEFING

THE ROAD TO THE RIVER

AND OTHER STORIES

ANTONY TREW

HarperCollins*Publishers*

HarperCollins*Publishers*,
77–85 Fulham Palace Road,
Hammersmith, London W6 8JB

Published by HarperCollins*Publishers* 1992
1 3 5 7 9 10 8 6 4 2

A catalogue record for this book is
available from the British Library

ISBN 0 00 223800 4

Set in Linotron Ehrhardt at The Spartan Press Ltd,
Lymington, Hants

Printed in Great Britain by
HarperCollinsManufacturing Glasgow

Contents

The Road to the River	1
The Lighthouse	10
Fran's Funeral	25
Stopover in Port Said	34
Destination Uncertain	54
Bushveld Shoot	70
Along the Towpath	83
The Cry of the Peacock	94
Nightmare	105
Tea at the Ritz	119
Philemon's Tank	141
Conduct Unbecoming	166

THE ROAD TO THE RIVER

The old man walked slowly down the road, the cardboard box he carried on his head swaying from one side to the other, his long stick flicking the earth at his feet into darts of red dust. Far ahead he saw the line of trees marking the river, dark in the late afternoon. Behind him the storm gathered and heavy black clouds came in from the Lebombos towards the Komati Valley.

He walked stiffly, for his back was painful and he felt the weight of the box. Fearful of the future, he thought about the long years of his life since he had left this place to seek his fortune. To his mother he had been Manuello but to the white people he was Lemon. He did not know where this name came from but it had been his for many years. In the gold mines he had been Hammer because he was strong with the jackhammer at the rockface; and sometimes in the compounds they had called him *Indulamathi* – the giraffe – because he was tall and had a long neck. Then, when he had left the mines after his back had been damaged in a rock-fall underground and he could no longer do that work, he had got a job as a garden-boy at a boarding house in Johannesburg. There the white woman had given him the name of Sixpence because he had asked for sixpence a day boys-meat and she had said it must be only threepence a day. But later this name Lemon had come and stayed and now he could not remember why that name had come to him. It was too far back in the years that had passed.

In his reference book was his native name, Manuello Ndhlovu. Ndhlovu, the elephant, the family name: Manuello from his childhood in Mozambique where he had been born in the years of the Great Queen. He was of the Shangaan tribe which had defected from the Zulus and fled to Portuguese East Africa long before his birth. Fearful of forced labour under the Portuguese, those of his father's kraal had crossed the border into the Transvaal near Ressano Garcia at the turn of the century. With a handful of scrub-cattle they had settled on the banks of the Crocodile River in the district of Komatipoort.

Here at Kubeni in the blistering and malarial heat of the Lowveld his people had begun a new but precarious existence. Huts of saplings, grass and clay were built, and thorn tree *bomas* thrown up to protect the cattle from the lions and other predators of the nearby Sabi game reserve. For Manuello's people the river was the life-force and along its banks they scratched the earth and raised mealies, kaffir corn, groundnuts and wild pumpkin for food. From the kaffir corn they also brewed beer. In time others of the tribe crossed the border into Kubeni; the people made Letsibe their Chief and resigned themselves to the old struggle in the new place.

Manuello spent his boyhood herding the cattle of the tribe in the long grass and thorn and fever trees of the Komati Valley. There he learned much of nature and the Lowveld, but little that was to help him later. When he was twenty the kraal could no longer support him, so with a new blanket from his father to cover his nakedness, and a red handkerchief from his mother for his provender, he set out on the three-hundred-mile walk to the gold mines of the Witwatersrand.

He would work there just long enough, he had planned, to save the money to buy the cattle he must one day give as *lobola* for the girl in Kubeni he wished to marry. Since these cattle would embody the spirits of his ancestors it was little enough that he should go forth and toil for them.

The old man worked methodically at the sink, washing and drying the things from the white people's table as he had washed and dried them for so many of the years of his life. He was tired and afraid, his back ached and his eyes hurt. He thought of the conversation that morning with the white woman and the doctor after they had seen the pictures of his back; pictures taken by another doctor at the hospital with a strange machine.

Manuello knew that this was the great crisis of his life. Soon the bell would ring and they would tell him what he already knew. He did not know what he should do; he knew only that he was old and afraid. If only the others had not gone away, the Wilson people. For them he had worked most of his life; perhaps more than thirty years. For the first ten years after he left Kubeni the work had been in the mines and at the boarding house and, later, in the house of the white woman where the name Lemon had come to him.

The Wilsons had been very good people. He had started with them as garden-boy at two pounds ten a month. Later he was houseboy, then cook/houseboy and afterwards, when they moved to the new house outside Johannesburg, he had the top job as cook. In the big war the man Wilson had gone across the seas and the family had moved to Cape Town; Manuello had gone with them and that train journey of a thousand miles to the south had been his Odyssey; his greatest adventure. There had been three Wilson sons, all born and grown to manhood and matrimony within the period of his service. The Wilsons had been the limits of his world, for them he had worked the best years of his life and they had been good to him.

But the shattering time had come when they said they must go over the seas to live, and they would not come back. They had found him work with the Mencken people in Parkwood, but it was not the same. For the Wilsons he had been cook at twelve pounds a month. Now he was cook/houseboy at eight pounds a month and the work was too much for him. He had struggled for nearly two years but he knew that he had failed. He made too many mistakes, he broke too many things. His back hurt him very much, so that he could not sleep in the nights, and his eyes were failing. The white woman was not pleased with him, he knew, and after he had been sick for the third time she had taken him to the hospital for examination. Now this thing had happened and Manuello trembled for the future. It would be very bad, he knew.

The bell rang. He looked at the telltale board over the sink before walking stiffly down the passage to the sitting-room door. He knocked discreetly, walked in and closed the door behind him. Then he stood submissively, feet together, head and shoulders bowed slightly forward, hands clasped against the middle button of his white coat. The frizzy, tightly curled hair white against the black face.

'Madam wishes to see me?' he asked.

'Yes, Lemon. Lemon, I have told the Master what the doctor said this morning. The Master wants to talk to you about this.'

The white man put down his newspaper; he looked embarrassed and uncomfortable.

'Lemon, it is very bad what the doctor says.'

'Yes, my Master. It is very bad.'

'What are you going to do, Lemon?'

'Master, the doctor has said that I am too old to work. So I must go.'

'It is not just that you are too old, Lemon,' said the white man. 'It is the pain in your back. That is a very bad thing. The doctor says you must rest. What are you going to do?'

'I do not know, Master. But I shall go.'

The white man frowned, scratched imaginary cobwebs from his forehead. 'Madam tells me that your kraal is near Komatipoort. We have discussed the matter. We think you must go there to your own people. They will look after you.'

Manuello was aware that the Menckens knew nothing of his family, his kraal or his people. These things had never been discussed; the white people were not interested and he did not expect them to be. He had worked for them less than two years. With the Wilsons it had been different. They had known everything about him. They knew that he could not read or write; that he had married a girl of the Letsibe tribe and that she had died in Kubeni bearing his fourth child. They knew that his mother had brought up the children while he worked on in Johannesburg, sending most of his wages home to her; that later his parents had died and that he had not returned to Kubeni for many years because his surviving children had left the kraal and disappeared. The Wilsons knew that he had, in the years since, lost touch with the tribe. They knew, too, that he had lived for many years with a woman in the Alexandra native township. She had given him solace and friendship and a place to go on his day off each week. But she had borne him no children and had died many years ago. In all those years he had given her most of his money for she was desperately poor and burdened with her daughter's children.

The Wilsons had known his weaknesses too. His love of gambling, fired in later years by his desire to have something put by for his old age – something that his wages and circumstances had never made possible. The Wilsons knew of his bets on horses that he never saw run; his hopeless preoccupation with the China Game; his simple faith in township lotteries and native 'bankers' who promised to double and treble his money and then unaccountably disappeared. The Wilsons knew that for these reasons he had, in all his long years of toil, saved no money.

But the Menckens knew none of these things and Lemon could not tell them how it was with him now. It was not for them. He knew he must go. He was old, he was ill and he could no longer do work that would please the white people. So to Baas Mencken he had said, 'Yes, my Master. I shall go as you say.'

Then the white woman had explained that in the next week they would be motoring to Lourenço Marques for a holiday and their road would take them by Komatipoort. Lemon was to travel with them and they would drop him near his kraal, so that he could go to his people at Kubeni.

The discussion was at an end. Manuello unclasped his hands, bowed and withdrew with short, backward steps, closing the door behind him. Back in the kitchen he finished washing up the things from the white people's table.

The big American car swept down the blacktopped national road from Nelspruit, through Kaapmuiden and Hectorspruit towards Komatipoort. In mid-afternoon the sun was high and the road shimmered with heat where it stretched out ahead, dividing the foreground of Lowveld grass, thorn trees and farmland into two equal parts. Over the Lebombo hills the clouds were massing; white in the east but dark and ominous in the south. To the left of the road a broken line of trees marked the distant course of the Crocodile River on its journey down to the Indian Ocean.

Manuello sat in the back with the coats and pieces of small luggage which Madam did not want to go in the boot. He could not see far, but the heat and humidity of the Lowveld, and the lush perfumes of grass and bush, clothed his senses like a warm coat and he knew that he was back in the countryside of his youth. But he knew, too, that he came as a stranger, for Kubeni was no longer home. He had been away too long and the ties had been broken too completely. Who there would now wish to see him, or even recognize him? Would they not look the other way? To whom could he go for food and shelter? For a few days, perhaps, some might take pity on him. But then . . . ? Manuello could not answer his thoughts, but he knew that things would be very bad for him. He was too old now. A man of his age must be cared for by his children; but where were his children?

The white woman was not pleased with her husband.

'We're terribly late,' she said. 'I hate keeping Sue and John waiting. When people put you up the least you can do is be punctual. You know we're to dine at the Polana tonight. It really is too bad.'

'I know. I'm sorry. But this trip is on the firm and I couldn't leave Nelspruit without seeing Du Plessis.'

'Well, I think it's most inconsiderate to say the least – especially as it's Sue.'

They drove on in silence for many more miles and the worst of the afternoon heat passed. But the clouds over the Lebombos grew larger and in the south lightning darted against the storm as it came towards the Komati Valley.

The white man turned his head: 'Lemon,' he said, 'we are in your country now. Komatipoort is about five miles ahead.'

Manuello looked about him; it was hard to be sure and he could not see far. It was many years since he had been in this country, many years before the national road had been given its blacktop. But he must answer the white man, so he said, 'Soon we should see a small road to the left, my Master. If we can stop there I can walk to the kraal. It is the road to the river.'

The white man spoke to his wife hesitantly, almost in a whisper: 'Shouldn't we take him to the kraal? That storm is coming up quickly and he has his box. And then his back, you know.'

'Don't be absurd, Geoff. You know what these people are. It may be miles to the kraal and we're already terribly late. We've still got to get through customs. We must hurry or we'll never make LM before dark.'

'Yes, but what about him? Think of him.'

'Oh, he's in his own country now. They'll look after him. There'll be others walking on the road.'

'And his back?'

'Geoff, he's had that for months – don't be emotional.'

'I still think we should take him to the kraal.'

The white woman turned to Manuello, smiled: 'Lemon, you are in your own country now. Your kraal is not far, is it? You'll be all right if we drop you near here, won't you?'

Manuello had heard the white people's conversation and although he had understood little, he sensed that he was now making trouble for them. They had brought him a long way. The train from Johannesburg would have cost him much money; perhaps three pounds. They had saved him that and he must not be a burden to them. Close ahead he saw a dirt road where it came in on the left, the reddish-brown earth bordered by stands of high grass which bent and shivered in the wind. He was not sure but he thought it might be the road to the river because the white man had said they were near to Komatipoort.

'This is the road, my Master,' he said. 'It is not far to the kraal. The Master can stop here.'

The car stopped. Manuello opened the door, took the cardboard box tied with string and pushed it onto the road. In one hand he clutched an old felt hat, in the other a long stick. He climbed out of the car and stood erect by the roadside, the box at his feet, the stick raised in salute.

'Goodbye, Lemon,' the white woman called to him. 'Your people will be glad to see you. They will look after you.' Her voice rose as the car moved away. 'And you must rest – you must rest,' she ended shrilly.

Manuello stood watching the car as it gathered speed and drew away down the long, black highway until it was out of sight. He picked up the box and balanced it on his head, steadying it against the wind with one hand. Slowly he set off down the road, to the river which he knew must be on his left. It could not be too far now to the kraal. He could be there, perhaps, in an hour – perhaps before the storm broke.

The wind-blown grass lining the road was green and lush though powdered with red dust. He walked on slowly, awkwardly, for a mile or so, the wind increasing. The scrub and thorn bushes began to give way to larger trees; to wild fig, euphorbia, lime-green fever trees – *nkelenga* in his language – and many others to remind him of his youth. Behind him the storm came in steadily from the southwest and the noise of distant thunder made him wish he could walk faster. But with the box and his back that was not possible.

As he went Manuello thought about the past. How strangely things had happened since he had been a boy here in this country. He wondered what had gone wrong with his life; how he could have made it otherwise. Now, towards the end of his years, after a lifetime of hard work, he was alone and without hope. The white woman had said that he must go to his people, but he knew that he had no people. Neither here at Kubeni nor in the big city. He belonged nowhere; he was no longer of the tribe and he was not of the city. There was no place for him. He could not understand how it was that these things were so, nor could he understand how he could have made them otherwise.

The dirt road curved and ahead of him, perhaps a mile away, he saw the line of trees that marked the river. Letsibe's kraal could not be far now, perhaps thirty minutes away, he thought. It was hot and dusty and the box on his head had become heavy and made his back hurt. He felt very tired so he sat down on a bank in the shade of a wild fig tree to rest. He must have been dozing for the noise of cattle lowing woke him. There were many of them, fine red Afrikanders, and they stirred up clouds of dust as they passed. Manuello knew that they were the cattle of Europeans and he was puzzled. Not here, surely not here on tribal land, he thought. Behind the cattle walked a young Shangaan wheeling a bicycle and carrying a stick. As he came near he raised the stick in salute. He stopped opposite Manuello where he sat on the bank and stood respectfully by his bicycle waiting for the old man to speak.

Manuello felt that this must be one of his people, one of the tribe. He tried to be calm and matter-of-fact, but he was filled with emotion.

'My son, is it far now to the kraal of Letsibe?' he asked.

The young Shangaan regarded him curiously: 'Letsibe's kraal is not here, old man. It is very far.'

'How far then can it be?'

'It is many days from here.'

'But it was here, I knew it well. It was here by the river.'

'Yes, before it was here.'

'And now . . . ?' The old man's voice trembled.

'For a long time it has been gone, old man. The baas from the Government came and told the people they must move to a new country, because this land by the river was now for the white people. Then Letsibe took his people to the new country the Government gave to them. It is very far – there towards Swaziland.' He pointed with his stick to the southwest, towards the distant mountains. 'It will take you many days to walk there, old man. It is too far.'

Manuello sat silent, stunned and uncomprehending, his mind unable to encompass the shock, the enormity of his disappointment.

The young Shangaan waited for a few moments before climbing onto his bicycle. 'Go carefully, old man,' he called as he pedalled away.

The clouds were overhead now and it had become darker; above Manuello the wind blew with increasing urgency through the leaves of the wild fig as the tree seemed to make itself ready for the storm.

Along the dusty road the Shangaan herdboy had caught up with the cattle and was again walking behind them, pushing his bicycle.

Manuello sat against the trunk of the wild fig tree, his knees drawn up towards his chin. He pulled the crumpled felt hat forward over his eyes, and drew the cardboard box close to his side to shelter it as best he could under the flap of his worn coat.

The first drops of rain came singly and heavy, little red spouts of dust marking where they fell. Steadily they multiplied until the drops became a dark curtain of water. Driven by the rising wind the storm broke and the rain struck like a lash across the Lowveld.

THE LIGHTHOUSE

Beneath the canopy it was all sound and fury, the big seas lifting the life raft on high, tilting it alarmingly on their summits, before hurling it down the long slopes into the troughs below; endless repetition varied only in quantitative terms of sound and movement, the scream of the wind and the thrust of the sea.

There was nothing to be seen, the darkness under the canopy as black and absolute as the storm-ridden night, the two bodies huddled together on the wet, heaving, rubbery floor silenced by the howling of the wind and the violence of movement. The man had tried to put an arm round his wife's shoulders but soon found that he needed both his hands to steady himself on the constantly moving floor.

'It's going to be all right,' he shouted. 'Don't worry.' If there was any reply he could not hear it, so he touched her arm in a gesture of reassurance. There was no response.

The illuminated dial of his watch showed 0237, almost four hours since they'd put the life raft over the side and struggled into it. He'd gone into the sea first, grabbed a lifeline under the canopy entrance and shouted to her to jump. She'd hesitated for long seconds but at last she'd done it and he'd been able to reach out with his free arm and grab the collar of her life jacket. The struggle to survive had given him the animal strength to push her up over the buoyancy chamber into the raft. He had clambered in after her, let go the rope that secured the raft to the sinking ketch, streamed the sea anchor and closed the canopy entrance.

The sea had been moderate then but an hour later the wind backed suddenly to the north and began to blow hard. Before long it had reached gale force, building up big seas. He tried to recall what had happened. It had been so sudden, so totally disastrous. The ketch had been running under jib and reefed mainsail on a westerly course with the wind on the port quarter; he at the wheel, Margaret asleep down below. Though there'd been a good deal of movement the following sea had made things reasonably comfortable.

He had been searching with night-glasses for a pinpoint of light he thought he'd seen broad on the starboard bow when there was a loud bang and the ketch had shuddered violently. He was thrown forward in the cockpit, there was a scream from the cabin below and seconds later Margaret scrambled up the companion ladder.

'Oh God, what's happened, Bob?' she'd shouted hysterically. 'The sea is flooding in below.'

'Inflate that life jacket,' he'd shouted back. 'I'll send a Mayday.' He'd made for the companion hatch, looked down it. The cabin light was flickering but he could see foam-laced water swirling, reaching up the steps of the ladder.

'We'll have to get the life raft over the side,' he'd yelled. 'Lend a hand. Not much time.'

And there hadn't been much time. No time for a Mayday. Soon after they'd drifted clear of the ketch he saw its dim shape disappear and realized she had sunk.

We must have hit something pretty solid, he decided. A water-logged container or the trunk of a big tree. Bows stove in below the waterline.

With his hands he searched in the darkness for the waterproof bag containing flares, compass and other emergency equipment but soon gave up. The wet, heaving floor was too much for him, and Margaret had begun to vomit. Somehow he had to help her. Only God knew how. When daylight came he'd look for the emergency kit. With a twinge of conscience he realized that it was a long time since he'd checked what was in the life raft.

Thank God the paddles are there, he thought. If only this bloody gale would subside. What a shambles this trip has become. Why did I worry about bloody Rockall? Must have been out of my mind. Poor Margaret. It's bad enough for me. What must it be like for her? Will we make it? God knows. At least the gale is blowing us towards Ireland.

That'll mean a lee shore. Pretty disastrous in this weather unless we can find a lee behind one of those little islands which dot the West Coast of Ireland. Mustn't let on to Margaret about a lee shore. I'll say a prayer. Ask God to stop the gale.

Though he hadn't been to church for a long time and had his doubts about God, he prayed; silently but fervently. The end of his prayer coincided with a vicious scream from the wind as the life raft reached the top of a great sea, tilted crazily and shook like a wet dog before beginning the descent down the long, unseen slope into the maelstrom below.

Margaret Ingram coughed, wiped the rime of vomit from her mouth and sobbed in despair. The ghastly thing that was happening was the end. Nothing could save them now.

I know, she thought, that one of these dreadful seas which lifts us so high, throws us so violently down, is going to capsize this awful little rubber raft – Bob and I will drown. It's typical of him to say don't worry, we're going to be all right. He's always madly optimistic about everything. Can't bare to face facts. I warned him about his crazy idea of visiting old wartime haunts, or whatever he calls them. Barra Head, Londonderry, Rockall – the stupidest of them all.

She recalled how he had reacted: 'Those places are an important part of my life, Margaret. Coming on that surfaced U-boat at night, the incredible excitement of it all. And the light at Barra Head winking away in the distance. I've got to see that again, recapture the moment. The fantastic fun and games at Derry. Those gorgeous Wrens. The parties we had. Must see dear old Londonderry again. You'll love it. Lough Foyle, Inishowen, beautiful country. And Rockall – an incredible great rock standing alone far out in the Atlantic. I've told you of the night we picked up survivors close to the rock. The night I dived over the side into that bloody cold water and pulled out that wounded sailor. Remember? I got a mention for that.'

Yes, of course I remembered. How could I forget? Bob has told the story dozens of times. And all the other stories, ad nauseam. But I understood. It must have been a wonderfully exciting time for people like him. But he's no longer an RNVR sub-lieutenant, nor is he twenty-one. He's a commodity broker now, and in his early sixties – like most of his gorgeous Derry Wrens, no doubt.

Oh, God. I'm going to be sick again. All over this wet, horrid, heaving floor . . . ugah . . . uger . . . ugah . . . It's no good. Nothing comes anymore. Just those ghastly retching noises. Oh, God, how much longer? Glad Bob can't see me – it's too dark – and he can't hear me because of the awful noises of this terrifying gale. He tries to hold my hand to comfort me but then he has to snatch it away again to stop toppling over.

When he told me what he'd planned for our autumn cruise I was terrified. Especially about Rockall. I said why go almost two hundred miles from Rothesay, where we keep *Sarka*, way out into the Atlantic, miles from anywhere to shelter if there's bad weather? He laughed, said I always worried too much, always saw the negative side of things. 'You'd enjoy life much more if you thought positively,' he said. If you assumed the best, not the worst. I said I just could not understand why we had to change our autumn holiday routine: the lovely sailing we've always had in the lochs and waters north of Arran and the approaches to the Clyde. Good winds, marvellous scenery, and never far from shelter if the weather turned nasty . . .

An unusually fierce gust of wind shook the life raft, depressed the canopy momentarily, releasing it with an explosive bang, the buffeted little raft twisting sideways until the pull of the sea anchor steadied it once more. She clutched wildly at her husband, missed him in the ebony black of the small compartment, fell sideways across his outstretched legs, her dishevelled head partially submerged in the water which sloshed about the floor of the raft. She felt his arms attempt to lift her as the life raft tipped over the crest of a sea and they rolled across the floor, ending up against the buoyancy chamber. He put his mouth to her ear and shouted, 'Don't worry, old girl. It's going to be all right. With daylight we'll . . . ' The rest of the sentence was lost as a sea lifted the raft and they were thrown back across the heaving floor.

Dawn came soon after five o'clock the next morning, the wind and sea moderating slowly until by noon it was evident that the gale had blown itself out or moved elsewhere. He folded back the flaps over the canopy entrance and for the first time light came into the raft. They could see and talk to each other; she predictably fearful and pessimistic, he, as always, cheerful and optimistic though their appearance and the state of the life raft seemed more in accord with her mood than his, particularly when a frantic search revealed that the bag containing the flares, compass and other emergency gear was missing. The flask of fresh water, the waterproof pack of biscuits and powdered milk, and the first-aid outfit were in the canvas pockets of the buoyancy chambers.

'So the yobs left us something,' he said with a cheerful grin. 'Only wish we had the compass. We'll have to rely on the sun and the stars. Like the early navigators.'

'*If* the sky clears.' The sad tones were husky. 'Could be days before that happens.'

He shook his head. 'It'll clear long before that. I feel it in my bones. We'll be safe and sound in Ireland in a couple of days. Or we'll have been picked up. Let's have some milk and biscuits. Nothing like food to raise the morale.'

The day passed into night uneventfully, the weather improving though the sky remained overcast. He judged wind and sea to be about force 4 which was enough to ensure that life in the raft was still uncomfortable though nothing like as violent as it had been. On two occasions in late afternoon they saw vessels on the distant horizon; fishing boats, he said.

With no compass and an overcast sky, he had no way of knowing from which quarter the wind was coming, nor on what heading they were drifting, and this worried him. Was the wind still blowing them towards Ireland or was it taking them further from the land? He had a rudimentary idea of the tidal streams in the region, based on what they had been in Londonderry and off the coast of South Uist. The prevailing current would, he imagined, still be the Gulf Stream. To what extent these factors would help or hinder his hope that land would show up ahead before too long, he had no idea. He was careful not to mention these problems to Margaret. She was already over-stressed with doubts and fears; to add to them would be disastrous.

His hopes were raised shortly before the onset of darkness that evening when he saw a sector of the distant horizon turn faintly pink – it was, he knew, light from the setting sun behind the overcast.

'Bloody marvellous,' he shouted. 'I can see where the sun is. Must be somewhere between sou'west and sou'west by west. That means the wind is northerly, probably with a bit of west in it. So we're being blown towards the land.'

'Good. But that means a lee shore. That will be dangerous, won't it, Bob?'

'Oh, for God's sake be positive for once, Margaret,' he said wearily, his patience gone. 'Why always think of the worst that can happen?'

'You said that before we left Rothesay. And look what's happened to us.' She was in tears.

He looked at her and felt suddenly guilty. Her hair hung about her face like tattered strands of seaweed, through which her nose shone moistly, a bruised cherry between darkly circled eyes. She was no longer young and he had bullied her into coming with him, knowing she hated being left alone in their house in the country. She was fearful of burglary and rape, a fear fed by the horrible experiences of her friend Edith, a distant neighbour, only a few months earlier. He knew, too, that he'd been selfish and foolhardy in venturing so far afield with only Margaret as crew, not that more crew would necessarily have prevented the disaster. In spite of the inevitable upsets and bickerings of matrimony they were deeply attached to one another.

'I'm sorry, old girl,' he said contritely. 'My fault that all this has happened. But don't worry. We're over the worst and we'll be on dry land before long.' Of that he was by no means certain but he was optimistic as always and he remained cheerful.

The night was as uneventful as it was uncomfortable. They saw a distant light but without flares there was nothing they could do and it had soon disappeared. Sheer exhaustion gave them uneasy sleep, broken by his efforts to ensure that one of them was always awake keeping watch at the canopy opening. Another day followed, the wind still blowing freshly from what he took to be a little west of north. In early afternoon the sky began to clear and soon the sun shone brightly, glinting upon the sea in flashing lines of gold. It also lit up the dark and watery interior of the life raft and lifted the spirits of its occupants.

Not long afterwards he shouted, 'Look, Margaret. There's a lighthouse ahead. It's on a rocky islet. If this wind holds we'll be close to it before long. There must be a jetty or landing stage of some sort in its lee.'

She mumbled a cautious, 'Oh, yes. I can see it,' followed with a sombre, 'We'll never be able to get up that huge rock.'

The lighthouse was, he estimated, only two or three miles away. During the next few hours they drew steadily closer and by the time the sun was low in the west they were, with the aid of paddles, able to manoeuvre the life raft into the lee of the dark jumble of rocks. Now sheltered from the wind they paddled furiously towards the flight of steps which led down to a barely visible landing stage. They reached it and bumped alongside. The concrete jetty, matted with seaweed, stood four or five feet above sea level, and Bob had difficulty in freeing a ringbolt for the raft's painter. That done, he hauled himself up onto the slippery surface. To get Margaret he knelt, seized her hands and pulled her up beside him.

They made their way slowly up the steps, clutching the old and rusted handrail, Margaret leading, he close behind in case she slipped. At the top of the steps they took to an overgrown path which led through the rocks to the summit. There, monstrously tall and sombre against the coppery glow of the western sky, stood the lighthouse, no more than a stone's throw away.

Margaret looked at it in disbelief, laughed happily: '*Voilà mes enfants*. There it is. The lighthouse.' She turned to her husband, threw her arms round him. 'Oh, darling. How marvellous. You are a clever man.'

The nearer they got to the lighthouse the more their minds were filled with doubt. Daylight was fading but there was enough to reveal the structure as weather worn and dilapidated. The glass surround to what should have been the rotating light at the top of the tower was broken in several places, the entrance to the tower at its base was doorless, a faded canvas screen substituting for the missing door.

'Looks as though it's no longer in use,' he said. 'But at least it's on dry land and we're safe here.'

'For how long, Bob? What about food and water?'

'There's still fresh water and biscuits in the life raft. Fishing boats are bound to come by, and the coast looks only a few miles away. We can get there in a couple of hours when wind and sea are right.'

'What? In that awful little life raft. Not for me. I'm staying on dry land.' She shook her head in defiance.

'That life raft saved our lives.' There was anger in his voice and in his tired, inflamed eyes. 'Come on. Let's explore.'

He led the way up the short flight of battered steps and was about to push the canvas screen aside when a voice from behind shouted something. They turned to see the dark shape of a man hurrying towards them, waving his arms. His face was heavily bearded, his hair long and ragged, the old overcoat he wore torn and patched. He carried a shopping bag in one hand and a coiled line in the other.

'What you folks doin' 'ere?' was his hoarse, unfriendly challenge as he reached them.

'Our ketch sank two days ago. Between Londonderry and Rockall. We took to the life raft and the wind blew us here.'

The tramp – for such he appeared to be – examined them with suspicious, piggy red eyes. 'What you stop 'ere for? The shore's only a few miles on. You'd be better off there, mister.'

'We've been at sea for nearly three days in a life raft. Mostly in a gale. Wind and sea are still enough to make landings on a lee shore dangerous – especially in the dark. And we're both exhausted. That's why we're here.'

'Well, more's the pity. There's little enough food for meself. 'Ave to catch what I eat.' Shaking his head, he regarded them uncertainly. 'Suppose I'll 'ave to make the the best of it then.' He came up the steps past them, held the flapping canvas screen aside and beckoned them in. He followed, made fast the screen, and fiddled with matches before lighting a hurricane lamp and hanging it on the wall.

In its flickering light the survivors took stock of their refuge and their host, and derived little comfort from either. The ground floor of the lighthouse was evidently the only habitable part of the decaying structure, its floor of faded red brick badly worn. There was no furniture other than a scatter of wooden and cardboard boxes; soiled blankets on a layer of old newspapers evidently served as a bed. Beside it lay a rucksack, the canvas stained and threadbare. A single-burner stove, reeking of paraffin and antiquity, sat on a wooden box; near it another box served as a kitchen table. A battered iron bucket of water stood against the wall close by. The overwhelming stench in the musty, crumbling space, encircled by inward sloping walls of flaking brick, was that of fried fish.

'Take some newspaper an' sit back t'er wall,' said the tramp, suiting his action to his words.

'Like to get rid of these first.' Bob peeled off his wet oilskins, helped his wife take off the life jacket she was still wearing and then her oilskins.

''Ang 'em on them nails on the walls. They'll dry out slow there,' advised their host.

When they had done that, they shed their soaking deck-shoes and socks, took wads of newspaper and joined him on the floor. The trio sat in silence until the tramp stood up, took a small silvery fish from the shopping bag he'd been carrying and put it on the box beside the burner. 'Catched 'im just afore you come,' he explained. ''Ave to do for the three of us.'

Bob made some sort of apology, explained that they hadn't realized the lighthouse was old and deserted. It was very good of him to share his food with them, they would see that he was well recompensed for his assistance. Perhaps help would come the next day. A passing fishing boat possibly. Or a yacht, cruising like they had been. Perhaps he could suggest something. The shake of the tousled head was emphatic. There was nothing he could do. He had no radio, no boat. Passing ships and fishing boats kept well clear. The new lighthouse, twenty years or so old, was further south, more to seaward. At long intervals a friend came off from the mainland in a dinghy, brought him a few things. ''E was over last week. Won't be comin' a while yet.' He scratched his head. 'Only thing for you folks is that life raft. Soon as the wind drops. Likely in the mornin'. Be ashore quick enough then, you will.'

'Where does your friend in the dinghy come from?' asked Bob.

'From the mainland.'

'What's the name of the place?'

The tramp shook his head. 'Don't rightly know. It's just cottages. Nothin' to it.'

He turned his back on them and began gutting and scaling the fish. Next he lit the burner, turned up the flame, sliced the fish and began frying it in a broken-handled pan which, like the water bucket, appeared to be as old as the lighthouse.

While he cooked the survivors made attempts at conversation but found their host taciturn and suspicious, so little progress was made. However, names were exchanged; he gave his as Jake. Margaret asked where the water in the bucket came from. A tank outside. It took rainwater from the roof, said Jake. After another silence Bob ventured the key question. Why did Jake choose to live in such an outlandish place? There was a long silence during which the question appeared to be under consideration. Eventually Jake turned his head, glared at Bob. 'Because I like it,' was his curt reply. The survivors looked at each other with dubious, questioning eyes which said there had to be another, more sinister reason.

Jake took a bread loaf from a tied plastic bag, potatoes and onions from a cardboard box, and put them in a battered pannikin of water scooped from the bucket with a chipped enamel mug. He worked in silence, the only sounds those of the sea breaking on the rocks, the flapping and banging of the doorway screen and, nearer at hand, the spit and sizzle of the fish frying on the burner.

Evidently satisfied that the fish was done he put the frying pan on the floor and the pannikin of vegetables on the burner. He cleaned the large knife he'd been using with a scrap of newspaper and slid it into the sheath on his belt. He pointed to the fish in the pan. 'I'll be warmin' 'im when the vegs are done. It's slow cookin' on the burner.' This observation was followed by several loud bangs from the canvas screen. 'Winds comin' stronger again,' he said. He went to the screen, lifted it and went outside. They heard him going down the steps.

Margaret looked at her husband with troubled eyes. 'So, what d'you make of it? He's most odd. Frightens me. Why is he hiding himself away in this godforsaken place?'

'Look Margaret, he's a tramp, living the life of a recluse the only way he can afford. That doesn't make him a criminal. There are many people who prefer that sort of life. Why not him?' He shrugged. 'Anyway, it's a lot better being here than in a life raft out there.' He jerked his head towards the banging screen through which came the sounds of wind and sea. 'I doubt if we'd have made it through this night on a lee shore.'

She clasped her arms across her breasts and shivered. 'We've no blankets, no pillows, nothing. There's nowhere to wash, no loo. We'll have to sleep on the floor. It's terribly grim, Bob.'

'Not too good. But at least we're alive. And it's only for a few days at most. If it wasn't blowing so hard, and such a climb up, I'd ask him to give me a hand bringing the raft up here. We could use it as a bed and get some privacy.'

'It's full of water, terribly wet.'

'I suppose so. Better to forget it, perhaps. He doesn't seem too enthusiastic about us. He may thaw by tomorrow.' Bob laughed. 'Get used to the idea of visitors.'

Before she could reply the canvas screen was pushed aside and the man they were discussing came in, fastened the flap, turned and stared at them in silence. In the uncertain light of the hurricane lamp the bearded, ghoulish face, the sunken red eyes, pitted skin, gappy stained teeth and long tousled hair suggested unfathomable evil to Margaret – to her husband, the scars of a hard life.

'You'll be losin' that life raft come 'igh tide. Best to 'aul it 'igher.' Jake took a torch from where it hung from a nail on the wall. 'You come along, squire. It'll take the two of us with this wind.'

Margaret got to her feet. 'Shall I come too?'

Jake shook his head. 'Not you,' he said gruffly.

The two men went out into the night, the sound of their footsteps soon lost to the roar of wind and sea. Margaret, nervous, cold and miserable, wandered about the small space swinging her arms and slapping her chest like a policeman on the beat. She rearranged the oilskins and her life jacket on the nails from which they hung, spreading them more evenly on the crumbling wall. She examined the vegetables in the pannikin, decided they were far from ready. She looked round disconsolately, moved over to the pile of old newspapers and paged idly through the top copy. She had stopped at an inner page, was fighting off a desire to scream, when she heard footsteps. Moments later Jake came in, alone. Saying nothing, ignoring her, he extended his arms, shook himself like a duck, and went over to the single burner.

Margaret Ingram was speechless. She'd just read the headline, *MAN WANTED FOR MURDER* and, in the dim, flickering light of the hurricane lamp, seen beneath it the Identikit picture. The notable features of the heavily bearded face were much the same as Jake's.

Controlling her voice with difficulty she asked what had happened to her husband.

Jake ignored her, went over to the single burner, turned up its flame and stirred the vegetables with his sheath knife. ''Appened?' he mimicked. 'Now't 'as 'appened.'

'What's he doing then? Why didn't he come back with you?' Her voice trembled with fear.

Jake continued to stir the vegetables, the long steel blade of the sheath knife reflecting the light from the hurricane lamp.

'Veg's comin' on good,' he said over his shoulder. 'Now as to yer 'usband. Well, I don't rightly know. Could be in for a surprise, I daresay.'

She huddled against the wall. Something terrible had happened to Bob, something ghastly was going to happen to her. There was menace, threat, terror in what had just been said. She shivered, felt her teeth chatter. Even Bob the optimist had said that Jake was not enthusiastic about having them there. Of course he wasn't. He was wanted for murder and this was his hide-out. He knew that if they got back to the mainland they'd go to the police. He'd killed Bob, murdered him. She'd be next. But first he'd . . . She tried not to face the thought, but obviously that was coming. Why else hadn't he already murdered her, instead of going on with the cooking as if nothing had happened? It was going to be like what happened to Edith. Now she, Margaret, was at the mercy of this evil, sullen brute who either ignored her questions or gave hoarse, disingenuous replies.

Unspeakable things would happen before the night was out. What could she do? She was utterly helpless. Oh, God, why had Bob risked going out into the night with such an obviously evil man? And now Bob was dead. Once again she fought down a desire to scream. She mustn't allow this vicious brute to know she was terrified, that she knew who he was. It could only make things more horrible. If only Bob had seen that old newspaper report – strong and resourceful, he would have been more than a match for this wicked man.

Her fears about Jake were soon confirmed. Turning from the burner he looked at her, gave her a lop-sided grin. 'Veg's done. I'll be warmin' up the fish now. Not much of it.' He wiped his mouth with his fingers. 'Didn't know I'd 'ave a lady for supper.' A smirk creased the unpleasant face. 'Could 'ave done with a fine lobster I reckon.' He coughed; a hoarse, throaty bronchial cough. 'Anywise, there's summat else we'll be 'avin'.' She shrunk from the suggestive stare. 'Charlie brought over some grog last time. Ain't opened yet. Been waitin' for a special occasion. Like as now.' He cackled quietly, as if to himself. 'A wee drop won't do nobody no 'arm, lady. Makes folks more friendly like.' He cackled again. 'Loosens tongues.'

Oh God, she thought. He really is evil. He was stooping over the single burner again, his back to her. She wondered desperately what she could do. Make a dash for the canvas screen, hide somewhere among the rocks in the dark? Hopeless. He'd catch her while she was unfastening the screen, or find her when daylight came. Perhaps she could escape in the life raft? Jake would find her long before she could get down to it. She'd have to wait until he attacked her, then fight for her life. She sat down, back to the wall, exhausted by despair but determined not to give way to her emotions. Her eyes searched left and right, her body motionless for fear of alerting Jake, as she looked for a weapon, any weapon. But it was hopeless. There was just nothing.

I'll have to use my fists and teeth and hit and kick and scream, and fight and struggle madly, she thought – my nails are sharp and strong . . .

As her thoughts darted about the corridors of hysteria she saw him put the sheath knife on the box beside the burner. Next he took a strip of newspaper, folded it into a pad and set about taking the pannikin off the burner. She supposed he would put the pannikin on the floor, and transfer the frying pan to the burner to heat the fish. He was bending over the burner, his back towards her, the sheath knife still on the box.

She concentrated on the knife as if it were a living thing – the knife he used for every purpose: cleaning the fish, slicing the bread, turning the fish in the frying pan, stirring the vegetables in the pannikin. A knife for . . . When he left the lighthouse with Bob it was in the sheath on Jake's belt. She shuddered, pushed the horror away. I'll go mad if I think of that, she told herself.

But the knife . . . ? She realized that it was now only a matter of seconds. She braced herself, moved her legs slowly to a position from which she could spring to her feet. The knife was ten or twelve feet from her. Jake had lifted the pannikin from the stove with his right hand and stooped to the right as he put it on the floor. He stood up, the frying pan in his right hand, and turned back to the burner. *Now*, she decided. Pushing her hands against the brick floor, her back against the wall, she raised herself to her knees, straightened up until she was standing, then launched herself forward, her right arm extended towards the knife. As her hand seized it Jake turned to face her, the sunken red eyes staring.

She was about to leap, the knife held high for stabbing, when a voice from the doorway shouted, 'For God's sake, Margaret. What's going on?'

She dropped the knife, rushed towards the canvas screen where he stood. 'Oh, Bob. Thank God you've come.' Sobbing, she threw her arms about his neck. 'I thought you were dead.'

'Dead? For God's sake, why should I be dead? I've been gone for less than half an hour.' He explained that while they were hauling the life raft up onto the rocks above the landing steps Jake had told him there wasn't really enough fish for three people. He said it wasn't too difficult to catch a lobster by torchlight.

'He took me down to a rock pool not far from the landing steps – that's on the lee side, of course – and showed me the drill. You shine the torch into the pool, the lobster comes out to see what it's all about and you scoop him out with a piece of wire, its end bent into the shape of a hook. No lobster showed up and Jake said it was the weather. I said I'd like to have a shot. He said okay, he'd come back here and get on with the cooking. Nothing happened at first, then a big lobster came up and I scooped with the wire. But he was too quick for me. I tried again after that but he wasn't having any more. I'll try again tomorrow night. It's great fun,' he chuckled.

'I'm sure it is fun.' With her fingers she wiped tears from her eyes. 'But Jake didn't tell me all that and I thought . . . ' She stopped, looked miserable, wiped at the tears again.

'But what on earth were you doing with that knife, Margaret?'

'I slipped when I was passing it to Jake. I'd taken it from there.' She pointed to the box beside the burner. 'To cut off a loose thread on my jersey. I was trying to give it back to him for turning the fish.'

Bob laughed with relief. 'Looked more as though you were trying to kill him.'

'I told you, I slipped. Had to raise my arm to regain my balance. *Of course* I wasn't trying to kill him. What a silly thing to say. Wasn't it, Jake?' She smiled at him.

He continued to stare at her with puzzled eyes. 'Was it?' he said, turning back to the burner. 'Only you know, lady.'

FRAN'S FUNERAL

Driving along the top of the downs in a remote part of Surrey I was reminded how beautiful the countryside could be in the vivid colours of autumn. I had not been in Surrey, indeed in England, for rather more than thirty years and although this brief business visit allowed little time for sight-seeing, I was using a few free days for what was, I suppose, a sentimental journey. A short leave with friends in Surrey during 1943 had left me with the happiest of memories. Although they had moved to Canada some years earlier I was determined to revisit Surrey, and had already spent two pleasant days exploring that attractive county; now, on the afternoon of this fourth day I was, somewhat unexpectedly, on my way to a funeral.

The day before, a notice in a local newspaper had jolted my thoughts back to Scotland, in particular to the beautiful country around the mouth of the Clyde – country I'd known a good deal better than Surrey – and which I would certainly have visited given more time. The funeral of Frances (Fran) Leigh Huntington would, said the notice, take place at St Mary's Church, Merrifield Down, on Wednesday, 25 September at 3 p.m. In a brief tribute to Miss Leigh Huntington's life and good works it recorded that she had served in the WRNS during the Second World War.

So Fran was dead and she had not married. That funeral notice had induced in me a sombre mood, a sense of guilt tempered by a feeling that I had been short-changed by circumstance – illogically, as it happened, for memory soon reminded me that I'd done nothing to keep the relationship alive when I returned to South Africa after the war. Indeed, nagged memory, I had broken a promise; I remembered that last night at dinner in the Bay Hotel in Gourock. 'I'll write as soon as I have a settled address,' I'd said. But for one reason or another I had put off writing; partly, I suppose, it was the excitement of getting back to the Cape, of once again being with my parents and friends, of beginning a new life as a mature student at Cape Town University – and then, in no time, I'd fallen in love with Sarah, my future wife. The longer I delayed writing to Fran the more difficult it became to think of a plausible excuse – in fact there just wasn't one. So, in cowardly fashion of which I was mortally ashamed, I broke my promise. For years my conscience troubled me. I had of course thought of Fran, but though inevitably at increasingly long intervals, I'd never forgotten her. Our relationship had been too close for that; two young people caught up in a wartime romance; one which had flared marvellously during the brief periods when my ship returned to our base on the Clyde, only to flag miserably when the exigencies of war took us to sea again. Always prone to jealousy, I used to wonder then if others took my place.

As time passed, my recollections of Fran and our times together receded until in recent years they were all but lost in the mistier recesses of my mind. For some time I had tried to salve my conscience by attributing my failure to keep in touch with her to the fickleness of youth, to distance and circumstance. She was twenty-one and I twenty-three when we'd said goodbye in Gourock; Scotland and the Cape were six thousand miles apart, and not long after I got back I'd met Sarah. I chose to assume that Fran was probably doing much the same sort of things with her life, that she was probably grateful I'd not kept in touch. These assumptions were, of course, a spurious attempt on my part to excuse the inexcusable. In this they failed lamentably.

My thoughts shifted to the extraordinary set of circumstances which had led to this journey to her funeral. If the car I'd hired had not broken down, delaying me for a day in Guildford, if I'd not during that day gone to The Wellington Arms for lunch, if in a moment of boredom I'd not glanced through the pages of the *Surrey Herald*, if the name Frances (Fran) Leigh Huntington had not caught my inattentive eye, then, but for all those ifs, I would most certainly not have been on my way to her funeral. Why was I going? Mostly, I suppose, because I knew no one in Guildford and had nothing else in particular to do that day, possibly because I might just chance to find an old naval friend there, perhaps someone who had been a Wren with Fran in Greenock. Behind this façade there was, however, a more compelling reason. She had been very important to me, the woman of my first real love affair, and I had not only broken a solemn promise but shamelessly let her down. By attending her funeral I was trying to come to terms with my conscience.

The road I was following turned and twisted through woodland, branches arching over the road, leafy canopies of gold, ochre and magenta, and for a moment the breathless beauty of an autumn day stilled my thoughts. But soon pictures of our times together once again flashed on the screen of my mind like a family slide show, some held for longer than others. Despite the thirty years, I often felt I could hear what we were saying to each other, almost as if the pictures had been dubbed with sound. These mental pictures covered a wide spectrum: parties at the Wrennery in Greenock, parties on board my ship, picnics *à deux* in the lovely country around the lower reaches of the Clyde, cycling to Largs on a burning summer's day, by ferry to Rothesay for a long walk to tea with cream-scones and strawberry jam at the end of it, a weekend with Fran at Windermere, climbing the fells overlooking the lake. So many pictures, so many memories, refreshed now by the immediacy of her funeral.

The sign for Merrifield Down showed up sooner than I had expected. I began the descent and not long afterwards another sign appeared – St Mary's Church. I turned into the lane and followed it down until, quite suddenly, the church appeared. It was old, small and beautiful, set in a frame of oaks, beeches and conifers, the surround of weather-worn gravestones, some broken or leaning awkwardly, completing what might have been a Constable picture had it not been so infinitely more compelling.

There were a number of cars parked outside the churchyard, among them a black Daimler hearse. I parked not far from it and joined the small file of mourners heading for the church. Following them through the oak doorway, cracked and grey with age, I made my way to a pew towards the back of the aisle, my entry attracting sidelong glances from several elderly ladies already seated there: checking my credentials, I thought as I knelt to pray.

When I'd finished I looked towards the altar and saw the flower-draped coffin in the chancel. It was difficult to imagine the vibrant, attractive young woman I had known lying in that coffin, and I had to remind myself that she must have been in her late fifties when she died. Somehow I could not visualize Fran at that age. In the pew reserved for family there were a middle-aged couple, two younger couples – three small children between them – and a grey-haired man. Since they all had their backs towards me I was none the wiser. I looked at those in the other pews. There were perhaps thirty or forty mourners, mostly ladies in old or late middle age, and I found this depressing. The Fran I had known surely deserved younger people. Again I had to remind myself that I was approaching sixty and we had been of much the same age.

I wondered who the people in the family pew were. It was weird to be such a stranger, to have come six thousand miles to this attractive little country church, so lovingly decorated with flowers, so quiet and peaceful, so used to baptisms, confirmations, marriages and funerals, so old and worn yet so much a testimony to a remarkable island race; the last thought triggered by a plaque on the stone wall to my left. It was inscribed, *To the Sacred Memory of Lord Charles Laverton, Marquess of Badham, a Vice-Admiral of the White in the Navy of Great Britain, died of wounds in a sea battle off Corsica, July 27th in the Year of Our Lord 1753.*

As the service progressed I became immersed in it, feeling that this was an act of homage which Fran would have appreciated could she but have known, and I sang the hymns with a gusto reminiscent of services on the messdecks of the destroyer in which I had served. But soon my mind began to drift, and I found myself wondering about Fran's life. Had it been a happy one? Why had a woman so attractive not married? Had there been lovers? To whom had she left her money, if she'd had any? Nephews and nieces and charities she'd worked for, I supposed.

The vicar, a tall, stooped man with an aesthetic face and pale eyes behind steel-rimmed spectacles, was delivering an eulogy; Frances Leigh Huntington had worked unremittingly for many charities and had, in particular, done a great deal for St Mary's Church. She had been a supremely kind and caring person, her shoulder always ready for those in need to lean upon. Fran was, he said, an exemplary character, there were all too few like her in this modern world, and Merrifield Down was all the poorer for her passing.

The service was coming to a close. The vicar announced that there would be a brief committal at the crematorium at which only family would be present, but it was hoped that Fran's many friends would go on to High Pines where Sir John would be awaiting them. There was a final prayer, the mourners rose to their feet and the organist played them out. The grey skies of early afternoon had given way to one of blue dappled with fleece-like clouds when I joined the slow-moving line of mourners, at its head the middle-aged couple from the family pew. I was wondering what I should say when my turn came and, having decided on something which seemed appropriate, I encountered a problem: what relationship did the couple bear to Fran? Were they Leigh Huntingtons? She used to speak of a brother and sister. Was it they? And who was Sir John? Lowering my voice I asked the matronly lady immediately behind me who they were. She looked surprised. 'Oh, you mean Fresca and Mathew Hartley. Such darlings, and so sad. They were devoted to her, you know.'

So was I, I thought. But a long time ago.

The couple ahead of me reached the Hartleys, spoke to them quietly for a few moments before moving on. I took their place, introduced myself. I was, I explained, on a brief visit from South Africa; I had seen the notice of Fran's funeral in a local paper the day before. I had met her during the war. 'We asked a number of Wrens to a wardroom party and your . . . ' Still uncertain of the relationship, I hesitated.

'Sister,' prompted Mrs Hartley, frowning as she shook my hand.

'Oh, yes,' I nodded. 'I see the resemblance. We met again after that, at long intervals, when my ship was in harbour.' I'm being too talkative, I told myself, holding up the line.

'It was good of you to come. After all those years. She would have been touched.'

'It's a sad occasion. You must . . . ' I shrugged, left the sentence unfinished. Mathew Hartley was holding out his hand to the couple behind me.

'I do hope you'll come back to High Pines for tea,' Mrs Hartley smiled. 'John will be going straight there. We'll follow later. We must have a little talk. A wartime friend of Fran's is so welcome. John's car is that black Mercedes.' She pointed. 'Next to the hearse. Just follow it.'

'Thank you – yes, thank you. I'd like to,' I said, feeling that I could hardly refuse; and in any event it would help pass what remained of the afternoon.

The drawing-room at High Pines looked out over terraced lawns and through a woodland vista to fields where cattle grazed. The lawns looked overdue for cutting, and the herbaceous borders somewhat neglected, too many weeds and too many old blooms in need of deadheading, notwithstanding that it was autumn. It must have been a beautiful garden in the days when gardeners earned a pittance, but nowadays . . .

A tall, grey-haired, military-looking man came up to me. 'Looking after you are they, old man?' he asked. 'I see you've got a drink. Sound choice. Safer than tea. Don't think we've met. I'm Fran's brother. John Huntington.' We shook hands.

'I'm Robert Bennet from Cape Town. Over here on a visit. I met Fran during the war. We were both in the navy. Very sad that she's gone. I saw the funeral notice in the *Surrey Herald* yesterday.'

'Good of you to have come. Fran would have been pleased.'

A man with apple-red cheeks beneath wild white hair joined us. 'Hullo, Sam,' said the tall man.

'Ah, Sir John. A sad day indeed.'

'Yes, yes. A great loss. But we all have to go sometime. Trouble is the best ones often go first. You've got a drink, I see.' He indicated me with a sweep of his hand. 'This is Robert Bennet from Cape Town. And this,' he inclined his head towards the man with apple-red cheeks, 'is Sam Moulton. He farms my land. Makes a better job of it than I could.' I shook hands with Sam Moulton. Sir John excused himself. When he'd gone we discussed farming, the weather, and were embarking on the news when Mrs Hartley appeared from nowhere. 'Now, Sam, you've had your turn. I want to ask Mr Bennet all sorts of questions about South Africa. Mrs Whitlock is dying to pick your brains. She has a problem with her sheep. She's over there. By the fireplace.' Sam grinned. 'That's an order is it, Mrs Hartley?'

'Oh, yes. Absolutely. Off you go.' She watched him go before turning back to me. 'Now Mr Bennet, you said, I think, that you knew Fran during the war. Tell me all about it, and do call me Fresca. Incidentally, what do your friends call you?'

'Bob, most of the time.'

'Then I shall call you Bob.'

'Please do. There's not much to tell, I'm afraid. My ship was based on the Clyde and Fran was at Bellaire, the Wrennery in Greenock. We met at a party in our wardroom. A number of Bellaire Wrens came to it. In due course we were invited to a party there. Fran and I met several times after that when my ship got back to the Clyde for boiler-cleans and refits. The Bellaire Wrens used to join us for picnics and cycling expeditions.'

'I see.' There was a hint of amusement in Mrs Hartley's brown eyes. 'So it wasn't a wartime romance?'

'Oh no. Nothing like that,' I protested. 'We didn't really know each other all that well. It was just a pleasant friendship. The sort of thing that happened during the war.'

'Well, well.' Mrs Hartley's expression changed from amusement to challenge. 'If you're nothing else, Benjy Bennet, you are certainly a most accomplished liar.' She had lowered her voice.

I stared at her in amazement. 'You . . . you called me Benjy.'

'So I did.'

'But . . . I mean . . . why?' I was astonished. Had Fran told her about me and if so how much had she told? The hard look in Mrs Hartley's eyes was not reassuring.

'Because it was what I always called you, Robert Benjamin Bennet.' The stern look gave way to a dazzling smile. 'Though you didn't like it at first, did you?'

'When? What d'you mean? I'm afraid I don't understand.' Nor did I understand. On the contrary I was utterly baffled.

'*When*? My dear Benjy.' She looked at me sadly, slowly shaking her head. 'At parties in your ship and at Bellaire. On our cycling trips and picnics *à deux*, and of course on occasions like the weekend at

Windermere. I know it was all a long time ago, Benjy, but surely you haven't forgotten?'

Puzzled, embarrassed, I put a hand to my forehead, half turned away. 'Good heavens,' I stuttered. 'You can't be . . . This is crazy . . . You can't be Fran? I mean, Fran's funeral? Your sister is Fran? You are Fresca? This is totally absurd.' I faced her again.

Mrs Hartley drew a deep breath. 'No, it's not totally absurd. Poor Benjy. I shouldn't have done this to you, should I? Obviously you didn't recognize me. Oh well, thirty years is a long time. And I'm afraid you don't look much like you did in those days.' She glanced round the room. 'I suppose I had better explain – and I'll have to be quick. Mustn't neglect my other guests. My sister and I were twins. Our parents had always said that if it was a boy it would be Francis, if it was a girl Frances. My grandmother was Frances and they both loved her dearly. So when twin girls arrived there was a problem. They solved it by calling my sister Frances, she actually popped out first, and I became Francesca. They made life easier for us by calling Frances Fran, and me Fresca. When I joined the Wrens and gave my name as Francesca, they called me Fran. My sister, Frances, was also a Wren, but she was in Portsmouth and I was in Scotland so there was no confusion.'

Now more amazed than puzzled, I said, 'This is unbelievable . . . ' I shook my head in bewilderment. 'Now I know why I saw the resemblance. Oh, Fran. I'm so pleased to see you again but I'm . . . I don't know what to say really.' I spread my hands in a gesture of despair. 'I'm terribly embarrassed. I behaved so badly.'

For a moment her brown eyes signalled disapproval. 'Yes, you did, Benjy. I was so unhappy at the time. Waiting and waiting for a letter which never came. It was terribly hurtful. I worried about you, thought something awful might have happened. But I had no address, no means of getting in touch. Yet I felt I must wait, although there were other men who seemed interested in me.'

'What can I say?' I hoped I looked and sounded as abject as I felt. 'I behaved abominably. I couldn't be more ashamed. It was a rotten thing to do.'

She laughed in an embarrassed way. 'But it doesn't matter now. I married Mathew a few years later. He's a marvellous man. Incredibly kind and considerate. We have two fine sons. They've both done well and married nice women who've given us three adorable grandchildren. You may have seen them in the church. They're over there. By the piano.'

She looked at me again with the keen penetrating glance I remembered so well. 'There wouldn't have been all these wonderful people in my life if you'd not let me down, nor the lovely life they've given me. So please don't feel guilty. We were very young, it was wartime and our . . . ' She hesitated, looked away, almost whispered. 'So it was all very natural at the time . . . in those circumstances.' She touched my arm and there was affection in the gesture and in those brown eyes. 'So thank you, Benjy, for letting me down. Now come and talk to Mathew and mind you keep on telling those appalling lies.'

STOPOVER IN PORT SAID

The wind, the *khamsin*, came out of Africa, cold and blustering, whipping the Mediterranean into short seas and ruffling their crests like old lace. Bows plunging, the ship lurched on her course for Port Said, wearily for she was old and had come a long way. An intruder, caught between sun and sky, she was out of place, the hulk of rusted steel, smoke issuing from its stack, its sides and upper-works glistening with spray thrown up by the bows, jarring the harmony of cloud, sun and water.

So wrote the author of an article in a magazine I had read while waiting to see my dentist. It dealt with the journey he had made from Istanbul to Port Said in a ship called *Chanticleer*, and his account so fired my imagination that I determined to follow his example. For this there were two good reasons: I love ships, real ships not five-star floating hotels, and this sounded like a real ship, and I had romantic memories of Port Said, last visited by me when a young man serving in the Royal Navy in the Second World War. Now a retired bachelor with adequate means and time to spare, I was fortunate in being able to exploit this whim. My local travel agent succeeded, after some difficulty, in getting me a leaflet from *Chanticleer*'s owners. It was encouraging: *Twelve thousand tons deadweight . . . this fine cargo-passenger ship offers spacious accommodation for twelve passengers . . . international cuisine . . . amenities include promenade deck, library, deck games . . . music and daily news sheets.* The ship would again be in Istanbul in January reported the agent.

In more modest terms the leaflet described the vessel as a twin-screw, oil-burning steamship, service speed 16 knots, registered at

Lloyds, with scheduled sailings details of which could be obtained through principal travel agents.

On other matters of some concern, mostly gleaned by me from Rufus Sprott – about whom more later – the leaflet was silent: for example, it did not explain why this Hong Kong-owned ship was registered in Panama; nor did it, indeed it scarcely could, mention the long haul which lay behind her when she arrived in Istanbul where I embarked: from Balboa, her port of registration, clear across the Pacific to Manila with calls en route at the Marquesas and Solomon Islands. Then, following an unseen trail, *Chanticleer* had steamed on for, owners' leaflet notwithstanding, this roving ship knew no scheduled sailings and went where cargo offered, without much regard, hinted Mr Sprott, to its nature or origin but with freight rates adjusted to the exigencies of either.

Thus, he told me, she tramped from port to port; loading here, discharging there; embarking a few venturesome souls as passengers in one place, putting them down in another, her accommodation rarely filled, for in spite of cheap fares there were few takers beyond itinerant missionaries, journalists, wrestlers, variety artists, distressed seamen and others obliged, or minded like me, to travel in so aged and unfashionable a ship.

But I have gone ahead of events and must return to Istanbul where I joined *Chanticleer*. It was late afternoon when a motor-launch took us off to where she lay at anchor in the Bosphorus; a drab, scruffy ship, deeply loaded, in dire need of paint and smelling like an oil refinery. There were others in the launch, passengers I presumed but for two nuns who I thought might be visitors to the ship which was to sail early next morning. I had arrived in Istanbul a few hours earlier after an uneventful flight from Heathrow.

As we drew near *Chanticleer* our Turkish coxswain put the engine astern, the launch drifted up to the gangway, a Chinese seaman helped us onto it and we climbed up to the iron deck where another Chinaman directed us to a companion-ladder which served the deck above, thence into an alleyway which led to a saloon where a rheumy-eyed man with tousled red hair and a barrel-like body sat at a table, clipboard in front of him, cigarette in mouth, ballpoint in hand and, for good measure, a pencil behind his ear. He was, I learnt, Rufus Sprott, purser, chief steward and medicine man. He was wearing a blue uniform reefer, unbuttoned and so revealing a crumpled shirt of much the same off-white hue as the faded paintwork of the dining-saloon. I was at the end of our small queue and thus well placed to observe my fellow passengers, the first to join for this voyage to Shanghai by way of the Suez Canal, Bombay, Singapore and Hong Kong. It seems *Chanticleer* had been lying in Odessa for two weeks loading agricultural machinery, most of it destined for China. All this I subsequently learnt from Rufus Sprott.

Our queue was headed by an athletic-looking man, tall, ramrod straight, with crew-cut hair on a well-shaped head. In the launch I had noticed that he wore a West Point fraternity ring. I was not surprised. He looked very much the magazine illustrator's idea of a US army officer.

'Name?' asked Rufus Sprott, without looking up.

'Maddison. Gary Garfield Maddison,' said the West Pointer. The deep voice, the firm incisive tone, evidently impressed Sprott for he lifted his head to see whence it had come before again focusing on the clipboard.

'Right. Your passport and ticket voucher, Mr Maddison.'

The West Pointer handed them over, Sprott examined them, looked at his list, placed a tick against a name, impaled the ticket voucher on a spike and put the passport in a filing basket. 'You get that back when you disembark in Hong Kong.' He coughed bronchially. 'Or earlier if you want to go ashore at ports of call. You're in Cabin number 3. Next please.'

Next was a small dark man with black, collar-length hair. In the launch he'd worn a wide-brimmed black hat but his face was now visible: deeply lined, hollow cheeked, with heavily shadowed jowls. His large eyes protruded and swivelled like a chameleon's. The purser went through his routine much in the manner of a desk sergeant committing an offender to the cells. In the course of it one learnt that this was Mr Kosta Kavaris, travelling to Shanghai. He was assigned to Cabin number 5.

Next in the queue were the two nuns. When they had been dealt with and assigned to Cabin number 1, they turned and I saw that the older, taller one had a long, horse-like face, grey and pitted, big hands and a deep voice. The younger, smaller one had mischievous blue eyes, cheeks like ripe apples, and a soft, appealing voice. With the right make-up she could have been a beauty queen. I had no idea what order they belonged to but they had spoken to Rufus Sprott in Italian, which language he appeared to handle with consummate ease. The nuns were bound for Bombay where, I had no doubt, they would find much to challenge their missionary zeal.

They were followed by a thickset, serious-faced German, Werner Haupt, whose white linen suit, Panama hat and sunglasses suggested he was bound for a hot climate. He would be leaving the ship in Suez, he told Sprott, whence he would travel by dhow to an obscure port in the Persian Gulf. He would, said the purser, join Mr Maddison in Cabin number 3. Haupt looked unhappy but accepted the verdict with a deprecatory shrug. He was an unusual man, I decided, to be taking on a journey which involved both *Chanticleer* and a dhow.

Rufus Sprott then dealt in quick succession with those still ahead of me in the queue: Solly Katz, a plump and cheerful individual in late middle age who was, I later learnt, a writer seeking material. Like me, he was to leave the ship in Port Said. After Mr Katz came a fresh-faced young American. The purser studied his passport closely before looking up. 'You certainly been around, son.'

'Yeah – I guess that's right,' said the owner of the passport whose name I didn't catch. He was to share a cabin with Solly Katz. After him came Nils Sandstrom, a calm-mannered Swede with serious eyes and greying fair hair. He was to share Cabin number 2 with me, said the purser. I didn't much like the idea of sharing a cabin at my age but, if one had to, Sandstrom was not a bad choice, and for that I was grateful to Rufus Sprott before whom I now stood.

'Name?' he said, blowing his nose vigorously and considering me in one and the same action.

'Geoffrey Simpson,' I said, passing him my passport and ticket voucher. He looked at them, then at me. 'You're the gent who wrote for a single-berth cabin, aren't you?' His expression was severe.

'Yes, I am.'

'We don't have no singles. Six twins.'

'Haven't heard you allocate Cabin number 6. Could I not have that to myself?'

'It's being fumigated, sealed off. Won't be ready for use until Port Said. Sorry. No can do.' The rheumy eyes smiled sympathetically. 'But you're sharing with the Swedish gent. He looks okay.'

Concealing my irritation and disappointment, I nodded, said: 'I see,' and went off to Cabin number 2 where I found Nils Sandstrom unpacking. It was a small dingy cabin, smelling of tobacco and long ago, but as I would have only a few nights on board I was not unduly upset. After a minimal unpack and a brief chat with the Swede I went up on deck and began to look round the ship. The light was fading but the upper deck was lit by cluster lights on the samson posts above the cargo holds. I ended up on the crosswalk above number 2 hold where bales of oriental rugs and carpets, boxes of dates and Damascene brassware were being loaded into the 'tween decks from a barge which lay alongside. I went down to the well-deck and stood at the hatch-coaming where I got chatting to the fourth officer, a handsome young Cuban whose name was Esteban y Camenos. I peered into the depths of the hold but could see nothing but large packing cases, all inscribed in Chinese characters.

'Motor cars?' I asked.

'No, señor. Agricultural machinery. For China.'

I left him and searched further afield but the more I saw of the ship the less it resembled the romantic image the travel writer had conjured up. I had cut that article – with my dentist's permission – and it now resided in the briefcase I had left in the cabin.

That night, after an indifferent dinner, I spent some time walking the small promenade deck and savouring the lights of Istanbul and Üsküdar until a cold veil of mist and rain closed over them and drove me back to the dining-saloon where, at its after end, there stood a small but well-stocked bar. Sitting at a table in the corner were Werner Haupt, Solly Katz and Maddison, the West Pointer. The young American was in the other corner writing a letter, a Coke at his elbow. I went to the counter, ordered a Scotch and soda and attempted but failed to engage the Chinese barman in conversation. Shortly afterwards Rufus Sprott came in and at once accepted my offer of a drink.

'The usual,' he said to the barman who had already begun pouring cassis into a glass of white wine.

We sat down at a table and for the next hour or so talked and drank, Sprott doing more of the latter. But he was an amusing man, a natural raconteur, and he warmed to an audience, however modest. It was from this conversation that I learnt much of what I have already revealed, but now he told me a good deal more: that the Captain was a difficult man, an alcoholic – 'Should've lost his ticket way back. But the owners are scared of 'im. Knows too much.' Sprott tapped his forehead knowingly and winked.

From what he said I gathered that the officers, the engineers, came from the seaports of the world; Malmo, the Piraeus, Liverpool, Naples, Balbao, Havana, Bremen, Glasgow and Cardiff. 'You don't sign on for a ship like this unless . . . ' Not surprisingly he left the sentence unfinished. However, if the officers were a mixed and dubious bag there was a nice homogeneity about the men for they were, he said, all Cantonese. But poor food and accommodation and a crapulous captain had strained their loyalties and most of them had deserted in Hong Kong where Tao Hu Sing, the new but heavy-fisted bosun, had recruited others in their place.

Sprott left me soon after eleven. When he'd gone the barman announced that the bar was closed, the dining-saloon emptied and I was the last to leave, reluctant to return to a stuffy cabin. When I got there I found Nils Sandstrom asleep.

Glad to leave the cabin and anxious to witness our departure I was up early next morning, my arrival on deck coinciding with sunrise. Making my way forward along the promenade deck, I went up the ladder to the boat deck and all but collided with a florid man with untidy hair and moustache, eyes like oddly coloured poached eggs – blue yolks and pink whites – and a blue-veined, alcoholic nose. The four stripes on his reefer told me that this must be Captain Olaf Pedersen about whom I had heard much the night before. He ignored me and went up a ladder to the bridge. I took up a vantage point on the crosswalk on the fore side of the boat deck. The derricks had all been stowed and the hatches battened down, but a barge was still secured to the starboard side abreast number 2 hold. A small tug was manoeuvring near the barge and there was some shouting between the tug captain and some *Chanticleer* seamen who were grouped round a very big Chinaman. I had no difficulty in identifying him as Tao Hu Sing, the bosun – 'He's a big bastard, twice the average size, I'd say. And tough as old rope,' Sprott had said.

The shouting and gesticulating went on, a young seaman threw a heaving line towards the tug. It fell well short, the knot-end landing in the barge. The tug crew yelled, its captain's shouts were drowned suddenly by bellowing from *Chanticleer*'s bridge. I looked up and saw that it came from a choleric Captain Pedersen. I was horrified to see Tao Hu Sing respond by felling the young heaving-line thrower with a wicked blow which sent him sprawling. When he eventually got to his feet his face was covered in blood. I had no idea what the problem was but in due course it was solved. The tug towed the barge clear, the windlass on the fo'c'sle began to turn, the anchor cable groaned and rattled up the hawse-pipe and in no time the chief officer shouted by loud-hailer that the anchor was aweigh.

So began *Chanticleer*'s undistinguished departure from Istanbul. The sun was higher now, playing magically on the ancient city's mosques and palaces, on their copper-sheathed domes and minarets, so that it was difficult to accept that a scene so beautiful could encompass the shack-like dwellings of the poor and countless beggars, cripples, piano-carriers and other human bearers of outrageous burdens.

As the ship turned to head northeast down the Bosphorus I took a long last look at the Blue Mosque, beyond it the Mosque of Suleiman. The beat of the engines quickened and Istanbul began to move slowly astern, the Golden Horn sliding into the background. Familiar landmarks passed by: the Park Hotel where I had stayed on my last visit, the stadium, and the Topkapi Palace, strangely beautiful in its cloak of early-morning sunlight; the only palace in the world, a Turkish guide had told me, that is bounded on three sides by water.

Not long after leaving Istanbul we passed from the Bosphorus into the Sea of Marmora and at that stage Mr Sprott arrived on deck and remarked rather sternly that breakfast was being served. It was Tuesday and I asked him when we would be arriving in Port Said.

'Latish Friday afternoon. Depends on the weather and the engines. Never know with this old girl.'

'Suits me. I plan to spend the night in Port Said. Go on to Cairo the next day and fly back to Heathrow a couple of days later.'

'All right for some,' grunted Sprott. 'Still can't understand why you've come on this old barge.'

'I told you last night. I love ships.'

Sprott shook his head. 'Plum crazy. Better get on with that breakfast. It'll be off soon.' I took his advice and made for the dining-saloon.

The next two days passed quickly. In that time we traversed the Sea of Marmora, passed through the Dardanelles and made our way down the Aegean, the Turkish coast and islands to port, and Lemnos and Thessaloníki to starboard. Not that we saw much for the Turkish coast was shrouded in mist and rain. But on the second day we were steaming down between the Cyclades and the Sporiades and though we seldom got close to any of them we were able to trace our course from the track which Esteban y Camenos marked on the chart in the lobby outside the dining-saloon. It showed many familiar names to starboard, among them Andros, Tínos and Náxos, and to port, Sámos, Kos and many others. In late afternoon we passed between Rhodes and Kárpathos, but we had only the chart to tell us this for visibility was poor, and wind and sea increasing. It was evident that *Chanticleer* was not making good the 16 knots promised in the owners' leaflet. Her failure was not for me unexpected. The engines were old, the ship's bottom long overdue for scraping and painting (*vide* Mr Sprott). I saw little of my fellow passengers several of whom, including the nuns, were said to be suffering from seasickness. Nils Sandstrom was a silent, self-contained man who spent most of his time reading. He was, he told me, an archaeologist and was bound for Luxor and Thebes which he was re-visiting in connection with a thesis he was preparing. It was this, too, that had taken him to Istanbul. Two passengers who seemed at pains to avoid each other were Maddison, the West Pointer, and Kosta Kavaris of the wide-brimmed hat. To what this apparently mutual antagonism was due I did not know. Possibly it was no more than that they were two very different people.

Solly Katz and Rufus Sprott played chess at odd moments when the latter was not busy – 'Me watch below,' he called it – while Werner Haupt and the young American, Don Short, engaged in long conversations while walking the deck or sitting in the bar. They were both serious men and from the fragments I overheard their discussions were serious: Vietnam, the consequences of the Six Day War – we were in the early 1970s – the moral decline of the West and other weighty matters. The weather had caused Herr Haupt to discard his white linen suit and Panama hat in favour of a dark tweed suit and Tyrolean headpiece.

The wind had risen, there was something of a sea running and by late evening of the second day *Chanticleer* was plunging and spraying in lively fashion. That night I took the travel article from my briefcase to remind myself what its author had said about the weather at this stage. It was not inappropriate:

> *Her cargo loaded, she headed back through the Bosphorus to the Aegean and, retracing her outward journey, moved tentatively through the Dodecanese, threading her way between the white and golden islands to Beirut where dates, carpets and other produce of the Orient were loaded.*

I felt cheated – we had missed Beirut – but let me quote him further, his descriptions are so much more colourful than mine.

> *Now Beirut lay astern and Port Said ahead, and seen from afar in this heroic panorama of sea and sky, sunlight shining on her wet superstructure,* Chanticleer *must have had about her something of the poetry of Masefield and Kipling. And so this noble steel horse of the high seas rode on to the south, hidden at times in a mist of spray, the great hull emerging suddenly to take on shape and substance, to be seen to be a ship, the home of men bonded together by their common love of the sea.*

Well, well, I thought, heady stuff in spite of the mixed metaphor, but he can't have had much discourse with Rufus Sprott – nor with the young Cantonese seaman whose bloodied face had so shocked me. But he'd evidently had much the same weather as we were having, though he put a more acceptable gloss upon it than I could.

In the bar late that night Rufus Sprott and the chief engineer, Angus McAndrew, got involved in an argument which ended in mutual abuse. It had been about malt whisky, of which both had drunk too much. The second engineer, a Mexican with an unpronounceable name, supported the elderly Scot, while Jean Luc, the French second officer, sided with Sprott. With each man talking at high speed in his own language the fiery discussion became as noisy as it was senseless. I finished my drink and went down to the cabin where Nils Sandstrom was snoring peacefully.

Next day the ship continued to battle with headwinds and seas, and the noon position Esteban y Camenos plotted on the lobby chart showed there was little chance of reaching Port Said before dark. This was later confirmed by the barman who said that we had already slowed down. 'Cheaper for night on sea than with harbour. We come to Port Said for morning. Is better.'

He was right. I was up early next morning, wind and sea had dropped and we were steaming at normal speed. The sun had climbed above the horizon in the southeast but it still glowed dullish red. I searched ahead for signs of land but saw nothing but the sea. It was not until some time later Port Said showed up. In the distance it seemed no more than a lighthouse or two pointing like fingers through the morning haze, with a few up-ended matchboxes for a backcloth; but as we approached it acquired the lyrical qualities of a Cézanne landscape with geometrical arrangements of beige, sepia and terracotta, and coppered domes and minarets dancing in the strong light of the desert sky, the sea spread before it all like a carpet of ultramarine shot with sunlight.

The pilot-cutter came out to meet us, the pilot clambered up the side, and we steamed in between the breakwaters where I missed Ferdinand de Lesseps who used to stand bronzed and unyielding at the mouth of his triumph. Now only the plinth remained.

There was over the harbour a complex odour of sea, spices and fuel oil, and a general fuss of waterborne traffic which suggested that here met the great trade routes of the world. Perhaps more than any other seaport, Port Said has about it a certain *je ne sais quoi* that no airport, however grandiose, can hope to match. There was movement everywhere, hurrying launches, graceful *feluccas* – their patched sails, tall and languid – stationary dredgers clanking and puffing, tugs shepherding lighters and water barges in some obscure unco-ordinated activity, and bumboats bright with merchandise hovering about the new arrivals. Every now and then fast launches of the Canal Authority creamed to and from Canal Headquarters, adding like cavalry a touch of distinction to the proceedings.

There were many ships, some working cargo, others, mainly tankers, waiting for the next convoy to enter the Canal, or to enter Port Fouad for repairs.

Taking her time, and with a good deal of noise from the bridge, *Chanticleer* found a berth on the eastern side of the harbour, near the floating dock, where we secured to buoys fore and aft. On the far side of the harbour the palms lining the waterfront stood like green soldiers guarding the city. I had no difficulty in identifying the Casino Palace, the principal hotel in my day, and Simon Artz, surely one of the world's most interesting shops, though they were both dwarfed by the white-hulled, yellow-funnelled cruise-liner which lay off the pontoons opposite the boat sheds. Way to the left the black and white ringed High Light reared up above the jumble of buildings like a giant salt cellar. It was all vaguely familiar and reassuring despite the years which had passed since my last visit.

Customs and immigration settled, I left the ship in mid-morning. Among others in the launch which took us ashore were Rufus Sprott, looking important with a briefcase of ship's papers, the two nuns, purring and modest, Maddison the West Pointer, Nils Sandstrom, notebook and camera in hand, Kosta Kavaris in wide-brimmed black hat and dark glasses, the young American, Don Short, and the ebullient Solly Katz. Once ashore I took leave of Rufus Sprott and the others, found a taxi, a vast disintegrating affair with missile-like fins, and bundled into it with my suitcase. The driver was a sad-looking Arab whose *tarbush* sat like a red pillar box upon his shrunken head.

'Casino Palace Hotel,' I said. It was no distance and we had soon squeaked and hooted our way there. I paid off the taxi, a commissionaire took over my luggage and in no time I had completed formalities and been shown to a room. It was not far from the one in which, many years before, I had spent a few madly romantic days with a lovely and most charming young lady from Greece. The Casino Palace – to Port Said what Shepherds was to Cairo – seemed quite unchanged, and to return years later was for me a delightful *frisson*.

After a light but delicious lunch, I spent most of the afternoon walking about Port Said, savouring once again its crowded streets and spice-laden atmosphere. It was during this re-exploration that I came upon the *Al Waha*, the nightclub I remembered so well. The discovery rounded off a nostalgic, sentimental afternoon during which my unseen companion, Cleo, the dark, sloe-eyed girl who had made my time in Port Said so memorable, never left my side. I had lost touch with her after the war but I knew she had gone back to Greece. Now in her early fifties, she was most likely to have married. She would still be beautiful. Carried away by recollection, and not withstanding my age, I resolved to visit the *Al Waha* that night. It would be my only chance. At noon next day I would leave for Cairo.

The dining-room that night was busy; many of the guests, my waiter said, came from the cruise-liner. I had a table to myself, something I much prefer. I find that being on one's own, and free from conversation with strangers, is far more rewarding. It provides opportunities for watching others, for speculating as to who they are and what they do. Though one usually arrives at the wildest conclusions, I find it an entertaining pursuit. On this occasion, however, there were several faces I knew and at least one surprise. Gary Maddison was there, handsome as ever, the West Point ring much on view as he ate. With him was a tall well-groomed Egyptian with greying hair, his dark eyebrows reminiscent of Omar Sharif's. Diplomat, I guessed or, perhaps more likely, Egyptian army officer. They talked a good deal but at no time did I see either of them smile. Some distance across the room Kosta Kavaris and Solly Katz shared a table. They talked little but ate voraciously; since Katz was a cheerful, bubbling little man I assumed that Kavaris was proving a dull companion. I wondered why they were dining together. Katz, like me, had left the ship in Port Said; Kavaris was going on to Shanghai, for what purpose I did not know. My guess was that Katz the writer had hoped to get a story of sorts from Kavaris who looked more than ever like a down-at-heel impresario. Why else would Katz dine with such an unattractive character?

For me the surprise was to see our two nuns sitting at a table in a far corner. The eyes of the older one, she of the equine face, were riveted on the plate of food before her which she attacked with zest. The young one with apple-red cheeks ate slowly, glancing occasionally at other tables. Once or twice I thought I saw her companion call her to order; or so I presumed, for apple-cheeks would switch her head back suddenly and fold her hands meekly. I wondered then about nuns as I always do. What is it that persuades them to abandon their freedom, usually at an early age, and enter voluntarily into an austere life of poverty, chastity and obedience – and sometimes silence? Was it, I wondered, due to some trauma – a hopeless love affair, fear of, or perhaps disgust with, the weaknesses of the flesh; or was it simply exemplary moral resolve? I had no idea but felt it unlikely that these two women, so very different, should have made the decision for the same reasons. It seemed to me, incidentally, somewhat out of character for nuns to be dining in such an expensive hotel, but they were bound for Bombay, and perhaps the opportunity of a really good meal before returning to the rigours of *Chanticleer* had been too good to miss. In any event I wished them well. Life could have few creature comforts for them and there would be more than enough poverty and austerity in Bombay.

After dinner I went up to my room and addressed a postcard to my sister; that done I lay on the bed reading the *Daily Telegraph* I'd bought during the afternoon. It was days old but it helped pass the time before I got up and made ready for my visit to the *Al Waha*; it was unlikely to come alive much before ten or eleven.

*

Nightclubs in seaports are pretty much the same the world over and the *Al Waha* was no exception. Nor had it changed in any significant way since my last visit. No doubt it had weathered and been refurbished during those thirty-odd years; and I did not recall the heavy maroon curtains which separated the reception area from the interior. Having paid my dues I passed through the curtains and made for the dimly lit bar where I asked for an ouzo from a barman I could scarcely see. A plump figure beside me in the half-light said, 'Didn't expect to see you here, Mr Simpson.' The voice was Rufus Sprott's.

'Sentimental journey. I knew the place during the war. What brings you here?' He seemed smaller out of uniform.

'Not much else to do in Port Said at night.'

'What'll you drink?'

He turned to the barman, pushed his empty glass towards him. 'Arak, Mustaf.' When the drinks had been poured and I'd paid for them Sprott said, 'Let's find a table. Been on me feet all day.'

He led the way down the left-hand side of the big room, past crowded noisy tables where the occupants were no more than dim shapes in the gloom. He found a table eventually at the far end, close to the small stage from which, in a blast of sound, guitars, saxophones, trumpets and drums came suddenly to life as strobe lights began to play on the oval dance floor, beat music and the lights combining to substitute fantasy for reality. The dance floor soon filled.

Where we sat the music was too loud for conversation and the lights beyond the floor too dim to see those at other tables. My thoughts went back to other times in the *Al Waha*, to magic nights when I had danced away the hours with Cleo in my arms. How marvellous, I thought, if by some strange circumstance she too was in Port Said. If she still had friends in the city, might she not, as I had, satisfy nostalgia by visiting the *Al Waha*, perhaps this very night. I was dismissing the thought as perverse when the music stopped and the lights went on.

'About time,' said Rufus Sprott, looking round the room and waving to someone. Moments later a young woman, dark-eyed and slim, came to the table. ''Allo, Meester Sprott. You want sumteeng?' she asked, leaning towards him, her hands on the table.

'Yes, darling. One ouzo, one arak.'

She repeated the order, hurried away.

'That's Natasha,' said Sprott. 'It's not only drinks she supplies. If you're interested.'

'I'm not.'

'Didn't really think you would be.' Sprott sighed wheezily, looked round the room. 'One of our lot there.' He jerked his head towards a table to our left. It was in a row nearer the dance floor. 'And a few passengers too.'

I looked in the direction he indicated, saw in profile the features of Tao Hu Sing, the Cantonese bosun, his big body overflowing the chair in which he sat. There was a scarlet-lipped blonde with him. At two tables between his and the wall on our left I saw other familiar faces; at the table nearest the wall were Gary Maddison, the tall Egyptian I had seen dining with him earlier, a strikingly handsome woman who might, I thought, be the Egyptian's wife and a teenage girl. At the table between Tao Hu Sing's and Maddison's were another pair of diners from the Casino Palace: Solly Katz and Kosta Kavaris, the latter wearing dark glasses which hid the chameleon-like eyes but somehow made him look more sinister; perhaps it was their conjunction with the heavily shadowed jowl, collar-length hair and sunken cheeks.

'Strange,' I said, 'that the *Chanticleer* people should all be grouped at this end of the room.'

Sprott focused a rheumy eye on me. 'I give 'em all *Al Waha* discount cards and tell 'em half-nine's the time to arrive. So they turn up more or less together and the girls show 'em to the tables.'

'You didn't give me a discount card.'

'You're getting on, Mr Simpson. Not your line, this.' He swept an arm round the room.

I was not sorry to have Rufus Sprott with me. On the way to the *Al Waha* I had wondered what on earth I would do there once I'd arrived: an elderly and not particularly convivial bachelor on his own in a Port Said nightclub was not a promising formula. Sprott was an extrovert, cynical and worldly-wise, but good company and, above all, English, which was a pleasant relief in a foreign country.

*

The night went on, the mixture much as before, the beat group and the strobe lights assaulting our ears and eyes; the chatter, the laughter and general noise level doing much the same in the intervals when the main lights came on.

Natasha was attentive and we were on our third round of arak and ouzo when, yet once again, the lights went out, beat music and strobe lights took over and the dance floor began to fill. Sprott had just remarked that time was getting on and he'd have to think about returning to the ship, when a vivid red flash crossed my line of vision from right to left. Shrill screams came from a table near the wall on my left, the lights went up and seconds later the music stopped. The girl at West Point's table was standing up, eyes wide with terror, one hand over her mouth, the other pointing to what looked like a hunting knife embedded in the woodwork a few feet beyond where she'd been sitting. Maddison had swung round to face the tables behind him, his right hand under the left lapel of his jacket. I waited for the gun, but it didn't come. The American just sat there, hand under lapel, frosty grey eyes watching the tables. Then the noise started, more of it now because those who could see the knife were telling those who couldn't where it was, and they weren't doing it quietly, the hubbub spreading wave-like through the big room, and down into the semidarkness round the bar. Like many others I stood up to get a better view of the proceedings. I looked at what I thought would have been the knife's line of flight – the vivid red flash I had seen – then moved a few feet forward until I judged I was on it.

Sprott joined me. 'For chrissake don't get mixed up in this,' he growled. 'Keep out of it.'

I assured him I would, adding, 'Just checking something. You watch the drinks.' Still growling he went back to our table. It was only a few feet away.

I checked the probable line of flight and saw that the knife could have passed over three tables set diagonally between a wooden-clad roof-pillar and the wall immediately beyond Maddison's table. The knife-thrower could have stood behind the pillar before stepping out to throw the knife or, judging by the streak of red light I had seen, it could have come from one or other of the tables between Maddison's and the pillar; that is, from Tao Hu Sing's or the one shared by Kosta Kavaris and Solly Katz.

The knife had been thrown just after the music began and the main lights dimmed – the red streak must have been reflections on the knife blade from the red exit lights on the wall behind us. The thrower had chosen a good moment. I saw that the knife was still in the wall where three men were examining it, one of them Maddison's impeccably dressed Egyptian guest. As I watched he took a handkerchief from his breast pocket, placed it carefully over the knife handle and then, with some effort, pulled the knife free.

Moments later a frowning Solly Katz brushed past me. 'Just missed us,' he hissed. 'But from Arabs what can a man expect?' An immobile Kosta Kavaris, shoulders hunched, was still at the table Katz had left. The girl who had screamed was sitting down now, talking to the Egyptian woman, smiling nervously as if to atone for the screaming, but her pallid face and restless hands betrayed the attempt to appear calm. As I moved back towards our table I saw three young Chinese sitting at one some distance behind the pillar near which I was standing. That they were seamen was apparent from their blue dungaree jackets and trousers. One of them had a jagged slash across his cheek, beneath a black and swollen eye.

I sat down again at our table. 'Most extraordinary,' I said. 'Did you see . . . '

Sprott's rufous eyebrows bunched menacingly. 'No I didn't. Crazy to get mixed up in this sort of lark.' He got up from the table. 'You coming? I'm off.'

I said, 'Yes,' and we left the *Al Waha* together. It seemed a good time to go.

In spite of, or perhaps because of, a rather generous intake of ouzo, I had a good and dreamless sleep during what was left of the night and woke wondering where I was. A knock on the door and the arrival of a *khadem* with morning tea soon reminded me. In no time I set about preparing myself for the day ahead. I would be leaving for Cairo at noon and there I would spend two days before flying back to Heathrow.

My only previous visit to Cairo had been with Cleo in 1944 when we spent a weekend at Shepherds. I had booked there for this visit. These were the thoughts in the forefront of my mind until their place was taken by those concerning the incident at the *Al Waha* the night before. For some time I puzzled about it – at whom had the knife been thrown, by whom and for what motive? The more I thought about it the more likely it seemed that Tao Hu Sing was the target, and the Cantonese seaman with the battered face the knife-thrower. He could have waited for the moment when the main lights faded, the drums and saxophones throbbed into life, and the strobe lights concentrated attention on the dance floor. At that instant he could have taken the few steps to the pillar, thrown the knife then moved back to the table where his companions sat. The knife, having missed Tao Hu Sing, must have passed close by those at Solly Katz and West Point's tables before impaling itself in the wooden wall. It had been a puzzling, exciting incident, something I would always remember, but now I dismissed it and my thoughts returned to what lay ahead.

Later that morning, having settled my account, I was in the foyer waiting for a taxi when a group of men bustled past on their way to the front door. The group included two uniformed policemen and, as it passed quickly by, I saw the metallic glint of handcuffs at its centre. Because of his size it was easy to identify one of the men in handcuffs as *Chanticleer*'s bosun, Tao Hu Sing. All I could see of the others in handcuffs were the backs of two shaven heads. The rear was brought up by the tall Egyptian, Maddison's friend, who had pulled the knife from the wall in the *Al Waha*. My thoughts were interrupted by an announcement from reception that my taxi was waiting. Followed by a grinning bell-boy carrying my suitcase, I left the hotel.

A knot of onlookers had gathered outside, near two police vans. At its centre stood the handcuffed prisoners, Tao Hu Sing arguing with the tall Egyptian who had been joined by Maddison and Kosta Kavaris. Moments later Solly Katz came out of the hotel carrying two old-fashioned travel grips, faded green canvas, strapped with time-worn leather. They looked familiar but I could not recall where I had seen them. I moved closer to the bystanders round the group, hoping to get a better view of the shaven-headed prisoners. I assumed that what I was witnessing had something to do with the knife-throwing incident of the night before. The owners of the shaven heads had their backs to me but, dressed in the sober grey, ankle-length frocks they had worn at dinner the night before, their nun's habits and headdresses now discarded, it was astonishing but not difficult to see who they were. It was then that I remembered where I had seen the two old travel grips. They had been in the passageway outside the door of Cabin number 1 the day we embarked in Istanbul. Nils Sandstrom and I shared Cabin number 2. The nuns were in Cabin number 1. I looked at them in disbelief. The older one, with the long boney face and big hands, was shaking an admonitory finger at the tall, Omar Sharif-like Egyptian. She was shouting hoarsely in Italian, but quite evidently making no impression for on a word from him the two women and Tao Hu Sing were bundled into a police van. Two policemen followed, and a third took the seat beside the driver. The van moved away with an escort of armed police on motor-cycles, sirens blaring. The tall Egyptian, Gary Maddison, Kosta Kavaris, Solly Katz and a uniformed police inspector engaged in animated discussion, after which Maddison and the Egyptian drove away in one car, while Kavaris, Katz and the police inspector did so in another.

The onlookers broke ranks and, as he turned towards me, one of them had a familiar face. It was Don Short, the young American from the *Chanticleer.* He was putting a notebook into a side pocket of his jacket.

'Incredible,' I said. 'Those nuns involved in whatever that was all about – *and* Maddison, Kavaris and Katz, plus the tough bosun. Seems to have been a *Chanticleer* drama. What d'you make of it?'

Don Short gave me a long, hard look before answering. 'No way were those nuns, friend. The older one with the boney face is a racketeer – Guiseppe Frascatti. They've been after him for a long time. Homicide, larceny, felony. He's big on narcotics these days.'

'What about the other one. The girl?'

'She's his sidekick, Rosmonda Fiori. Not too kosher either.' He stroked his chin as if checking for beard growth. 'But it's great to see our FBI and DEA boys teaming up with the locals.'

'I know FBI but what's DEA?' I asked him.

'Drug Enforcement Administration.'

'And Tao Hu Sing. Where does he fit in?'

The young American frowned, felt his chin again with thumb and forefinger. 'I guess he fits in some place. When it comes to trial we'll learn.'

I looked at him with fresh interest. 'How do you know all this?'

He seemed undecided, looked at his wristwatch, then back at me, the steely grey eyes challenging. 'Because it's my business, sir.' He checked his watch again, said, 'Guess I'll be moving,' and with that he was gone.

In the taxi on the way to the station I decided that he was probably a media man who had travelled in *Chanticleer* on the strength of a tip-off. I realized, too, that what I had seen and heard involved endless permutations of who threw the knife, at whom, and for what reason. I would have to work at it in the train on the way to Cairo – it would help pass the time.

As a ship *Chanticleer* had fallen somewhat short of the claims made for her in the owners' leaflet but I did not feel short-changed for though she was in fact a tired old tramp steamer I shall always regard my brief voyage in her, the strange collection of passengers and crew with whom I shared it, and the dramatic happenings in Port Said, as among the most vivid and extraordinary of experiences.

Looking back upon that voyage I see *Chanticleer*, the provider of realities so far removed from ordinary life, as a truly romantic ship and I shall always be grateful to the writer of that article in the travel magazine, notwithstanding certain of his literary extravagances.

DESTINATION UNCERTAIN

Driving the big white Rolls-Royce with its amusingly personalized number plates out of London's traffic-snarled streets on a dark winter's night, Oswald Kettman – OK to his friends, Ossie to his intimates – was obliged to yield a part of his hyperactive mind to the exigencies of the moment, to exiting the metropolis with car and person intact. This called for concentration, alertness and judgement while in the throbbing, fuming, dazzling streams of traffic; moving, stopping and moving again, ineluctably forward, like marching columns of glaring-eyed, red-buttocked ants. Charlie Baker, his driver – Mrs Kettman, always sensitive to changes in the social climate, called him 'our chauffeur' – normally bore this burden but he had been given the day off.

That part of Kettman's mind not involved in surviving the traffic farrago would on most occasions have given priority to his business problems, for him almost always more pressing than those concerning his private life. But on this occasion a private problem was at the head of the mental queue for the very good reason that it had confronted him within the last hour. Soon after leaving his office in the City that evening he had stopped off in Chelsea to see Margritte, the young woman who lived in a flat he had made available to her. Its rent was a charge against the property company which owned it, one of his many subsidiaries.

The visit had not been a success. On the contrary, for Margritte had wanted money for something. This was not surprising for she often wanted money for something. But her wants had become more frequent and more costly as the year proceeded: redecorating the lounge and her bedroom, a chaise longue for the latter, a bigger and better music console, several trips to Düsseldorf to see her mother, another to Canada to see her sister, and other wants he could not recall. The initial pleadings for these were always conducted with discretion; no more than a brief reference, often an oblique one, to what she had in mind. Days would pass before Margritte took the matter further. Then, having planted the seed, she would state her want more succinctly, her manner always gentle, even wistful, as if she were the sad little poor girl starved for the good things of life which, her manner implied, he could so easily provide with his great wealth. These second-phase pleadings were always staged over drinks in the attractively furnished lounge against a background of romantic music, suitably pianissimo. Once he had produced his cheque book – a sure signal that her plea had succeeded – she would sit in demure silence, hands folded on her lap, until he had written the cheque and passed it to her. At that point she would jump up, emit a little squeak of pleasure, clasp her arms round his neck and kiss him passionately. 'Oh, Ossie. You are the most lovely man. You really are *wunderbar mein Liebchen*.' Then, holding him away from her, she would smile enigmatically. 'And so, *Liebchen*. What now? To the boudoir, I think. There my thank you will be the way you so much like. To make you happy after the – how do you say? – the tycoon's hard day of business. *Jawohl*.'

But tonight's visit hadn't ended like that. The Escort Cabriolet he had given her less than a year back was too noisy, too ordinary, she'd said. Not quite in those words but he was nobody's fool and that was what she was telling him. Everybody had Escorts. Did she not deserve something with more character? 'You always say that I am beautiful. Do you not think your beautiful mistress should have something more exciting? Something that shows how rich and generous her lover is?' This had been said gently, alluringly, her hand on his knee.

'Like what?' he'd said abruptly, thoughts of the bedroom receding rapidly.

She'd smiled, hesitated, dropped her voice so that it could just be heard over the sensuous whispers of *Music from the Andes*. 'Like the little BMW Cabriolet. It is really fabulous, Ossie. In white I would like.' It had been a long worrying day. One problem after another. Ganza Containers plc had said they couldn't repay a long-outstanding loan.

The banks were unco-operative. If Ganza were pressed they'd have no option but to call in the receivers. There had been a complaint from the shipping agents; the last consignment to the West Coast had arrived with many leaking drums, the insurers were disputing the extent of their liability – just one of those days. And he was tired, physically, mentally and emotionally; tired in truth of Margritte and her endless needs. He'd pushed her hand off his knee and, mimicking her voice, said, 'No. I do not think you need something more exciting.' For good measure he had added. 'If an Escort Cabriolet is good enough for Shirl it's bloody good enough for you.' Mrs Kettman's first name was Shirley.

That had led to tears and recriminations, notably that he was only interested in her body. When he'd asked what else she expected him to be interested in she'd run into her bedroom and locked the door. Tired, angry and frustrated he'd left the flat, got into the white Rolls-Royce and resumed the journey to Silver Birches, the house in Berkshire where his wife and children would be waiting for him. He looked forward to getting home. It was the background to the more tranquil side of his life, one that made him wonder why he ever bothered with other women, particularly with a knighthood in the offing.

It had begun to rain when he turned off the M40 at Junction 2 and he drove more slowly, the windscreen wipers dispelling the blurred images of the night which regathered with endless persistence after each swishing stroke of the spider-like arms. His thoughts returned to Margritte. The relationship with the German girl was wearing thin, very thin. In part because she was too demanding, her materialistic tactics too transparent, in part because he was too easily bored. She was costing him more than any of her predecessors and certainly more than he thought she was worth. One of the things Ossie Kettman prided himself on was his ability to value goods and services, an ability to which he ascribed much of his success. The German girl had become a problem and he resented that. There were quite enough problems in his life without Margritte adding to them.

He'd have to get rid of her. 'Pay her off, pronto,' he said aloud in a firm voice which reassured him that he'd made the right decision. 'Conditional on vacation of the flat within two weeks, furniture and contents as per inventory to be left in place and intact,' he added. Bosman, his solicitor for property matters, would see to that. Good man, Bosman. It was he who had warned against the dangers of giving the Margrittes of this world the status of tenants. The ladies concerned had always to sign a document confirming that they were Kettman's guests, enjoying his hospitality. Yes, he reflected, no problem. What's more it would be in her own best interests. It was about time she got off her backside and did something for herself. She was in her thirties, approaching her sell-by date for the way of life she fancied. She'd have to watch it. He and others like him were not easy to find, and certainly more difficult to keep. The competition was tough. All in all he was doing her a good turn. She would have to return the Escort. It was registered in the name of one of his companies, but he'd be generous – give her enough to get along comfortably for six months. After that she'd have to get out there and get stuck in. Like he'd done. Not that anyone had given him the sort of start he was giving her.

That thought caused him to think briefly of his beginnings: he'd come from what the social workers called an underprivileged background. Not that he thought of it like that. Sure, he'd been brought up in the East End of London, his dad was a docker, his mum a council cleaner. Both hard workers, a quality their genes had passed on to him. There were no books in the house and little else to read, he'd not done too well at school, left it at fifteen and gone out onto the streets to complete his education. By his early twenties he'd established himself as a street-trader, a streetwise young man who knew a lot more about how to get to where he wanted than he would have had he stayed at school and somehow got to a university. So he never felt in any sense underprivileged and resented the tag. By his thirties he had gone on to bigger things and before long become known in the City as a successful import/export merchant, one whose achievements, though not always his methods, were well regarded. His wife, Shirley, aware of his potential and her own social ambitions, had taken a protesting Kettman to private elocution lessons, had overseen his wardrobe and generally groomed him for what she believed lay ahead. For her part she took an active interest in Tory constituency affairs, having industriously researched the route to a knighthood for her husband; a reward which, with his generous contributions to party funds, should, she felt, be well within reach – if he kept clear of scandal. Sadly but philosophically aware of his penchant for younger women, she held out the carrot of a knighthood to discourage this tendency. Unsuccessfully as it happened, but at least she had made him more circumspect, more calculating, in that regard.

Short of Coleshill he turned right into the country lane towards the end of which lay the entrance to the drive leading to Silver Birches. He had gone the best part of a mile when, rounding a corner, he saw ahead of him a yellow Mercedes parked close to the hedgerow which lined the lane. There was not room enough for him to pass so he stopped the Rolls short of the parked car and saw for the first time that its bonnet was up. Through the rain-misted rear window of the Mercedes he could see that there was someone in the driving seat and for some moments he sat there waiting in the expectation that the arrival of the Rolls would lead to action. To encourage this he switched his headlights to bright. Almost immediately the driver's door of the Mercedes opened and a raincoated figure climbed out into the lane and came towards the Rolls. He saw then that it was a young woman, singularly good-looking in spite of her rain-soaked hair. He lowered his window. 'Hullo,' he said. 'What's the problem?'

'I don't know. It started spluttering then stopped. It's not fuel. The gauge shows more than half a tank still left. Terribly sorry. I pulled in as far to the left as possible but I'm afraid there's still not room for you to pass.'

'Nor to turn. I'll have a quick look under the Merc's bonnet. I used to know my way around in there but they've got complicated these days. Too much hi-tech. He took a torch from the glove box, opened the door of the Rolls and got out into the lane.

'That's terribly sweet of you,' she said. 'You'll get very wet, I'm afraid.'

'No problem. I'm almost home. If I can't spot the trouble quick I'll phone Murray. He knows me and he'll come right away.' He looked at her, the rain streaming down her cheeks, and thought how well this lovely, pink-cheeked young English woman compared with Margritte. Name, phone number, address? He'd get those before they parted. Not difficult in the circumstances.

They went to the Mercedes. 'Sit in the driving seat while I check under the bonnet,' he said. 'Leave the door open so that you can hear if I shout.' She got into the Mercedes and he moved forward, hating the rain. The light under the Mercedes bonnet was off, so he shone the torch light onto the engine and was wondering where to begin with so much that was unfamiliar when there was a blinding flash and he felt a heavy blow on the back of his head.

It was some time before he was able to rationalize the sounds and movement, the steady but subdued roar, the sudden movements, unexpected because they were without rhythm. Lying on his back, his hooded head on something soft, a pillow perhaps, his handcuffed hands under some restraint which held him to the floor, he could neither see nor move. At first he had thought he was in a van but soon discarded that for a motorboat until he realized that the sudden changes of trim and attitude, and the steady power roar, could only mean that he was in an aircraft. Why? Going where? What the hell had happened? He tried to recall events but his head ached fiercely and everything was hazy; his last recollection was of sitting in a car in a narrow lane and a pretty young woman standing in the rain talking to him. When that had been and where he just could not remember. How had he got from there into this aircraft? He was making desperate efforts to solve this problem when he heard muffled voices saying something. He felt pressure on his left wrist, somebody holding it, then he lost consciousness.

It was dark when he woke and silent but for the distant barking of a dog. The hood was still over his head but his hands were free and he found that he could sit up. He still felt fuzzy and the pain in his head persisted though it was not as intense as it had been. He tried more movement and found that he could crawl but his limbs were stiff and painful. He sat still for a while trying to put coherent thought together. If only he could see. He tugged angrily at the hood, felt the knotted cord under his chin, fiddled with the knot until it was loose and pulled the hood from his head. He had exchanged one degree of darkness for another. He would have to wait for daylight to examine his surroundings properly. His wristwatch had gone and the clothes he must have been wearing; all he had on now were shorts and a T-shirt.

'Christ,' he muttered. 'For Jesus Christ's sake, what have those bastards done to me? And why, why?' But which bastards, he asked himself, and at that point the answer presented itself. Kidnap, that was it, kidnap. And that answered the why too. Ransom, that was what they were after. His money. The thought made him tense his muscles, brought out his deep-seated antipathy towards anyone who attempted to get at his wealth or interfere with its sources – his entrepreneurial activities. 'I'm a wealth creator, a Thatcherite man,' he would sometimes say when asked what drove him, to what did he ascribe his success.

While waiting for daylight he found his mind clearing to some extent so that he could remember the row with Margritte and getting into the Rolls and setting off for the drive home.

He was slowly putting together recollections of that drive when he heard a noise behind him, turned quickly to see a square of dim light just above floor level and a bucket being pushed through it.

'Hey, hullo, you,' he called desperately. 'What's going on?'

There was no reply. The square of dim light disappeared. Somewhere in the distance a cockerel crowed and a dog barked. Early daylight, he told himself. That's what the light was. He examined the wall where the bucket had come through. His fingers told him that there was a square aperture there, about eighteen inches across. There was an outside cover over it but it would not yield to pressure. The bucket had a lavatorial odour but it had arrived too late. He'd already urinated on the earthen floor. But it was good to know that someone out there was attending to his needs.

He was still thinking about his unseen jailer when he heard movement at the aperture, it opened again and weak daylight showed for a brief moment as a small pot was passed through onto the floor. Kettman again called out, tried to make verbal contact, but there was no response. The cover was closed and secured and he heard the gentle pad of footsteps departing. He examined the contents of the pot by feel and smell. Whatever it was smelt good and was warm. It felt like stodgy porridge with a few small lumps of what his nose told him was well-grilled meat. He had not realized how hungry he was. Squatting on the floor he ate ravenously. The meal finished, his thirst took over. He was worrying about this when the cover over the aperture opened again and a gourd was passed through. The water in it was tepid and brackish but it relieved his thirst.

As the morning grew, more light filtered in through cracks in the walls and by way of a circular hole in the roof. No more than eight inches across, it was covered on the outside with thick strands of wire. With these few sources of light he was able to examine his cell more closely. It resembled an inverted circular basket, with horizontal layers of closely woven branches, the interstices packed with hard brown clay, the floor of stamped cattle dung and not of baked earth as he had thought. An African hut, he decided, probably sub-Saharan, possibly West African. Kettman had not visited that country but he had business interests there. He realized, however, that it might be East Africa or, for that matter, North Africa.

There were more distant noises of poultry and barking dogs now and, occasionally, the far-off cries of children.

The days passed, insufferably hot days, but the routine never changed, anonymous brown hands collecting and returning the bucket each morning through what Kettman now thought of as the trap door. The pot and gourd were delivered and collected in the same way, morning and evening, while twice weekly a slither of soap and a bucket of water came through the aperture. With these he managed some sort of hygiene and was able to wash the T-shirt and shorts occasionally, passing them to brown hands whose owners hung them out to dry. In that climate the naked Kettman was never kept waiting long for their return.

He had after some time achieved a fairly complete recollection of the drive home and his attempt to help the woman in the yellow Mercedes. It was clear to him now that the breakdown was part of a meticulously planned operation carried out by people with an intimate knowledge of his movements that day. He'd most likely have been followed from his office in the City to the flat in Chelsea and then, for most of the rest of the journey, the shadowing car advising those in the Mercedes, waiting somewhere ahead, of his progress. The woman in the Mercedes had probably had a couple of strong-arm men with her. They'd have hidden in the hedgerow close by. Easy on a dark night, especially with rain falling. Something like that, he decided, shaking his head in the darkness. If only Charlie Baker had been driving the Rolls that night. Charlie, an ex-policeman, was as much his bodyguard as his driver. A burly man who, at Kettman's insistence, always carried an automatic.

The persistent question in Kettman's mind as time wore on was, who organized the kidnap? He was still certain that ransom was the motive. But who were the bastards and what would they be asking? Fortunately nobody knew what he was worth, not even Shirl. He'd always liked the City's 'No man who knows what he's worth can be seriously rich', and had always shrugged off questions on the subject, though he had a pretty shrewd idea of his worth. Most of his personal wealth was offshore, principally in the Caribbean. Certainly not on any records available to Inland Revenue, nor to anyone else for that matter. Negotiations were probably taking place in London right now. Had the police been informed? Almost certainly. Shirl would have raised the alarm that night when he didn't get home. He'd phoned her from the Rolls soon after leaving Chelsea, saying he was on his way. The Mercedes lot would have taken the Rolls and left it in some remote part of the country. Or flogged it if they were downmarket villains. There'd have been enquiries at Margritte's flat and she'd have co-operated up to a point, particularly as she didn't yet know that he was going to pay her off. Dyason, his right-hand man at Head Office, would be handling things, working closely with Karpman and Zetter, Kettman's personal attorneys.

Time dragged on, days passed into weeks. Confined as he was in semidarkness, in limited space where he spent most of the time squatting or crouching because the roof was too low for him to stand upright, he began to lose count of time. Without his watch, he had a rough idea of the time on sunny days, but virtually none if there were clouds. At first he had tried to count the weeks by the number of times the bucket of water arrived but he soon discovered that it was coming days late or early and he became confused and gave up. He had nothing with which to scratch marks in the hard, stamped-dung floor and no other means of recording the passing of each day so lost count of the passage of time. Loneliness, helplessness, and impotent rage larded with self-pity sometimes led to tears. He felt deeply humiliated as he crawled or crouched his way round the hut. They treat me worse than a bloody animal, was his constant reproach. He never gave up trying to communicate with his jailers but they never responded. He tried talking what he imagined was pidgin English but without success. If only they had spoken to him in their own language it would have meant something, a reassurance to him that they had heard him even though they could not understand what he said. Their silence frightened him.

The intense heat, the humidity, were affecting his health. He suffered severe skin rashes, scratched himself endlessly, his beard and hair grew long and collected pools of sweat and what he thought were lice from the constant irritation they caused. There were bouts of nausea and severe headaches. Twice recently he had vomited. He ascribed the deterioration in his health to his living conditions and his diet, the water in particular with its tepid, salty flavour was suspect. But he had to drink it.

So far as he could judge it had not yet rained and he concluded it must be the dry season. But many parts of Africa and the Middle East had dry seasons so that was no clue as to where he was.

At times his thoughts grew confused. He put this down to the sleeplessness which afflicted him to an increasing degree, and to the marked deterioration in his health. When he did manage sleep he was almost always plagued by nightmares and would often wake in a sweat of fear.

Most of his waking time was spent rethinking thoughts which had long since become stereotypes. Why had this horrific, dastardly thing been done to him? If the perpetrator was not Salvi, who else could it possibly be? And if someone else, why, why, why?

Always he came to the same conclusion: it could only be Salvi, and the why of that was the tie-up with Barrera. But Kettman could not think of anything he had done to anyone, including Salvi, which remotely justified the savagery and viciousness of the treatment to which he was being subjected. Of course he'd been successful in a big way, built up a powerful group, become an important figure in the City and made a lot of money – his life style made no secret of that. But he hadn't done anything criminal, broken any laws. It was his brains, his hard work, his contacts, which had exploited a market that was open to all. Of course success and riches led to envy. But who, out of envy, would run the risks and spend the money involved in his kidnapping and imprisonment in a foreign country?

And so the days, the weeks – the months for all he knew – came and went, each day a replica of the day before, so making the passage of time meaningless, the only apparent changes the light in the hole in the roof, and the state of his body and mind. Anger, fear and desperation had long since given way to despondency, to a belief that he could not last much longer, that he was dying – dying like a sick dog.

One morning he was sitting, comatose, his knees drawn up to his chest, his head bowed when, at an unusual time, the trap door opened for an unusual reason. To the accompaniment of unintelligible grunts, two brown hands proffered an envelope. He snatched at it, the trap door shut and he crawled to the centre of the hut where a shaft of golden sunlight lay, pole-like, aslant the dung floor and the small hole in the roof. Trembling with excitement, stomach muscles taut, he opened the envelope and took out a small sheet of plain paper. He crawled towards the shaft of sunlight, held the sheet under it. The message read:

Your return journey begins tomorrow. On arrival proceed to Fiumicino Airport where you will find a sealed envelope on the letter rack in the first-class lounge.

He let out a hoarse shout of delight, did a number of crouching jumps and fell to his knees mumbling, 'Oh, thank God! Thank God!' But the moments of ecstacy and wild excitement soon passed and more sombre, angry thoughts took over. So it *was* Rome. Had to be that bastard Enrico Salvi. Salvi had the means and the motivation to have organized the kidnap and what followed. He recalled the last time he'd heard the Italian's voice, the phone call from Naples when Salvi had received the fax terminating their business relationship, the Italian blustering, pleading, reproaching and finally, Kettman now realized, threatening. Not that it had sounded like a threat – 'You'll live to regret this, Ossie' – more like a suggestion that Kettman's business interests would suffer without Salvi. 'You bloody fool, you total bloody twit,' Kettman rebuked himself. Of course it was Salvi. The man was a Sicilian, had often boasted that his family were Mafia, proud unforgiving people.

So Salvi and his associates had done it. It was a bloody wicked thing to do but those sort of people had no scruples. They'd be saying they'd let him off lightly, that a bullet in the neck was what he deserved for dropping Salvi. But business was business. Barrera had shown that he was a lot more valuable to Kettman than Salvi could ever be, and the new markets recently developed had been Barrera's brainchild, not Salvi's. Barrera's outfit was not only producing a lot of new business but it fitted like a glove into Kettman's group. As Simmons, group finance director, had put it in his poncy voice, 'The synergy is near to perfection.'

So the return journey was to begin tomorrow. 'Bloody marvellous,' Kettman chortled aloud, his red eyes streaming with tears. He began another crouching caper which ended with an attack of dizziness. He leant over the slop bucket and vomited.

Well before daylight next morning the door of the hut was opened for the first time during his captivity. Two men came in, both hooded, and a bag was placed over his head.

'What's going on?' he asked, not aggressively for he realized this was the beginning of the return journey. His left arm was seized, held in a firm grip, and he felt the prick of a needle briefly before losing consciousness.

At some stage or other he became aware that he was once again in an aircraft, his hands tied and his movement so restricted that he could not sit up though he could turn on his side. He tried to call out but, too dazed for coherent speech, managed no more than grunts. He became aware of a shape bending over him, of pressure on his left arm, followed by a faint prick there, after which he passed out again.

When he regained consciousness it was dark and his first desperate thought was that, once again, he was back in the hut but the steady roar outside, peppered with the shrill blasts of cars' hooters, soon assured him that he was not. His hands were no longer tied. Feeling round him in the dark he found that there was a pillow under his head and a mattress and bedclothes under his body. He fell asleep. When he woke there were chinks of light at the curtained window. Slowly because he was weak and his limbs were stiff, he got off the bed and went to the window. He pulled the curtain aside and daylight flooded in. The room was small, sparsely furnished, the walls and curtain faded. From the window he looked down on the street, at the steady stream of traffic, with a sense of elation. He was at last free and back to civilization. It was a marvellous feeling. The signwriting on the commercial vehicles and the advertisements on the hoarding on the far side of the road told him that he was in Italy, almost certainly Rome since he had been instructed to go to Fiumicino Airport.

So his abductors had been true to their word; he *was* in Italy on the first leg of his return journey and for a moment he experienced an illogical sense of gratitude as he turned away from the window and began examining the room. Next to a small washbasin in the corner he found scissors, razor, toothbrush, toothpaste, hairbrush and comb set out neatly on a small table. In a rickety wardrobe facing the bed he found the clothes he'd been wearing at the time of the kidnap. The suit had been cleaned and pressed and in the breast pocket of the jacket he found his wallet. He went through it. The banknotes, credit cards, everything was there just as it had been. Nothing was missing. He was mystified. Was all this part of the terms which had been negotiated for his release? Surely those representing him would not have worried about such detail? Again he felt a weird sort of gratitude to his captors, but a brief spell of nausea soon brushed it aside and reminded him of the dreadful conditions he'd had to endure for all those long weeks. No way had he anything to feel grateful about. He'd been humiliated, frightened and his health had been severely damaged. Perhaps it was Enrico Salvi's idea of a joke, the sort you played on somebody if you hated their guts. If so it was a bloody silly, dangerous joke. If he could establish that it was Salvi, the Italian was in for real trouble. Nobody took that sort of liberty with Ossie Kettman and got away with it. Kidnapping was a serious crime. Salvi could end up with years inside if Kettman got busy, and Kettman was prepared to devote considerable resources to that end. He concluded this mental outburst with a muttered, 'So look out, Signor Enrico bloody Salvi, you don't know what's coming to you, boyo.'

Feeling all the better for the invective, he took the scissors, went to the wardrobe mirror and cut off his beard and as much of his overlong hair as he could manage. He then shaved, had a really good wash, towelled himself down, got dressed and put on his brightly polished shoes.

At the end of it all he felt marvellously refreshed and whistled a tuneless but cheerful refrain. Leaving the shorts and T-shirt on the floor, and the toilet gear on the table – there was a barber's shop at Fiumicino which he'd often used – he left the room and went slowly down the poorly lit stairs. An elderly concierge was sitting at a small table inside the main door, knitting. He greeted her, the first person whose face he had seen since meeting the woman in the yellow Mercedes. But the old lady shook her head. 'No inglese,' she muttered. 'Italiano,' and went on with her knitting. He went out into the street to flag down a taxi.

On arrival at Fiumicino Airport he bought a first-class ticket to London by the first available flight, it involved a wait of less than an hour, and now eligible for the first-class lounge he made for it. Once he'd got the letter he would go to the barber's shop and then, time permitting, he'd put through some calls to London. He was not hungry; excitement, waves of nausea, a queasy stomach and attacks of dizziness offset appetite. His compelling need was to read the letter. It might, he felt, provide a clue – a lead perhaps to the perpetrators of his abduction, Enrico Salvi and his strong-arm men. Kettman was now in the grip of an obsession, determined on revenge for the wrong that had been done him.

He went into the first-class lounge and made for the letter rack aware that his heartbeat was well above its normal rhythm. There were a number of letters and messages on the rack and he panicked when he could not see anything with his name on it. Eventually he found a white envelope two down in the cluster of Ks, pulled it out and saw his typed name over the address, Fiumicino Aiport. There was no postage stamp or franking mark. That meant it had been placed there by someone with access to the first-class lounge. Salvi, of course. Kettman opened the letter with shaking hands, pulled out the white sheet of paper and read the message typed upon it:

> *You have spent six weeks on the outskirts of an African village. Your hut was near a dump of drums filled with toxic waste, some leaking. This was one of your earlier shipments. There have been many since. If you continue to behave as if it were clever to get rich at the expense of helpless and impoverished people more hazardous experiences await you. That is if you survive your recent close encounter with those commodities which are evidently so important to your wealth-creating activities. Many of the African villagers, especially children, have not.*

Kettman shook his head, grimaced, as fear, icy and total, took over. So that was what caused the skin rashes, the nausea, the vomiting, the sore eyes and the frequent spells of dizziness. That was where the horribly foul smell had come from. Christ Jesus! And they had done *that* to him. It was more than abduction, it was attempted murder, could still be murder. So it wasn't Salvi after all. It was bloody obvious now who it was. Who else could do such a stupid, wicked thing, write such a cheeky, pompous message but the Greens? Those starry-eyed, jobless sons of bitches who couldn't keep their noses out of other people's business. Back in London he'd consult his legal team, get the opinions of several senior counsel, see how he could teach these people a lesson they'd never forget. Second thoughts told him there might be problems – if the matter were brought to trial the publicity would not do him nor his interests any good. It was only certain people in Government and the City, and of course those in the industry itself, who understood the problems of toxic waste disposal and its economic importance to Britain – only they would sympathize. He would have to be careful.

A disturbing thought occurred to him. Was it really the Greens? Or was it that cunning bastard Salvi? He could have been responsible for the message, diverting suspicion away from himself. Kettman read the message again, was placing it in his wallet, when he was overcome by an attack of nausea, the second that day. With his hand pressed to his mouth he hurried to the lavatory off the lounge, vomited noisily into a handbasin. A dark-skinned attendant came to him with a towel, spoke soothing words in Italian.

Kettman's bloodshot eyes were wide with fear. 'I'm very sick,' he said brokenly. 'I must see a doctor.' Using the towel the attendant had given him he wiped vomit from his chin and tie and shirt.

'Ah,' said the black man. 'Signor ees Eengleesh, *si*?' Ees bes see doctor. Mus' see heem queek, hey.' With a friendly grin he went back to his little office.

BUSHVELD SHOOT

The dying campfire glowed in changing patterns of reds and golds, all hissing and spitting done but for occasional sparks and crackles as some last twigs and branches surrendered their store of thermal energy. In the darkness beyond the brief circle of light cast by our fire we could see the hazy outline of the three Africans squatting round theirs, the murmur of their voices rising and falling like the distant sound of breaking waves, an invisible opiate, the aroma of coffee and wood smoke, drifting down to us.

It was still early winter but there would be frost in the morning and we were sleeping rough, so there was no eagerness to leave the fire for the palliasses and blankets which the Africans had laid out for us. As it was we sat there sipping brandy-laced black coffee, chatting about the day's shoot and the prospects for tomorrow's.

There were five of us and we had over the years had many shoots on Blaauwkrantz, the four thousand hectares of Bushveld in the Western Transvaal where Bill Johnson farmed cattle and cash crops. His brother, Andy, organized the shoots and like the rest of us worked and lived in Johannesburg. Bill joined us occasionally but had opted out of this shoot on the grounds that he was too busy.

So it was the usual gang: Andy Johnson, Pete Claasens, Henry Hopkins, Karl Haussman and myself, Don Wilkins. We were all in our late thirties/early forties in this winter of 1947, and this was our seventh shoot since the end of the 1939–45 war.

We'd made camp where we always did, in a big clearing under fine old camel thorn, karee and wild olive trees at Connell's Drift, half a mile from Bill's farmhouse. The drift ran across a watercourse, almost always dry in winter, but there must have been plenty of underground water because the bush and trees flourished there in summer. But with winter now come all but the evergreens were stark and brittle, the veld grass brown and dust laden, the crisp night air beyond the fire pungent with odours of dry earth, cattle dung and frost-bitten vegetation.

A light breeze teased the leaves in the branches above us allowing brief glimpses of the star-filled southern sky where the absence of cloud promised heavy frost. But for the voices round the fire the only sounds were those from the bush: the distant howl of a jackal, the croaking and chirping of frogs and crickets, and the occasional hooting of an owl to which other birds responded with nervous twitterings.

Klaas came over from the Africans' fire and stood near us with clasped hands waiting to be noticed. Andy Johnson interrupted our conversation. 'What's the problem, Klaas? Reckon it's time for us to turn in?'

'The fire is low, my Baas. I must put more wood to make it big for the night.'

'You're right, Klaas. Come on lads, time for bed.'

We stood up, moved back and chatted while Klaas laid more logs and branches on the dying fire. Henry Hopkins, who claimed to have sprained an ankle during the afternoon's shoot, did a short and manifestly exaggerated limp round the fire before announcing that he'd be no good for next morning's shoot. As it was to be the last day he would like to leave early. 'No point in hanging about here with this ankle,' he said with a grimace of pain, 'is there, Pete?'

Peter Claasens, who was a doctor and had examined the ankle, grinned at us discreetly. 'None,' he confirmed.

Since Henry had come down from Jo'burg with me in my station wagon I felt that something was expected of me. 'Sorry about the ankle, Henry,' I said, 'but I was rather looking forward to tomorrow's shoots. I wonder if any of you people,' I waved a hand in the general direction of the others, 'are thinking of getting back early tomorrow?'

Karl Haussman said he was. 'I've a lot to do. Board meeting on Monday.' He shot me a dark look. 'As Don well knows. So I'll be pushing off after breakfast. If that's okay for you, Henry, I'll be happy to take you back.'

It was okay for Henry so all was well, but Karl's dark look had irritated me. We worked in the same mining house in Jo'burg where he was not only head of the finance department in which I worked, but was on the Board having jumped up the promotion ladder during the war while those of us who'd volunteered for active service were having what he called 'fun and games up North'. Because I'd come back with an MC and Bar, relics of Sidi Rezegh and Monte Cassino, he would at those early-post-war parties, if he was anywhere near me, say in a loud voice, 'Yes, he had a good war. They say the Bar was for looting chianti for his colonel. Ha-ha-ha!' He would then add in a lower key, 'I'd love to have gone but some of us couldn't get released. Had to keep the wheels of industry turning. If we hadn't, people like Don Wilkins wouldn't have had anything to come back to.'

I happened to know that he'd moved heaven and earth to be classified as a keyman. For these and other reasons, some more cogent than others, I did not like Karl Haussman. The fact that he was of German origin didn't help so far as I was concerned. Though we may have appeared to others to get on well enough the reality was otherwise.

Klaas had all but finished building up the fire when Karl Haussman said, 'I'll be glad to get my head down. Early start tomorrow and I'm damned tired.'

Henry said, 'Me too,' adding after a noisy yawn, 'You'll have to keep a sharp lookout on that Swartruggens-Rustenburg section. We had a near miss coming down. That bloody awful red dust. Thick as a sea fog.'

'You're exaggerating again, Henry,' I said. 'I saw that truck in plenty of time. No trouble, no near miss.'

'Why the bloody great swerve then – and the obscene language?'

I shook my head, said, 'Let's change the subject.'

Henry was a journalist. We all liked him but he had a vivid imagination and was by nature and occupation predisposed to embroider the truth.

'Sounds like a near miss to me,' said Karl.

'I daresay you think it's a pity I swerved.'

The flames from the burgeoning fire lit up Karl's face and I saw the muscles of his jaw tauten like drawn elastic.

'What exactly does that mean, Wilkins?' The use of my surname was the measure of his anger.

'Exactly nothing,' I said, looking into the fire. But we both knew that I was lying.

'High time they put a blacktop on that section,' said Henry. 'Grader-maintained roads can't cope with modern traffic. They're nothing more than dust generators.'

I'd no doubt the subject would be dealt with in next Wednesday's *Daily Informer*, written round a lurid account of the near miss. Henry's column appeared on Wednesdays.

Klaas had finished his work at the now roaring fire, the dogs had been bedded down in the back of the station wagons, we'd all come back from urinating behind the bushes and before long we were tucked into the five sleeping-bags which ringed the fire. The scene reminded me, as always, of shapeless corpses in body bags laid out for burial in the shadows of Monte Cassino.

Klaas called us at six next morning, the best part of an hour before sunrise, and we gathered round the fire he'd revived to drink strong coffee and warm our hands. After that we busied ourselves making ready for the early-morning shoot. Guns were checked, ammunition belts and game bags, water bottles and the other paraphernalia of a shoot were loaded into the station wagons, followed by Klaas and Esau, his son, who got into the back compartments with the dogs – Jake, Andy's English setter, and Caspar, Karl's pointer, both good gun dogs. Finally, we got in with our guns and the two vehicles set off, bumping and lurching along the farm track which led eventually to Spitskop where Andy had decided we should make our first beat for guinea fowl.

It was intensely cold, there'd been a heavy frost, and as our vehicles negotiated the rutted, potholed road the rim of the eastern sky began to glow pink and promising, and sleepy partridges along the track blinked their eyes and stretched their wings but did not fly as we passed. By the time we reached the foot of Spitskop the sun was half over the horizon, laying delicate washes of salmon and gold over the Bushveld.

The farm road had led us past the arable lands where it ended and now we were travelling on a cattle track running parallel to the dry but well-timbered watercourse which traversed this part of the farm, the dry veld grass, taller than our wheels, brushing them with the swish-swish of a pop drummer. Eventually we parked beside a clump of camel thorn trees, the station wagons shed their loads, ammunition belts were strapped on, game bags slung over shoulders, the dogs let off their leads, and we gathered round Andy Johnson with our shotguns. He gave us our orders for the first beat, we took up our positions, loaded our guns, checked safety catches, and the line moved slowly forward, climbing diagonally across the lower slopes of Spitskop, the dogs casting ahead, Klaas and Esau following us.

We'd not gone far when Caspar stopped, rigid from muzzle to tail as he pointed. Before long the bobbing heads of scurrying guinea fowl showed through the grass ahead of him. Karl, the nearest gun, hissed, 'Seek,' the pointer raced forward and the guinea fowl took to the air with a noisy flurry of wings. There was a ripple of firing and several birds fell. Predictably, two of them to Karl Haussman's gun and none to mine. He was an excellent bird-shot, I an indifferent one, there more for the occasion than the kill.

There were a lot of guinea fowl on the hillside that morning and now that the shooting had started our pace quickened as we tried to keep up with the fleeing birds which kept settling fifty yards or so ahead of us. Jake, the English setter, was particularly good at finding birds which had broken away from the main flock so there was no lack of activity. We managed another beat before 7.30, along the upper slope at first, then down towards the parked station wagons. There we counted the bag: twelve guinea fowl, three pheasants and two hares. The latter, as always, going to Klaas and Esau for their hard work. We drank from the water bottles, watered the dogs who lay panting beside us, filled gaps in our ammunition belts and made ready for the final beat along the *donga*, the dry watercourse which ran through the farm from northwest to southeast, bordering our campsite at Connell's Drift. It was a fine beat, one to which we all looked forward, the well-wooded *donga* much favoured by pheasant and partridges as the day grew warmer.

When we reached the *donga* Andy Johnson gave us our stations: Pete Claasens on the right bank, Andy and Karl in the *donga* with the dogs and the Africans. He put me on the left bank which was a good place to be. The arable lands would be on my left and it was towards them that birds flushed in the *donga* tended to fly. Andy's last instructions to us were the customary ones: 'Keep the line straight. Bank guns must only take birds which have flown well clear of the *donga*. Karl and I will only take birds flushed ahead of us. We'll keep our line of fire clear of the guns on the bank. Bank guns will keep their fire clear of the guns in the *donga*. Okay? Let's go.'

When we'd taken up our positions, Andy shouted 'Forward', Klaas and Esau released the dogs and the line of guns moved slowly ahead. From time to time we caught glimpses of each other through breaks in the trees and vegetation, each gun concentrating on those nearest him. In my case it was Karl Haussman down in the *donga* on my right. He wore a bush-hat with a leopard skin band and he was tall so not too difficult to see when the breaks came.

The sun was well up now and there was an earthy smell about the warm air rising into a cloudless sky. Near me an about-to-emigrate Diederik cuckoo was singing its unmistakable song, *dee-dee-deederik*, and from the fallow lands on my left came the *chwee-chwee-chwee* of a Dikkop plover. In spite of much that was worrying me at that time I thought once again how fortunate I was to be alive, living such a privileged life in so wonderful a country.

These congenial thoughts were interrupted by a burst of firing from the *donga*. A flushed pheasant showed briefly on my right, well within range, but Andy's 'Bank guns will keep their fire clear of the guns in the *donga*' prevented me from doing anything about it.

Looking down to my right I saw the leopard skin hatband through a gap in the trees. It had moved ahead of me and I quickened my pace in order to catch up. Then I saw Haussman himself, no more than twenty yards away, stooping to pick up a bird. Probably the pheasant that had flushed on my right.

We moved steadily forward, the firing intermittent, one or other of the dogs scrambling up onto the banks at times only to be called back by sharp commands from Andy and Karl. Once or twice I'd seen Pete Claasens on the far bank but there was usually too much vegetation between us to make this possible. Quite often Klaas and Esau showed up behind the gun line and occasionally I saw Andy, but it was Karl and the leopard skin hatband I had to look out for to keep my place in the line.

Hard as I tried to forget it my mind kept harking back to the conversation I'd overheard in the club a week earlier – a conversation which had suddenly and unexpectedly confronted me with a problem which was fast becoming an obsession. I had begun to recall what I had heard, when a partridge flushed almost at my feet and flew left towards the fallow land. I missed with the right barrel but got it with the left. When I'd picked it up and put it in my game bag I went back to the cattle track along the bank. Though I'd fired a dozen rounds so far I'd got no more than two pheasant and this partridge. This didn't worry me, I came on these shoots for the sheer pleasure of being in the Bushveld with congenial companions. If anything, the killing of wild fowl worried my conscience more than I would have cared to admit. Why did man, the most lethal predator of all, derive such pleasure from killing innocent creatures? Why was man the only natural species which planned the mass destruction of its own kind? These were questions I had often asked myself since the war. The only answer I could come up with was that man was a natural killer, but this was neither profound nor satisfying. I had to admit to myself, however, that I was a killer. I had killed men because I had been told to do so and believed that the cause was just; but I killed innocent wild creatures like game birds, not for a just cause but because I enjoyed the companionship and ambience of a Bushveld shoot.

Yet once again my thoughts were interrupted. This time by a leguuan, a lizard-like creature some three or four feet long, which had been sunning itself on the cattle track. Suddenly awakened, it had crashed away through the scrub a few yards ahead of me. I tried to concentrate on the shoot but my mind kept returning to man's predatory instincts. Perhaps I sensed that there was in this characteristic a possible solution to my unpleasant problem. I had, of course, thought of solutions, some more absurd than others, but they were no more than ventures into the wonderland of fantasy.

A burst of firing in the *donga* and another on the right bank brought me back to sober reality. Below me through a chink in the screen of trees I saw the leopard skin hatband, beneath it the shining barrels of his shotgun as Karl Haussman fired both in rapid succession. I could not see at what but I heard Andy Johnson's, 'Well done, Karl,' and guessed he'd got a bird with each barrel. When we get back to camp, I told myself, Haussman won't fail to mention that. Modesty is not one of his notable qualities.

I began to feel weary. The earlier beats on Spitskop, through the long grass and mostly against the slope, were beginning to tell. I was pleased that the boundary fence at the far end of the mealie lands would be showing up soon. A hundred yards or so beyond it we would finish the *donga* shoot, go back to the station wagons and make for Connell's Drift and breakfast.

I plodded on, my thoughts in limbo, until I heard a scrambling noise coming up the bank ahead of me. It was Jake, the English setter, in pursuit of a hare. He raced across the path and weaved his way through a clump of *withaak* thorn bushes onto the mealie lands where long lines of stalks from last year's crop stood cobless, tattered and withered like some shattered battalion. At that moment a pheasant flushed from the dried grass a few feet ahead of me. Its sudden screech and whirring wings startled me, so that I was slow and late and missed with both barrels. From the *donga* came Andy Johnson's shout, 'Get that bloody dog back, Klaas.' My thoughts wandered again.

It would be quite possible, I decided. Like Donald Blane's gun accident near Hammanskraal last year. They decided that he had broken his gun but failed to unload. Then, getting through a barbed-wire fence, trailing the gun, a barb had snagged under the trigger-guard, the gun had snapped shut and the barb had caught on the triggers and fired both barrels.

There was another burst of firing from the *donga*. No birds came up. Not surprising, Karl and Andy both super shots, and Caspar a fabulous and untiring worker. Where was I? Oh, yes. Gun accident at a fence. Always a risk. There'd been a good many. There'd be more. The pattern varied. One man failed to break his loaded gun – damn these bloody horseflies, and the sweat; should have taken my jersey off after the Spitskop beats – yes, left the shells in, tripped at the fence, fell – must then have pushed the safety catch to ON – both barrels fired and he killed one of his party. Bloody awful sort of accident. Sheer carelessness the cause. Bet he was never invited again. Perhaps it wasn't an accident? That's quite a thought.

More shots in the *donga*. Nothing coming my way. Would be different if drought hadn't burnt up the mealie lands. A single shot from the right bank. Good old Pete. Hope he's done better than I have. Such a decent guy. There's the fence, can't be more than a hundred yards ahead now. It's the only answer. Can't go on as we are. God, can I? Of course you can. It's a fabulous opportunity. Remember the drill. Break the gun, leave the shells in, safety catch at SAFE, climb through the fence, right foot first, right hand lifting the upper strand, gun trailing in left hand behind half-turned body. Body through, gun still trailing, pull gun through, snap it shut, slip safety catch to ON, aim at imaginary bird, left trouser leg caught on barb, prepare to stumble, shift target to leopard skin hatband and fire both barrels, stumble heavily with left foot still caught in barb . . . Fence twenty yards ahead now, more shots in the *donga* and two partridges flutter down like autumn leaves falling on a windy day . . . Remember the drill, and show emotion afterwards. I'll probably feel it anyway. Terrific tension now, heart leaping about like a mad thing, breathing like a steam train, wet with sweat, worse than on the beach at Anzio. Fence five yards ahead now. Check action in the *donga*. Trees and bush still pretty thick here. There's Andy, should be able to see Haussman. Wait a moment, yes, there's the leopard skin band. Range? Say twenty yards. What's that noise on my right? Jake gone mad in the mealie field, racing through the stalks after something. Andy will raise all hell about that. Poor Jake. Christ! Here's the fence. I nearly walked into it. Break the gun, don't remove the shells. Now lift the upper strand. Right, bend down, get that right foot through, trail the gun. Now get the body through. Good, now the left foot, watch out for those barbs. That's right. Bring the gun slowly forward, carefully, don't want to kill yourself, slowly, slowly . . .

'Look out, my Baas,' called a voice immediately behind me. 'Fence very bad with shells still in gun. Wait. I help you.'

I turned. It was Klaas, five feet away, gappy white teeth grinning in the leathery brown face. He reached me in seconds, put out his hands for the gun. But I'd already got it clear of the fence, snapped it shut and checked that the safety catch was at SAFE.

'Thanks, Klaas. You're dead right. Careless of me,' I said. 'I was hurrying. There was a bird ahead of me on the bank. I wanted to get it. No excuse. I should have taken those shells out.' I smiled woodenly, tried to quieten my noisy breathing, hoped he wouldn't spot the symptoms of high emotion. Klaas is an old man, a wise old African with no education but plenty of intelligence.

'Bad to hurry with loaded gun, my Baas.' The leathery old face broke into another grin.

'Anyway, what are you doing up here, Klaas? You should be down in the *donga*.'

'Jake run away to chase hare in mealie fields. Baas Johnson too cross. Tell me, "Get that bloody dog back." So I come up. Now must catch Jake.' Klaas moved off, picking his way through the cordon of bush on to the mealie fields.

The line of guns had moved ahead while we'd been talking so I set about catching up. Horrified at what I'd almost done I realized that I had been close to madness. Then, quite suddenly, I was at peace with myself, all tension gone. With feelings now of doubt and unbelief I asked myself how a man's mind could be so twisted towards violence . . . but it was an insincere question because I knew the answer. It was, beyond all question, due to the conversation I'd overheard in the club between the men at the washbasins while I was on the lavatory seat behind the locked door. My overwhelming emotion now was one of immense gratitude to Klaas.

The rest of that day seemed to pass quickly. Back at camp at Connell's Drift we found waiting for us the splendid breakfast Ephraim had prepared. There was the customary chat about the morning's shoot, Karl Haussman told us about that right and left – 'Fabulous really at that range, though I say it myself.' As always he'd killed more birds than anyone else. Klaas and Esau hung the birds on a line stretched between two trees, we stood in front of it with our guns, Klaas, Esau and Ephraim at our feet with the dogs, and Henry, his limp now forgotten, took the customary photograph.

Karl and Henry packed up their gear, took their share of the bag, got into Karl's station wagon with his pointer in the back and drove off in a cloud of dust while we waved and shouted goodbyes.

After shaving and bucket-washing, we spent the rest of the morning cleaning our guns, replenishing ammunition belts, lounging about and chatting. At noon we drove over to Bill Johnson's farmhouse where we had drinks and lunch before getting back to Connell's Drift. We rested there until 3.30 when we set out on the afternoon shoot. One beat on the lower slopes of Kaalkop, the rock-strewn hill which bordered the eastern side of the arable lands, and a final *donga* shoot. With only one dog and three guns the bag was nothing like the morning's, and of course Karl's absence made a big difference though it pleased me. In fact I thoroughly enjoyed the shoot. There is a harsh, arid beauty about the Western Transvaal Bushveld in winter: the air crisp and fresh under azure skies, the swathes of brown veld grass rising and falling in the wind like ocean waves. With my newly found peace of mind all this was more magical and enchanting than ever before.

The winter sun set early and, after hot coffee and snacks back in camp, we packed my station wagon, put the disgraced Jake in the back, tipped Klaas and the other Africans and thanked them for a wonderful shoot. With Andy and Pete as passengers, I drove off from Connell's Drift and made for Jo'burg.

Back in Jo'burg I dropped Andy and Pete at their homes in Dunkeld and Melrose and got back to my own place in Bryanston soon after ten that night. I parked the car in the garage off the drive and hooted. In no time Amon, our cook, came out and helped me bring in the gear. Normally Carol would have come to greet me but there was no sign of her. I asked Amon where she was.

Looking anywhere but at me he said, 'I think Madam is sick, Master. She go to the bedroom early.'

I went through to the study, put my twelve-bore in the gun-rack, the ammunition in the wall-safe, and locked both of them. Having dumped the rest of the gear in my dressing-room I made for the bedroom. The room was in darkness. I turned on a light and saw Carol slumped on the bed, her face buried in the pillows. She hadn't undressed. It was quite unlike her to do this. I went across to the bed, touched her on the shoulder, said, 'You all right, Carol?'

The only reply was a shake of her head, her face still in the pillows. I put my hand more firmly on her shoulder. 'What on earth has happened, Carol? It's not Jim or Charlie, is it?' Our sons were at boarding school in Natal. Again there was no reply, just that shake of the head.

'Then tell me, what's the trouble, darling?' I insisted.

She lifted her head, propped herself up on an elbow and looked at me. Her face was chalk white, the red mouth and bloodshot, darkly circled eyes giving her a Pierrette-like appearance. I saw at once that she had been crying.

'Haven't you heard?' she said in a strangled voice.

'Heard what?'

'Mary's ghastly news.'

'No. What is it?' I suppose my manner was stolid, but I was tired, it had been a long day, and I was used to Carol's drama-flavoured moods.

'Karl and Henry are dead.' The words burst out of her explosively, almost as if she were firing a gun at me.

'Good God? What happened?'

'The police at Koster phoned Mary just before lunch. Karl had a head-on collision while overtaking a railway bus.' Her voice broke and she put a hand over her eyes. 'The police said . . . they said . . . they . . . they were both killed instantly. The driver of the other car too.' She lay back on the pillows. 'It's too awful.' There was a dry sob. 'Too awful to think about.'

'Good God,' I said, adding quite involuntarily, 'Poor old Henry.'

Carol sat up on her bed then with the unexpected spring of a jack-in-the-box. Seeing the sudden fury in the moist red eyes I added, rather lamely I suppose, '*And* Karl, of course.'

'Is that all you can say?' Her voice was harsh, unforgiving.

I thought for a moment, fought back a desire to laugh or at least to smile. 'In the circumstances, yes.'

'What circumstances?' she challenged, her voice tinged with hysteria.

'The tragic circumstances, I mean.'

She looked at me with doubt and something close to hatred. 'You've always been jealous of Karl, haven't you?'

There was no point in going on in that vein, so I shook my head and left the room. I could hardly have told her that, but for dear old Klaas, I'd have shot her Teutonic lover that very morning.

The police at Koster had phoned. So Karl Haussman had taken the road through Koster, not Rustenburg as we had. That explained why we'd not seen any wreckage along the road. It was sad that Henry should have been involved. Such a decent chap. Had he survived he would have loved to write the story. But this time it couldn't have been about a near miss.

ALONG THE TOWPATH

The patchwork sky of whites, blues and greys was mirrored by the river, transforming the muddied waters of the Thames into something like the picture postcards on sale in the High Street. The illusion was heightened by the undergrowth and trees which lined the banks, casting abstract patterns of light and shade, presenting a Monet-like picture to the man who walked along the towpath, a solitary figure, his sober attire effective camouflage in those surroundings.

John Barrett was a retired shipmaster, a quiet man used to the exercise of authority and the loneliness of command at sea. It was that time between late afternoon and early evening when the light began to soften, to become limpid, diminishing the shadows which lay upon the towpath and the river it hugged. There was for Barrett a special appeal about walking along the towpath at such a time when there were few people about; indeed, along the stretch ahead of him, ending only where the path was lost to view as it swung right to follow the course of the river, there was no one to be seen. He would have appreciated the company of some congenial soul, man or woman, but he was only recently arrived in Weybridge and had as yet made no friends nor indeed met anyone beyond the bank manager, the doctor to whom he had been assigned, Mrs Wiggin who cleaned and tidied his apartment twice a week, the nearby newsagent, the postman and milkman and those others who attended to his needs when he went shopping.

Several reasons had led to his decision to live in Weybridge on retirement. As a youth still serving his apprenticeship in cargo steamers, he had spent the leave periods between voyages with an elderly spinster aunt in Weybridge; his own family lived in South Australia, too distant in terms of time and money. He had always had pleasant memories of those far-off days of his youth in Weybridge when Aunt Isobel had lavished so much care and concern upon him, becoming in a sense his surrogate mother. Not long before his retirement she had died, leaving to him her Weybridge house, by then divided into four flats. The only other surviving member of his family was his brother who still lived in Australia, a country with which Barrett had long since lost touch. Once settled into the Weybridge flat he had made no attempt to trace any of his aunt's friends, most of whom would no longer be alive for she had lived to a considerable age. It was early days yet, he had told himself, and he was no stranger to loneliness.

He looked at his watch and decided there was time enough to make the second bridge before turning back. It was his usual walk, some two miles, and there was more than enough light to see him home before dark. As he walked he thought about his loneliness, not in any sense of self-pity but out of curiosity as to how it might end. Should he take up golf, have lessons at a driving-range and progress from there to membership of a local golf club? Or should he learn to play bridge? He had heard from Mrs Wiggin that it was taught at Adult Education. Either way he was bound to get to know people. Not that he was good at that; years at sea in cargo ships, the last twenty of them in command, had conditioned him to a remote way of life. He had never married though in his time as mate of a coaster on the South American run he had taken up with a woman in Valparaíso where the ship was based. Spanish and darkly good-looking Margarita had meant much to him; she was intelligent, good-humoured and caring, attending to his needs in what had been a warm and comfortable relationship. Since they had not seen each other during those long and frequent absences when he was away at sea, the freshness had endured. He had suggested marriage but had soon learnt that it was out of the question; Margarita was a devout Catholic and though her husband had long since left her she had not been prepared to countenance divorce. 'Why so?' she had challenged. 'We are happy like this.'

The relationship had ended when he was promoted to the company's bulk carriers trading principally between Southern Africa and the Far East; they had kept up a correspondence for some time but the periods between letters had lengthened, ending suddenly when a letter came from a mutual friend in Valparaíso telling of her death in a road accident. He had been shocked and deeply depressed at the time; but that had happened many years ago and was now remote, blanketed by the march of time. His thoughts were diverted by movement on the river ahead. A small tug towing a laden barge had come round the bend and was chugging upstream making slow progress against the ebbing flow. When it was close he stopped walking to watch it pass; a scruffy, rusted little tug, rubber tyres strung in unseamanlike fashion along its sides, two men in the wheelhouse, one smoking a pipe. Skipper and mate, he decided. The barge was loaded with metal scrap. He wondered where it was bound for and for what purpose it could be used? Recycling? That was the thing today. In what form would it appear next? Children's toys, containers? Plastics must have limited the market for that sort of scrap. But they wouldn't be shipping it upstream unless it was wanted. He gave up the problem and walked on.

Soon after the second bridge came into sight he saw a distant figure coming towards him. As it drew closer it took shape and form; a woman preceded by a large dog which bounded ahead casting to left and right of the towpath, disappearing at times in the undergrowth, stopping only when she called to it; then it would turn, face her with a questioning stance as if waiting for some further command and, when none came, racing ahead again.

The woman and her dog were nearer now and he saw that it was an Alsatian, fully grown and very aware of his approach as it walked slowly towards him, tail rigid, ears pricked forward. The woman called, 'Heel, Ludwig, heel!' The Alsatian, well trained, at once turned and trotted back to her with lowered tail and ears laid back. It came to heel and she commanded, 'Sit, Ludwig.' She leant down, clipped the end of the reel-lead onto the dog's heavily studded collar and came on down the path, the Alsatian once again ahead of her and straining at the lead. It stopped a few yards short of Barrett, bared its teeth and began to growl. The woman jerked hard on the lead, shouted something in what sounded like German, the growling stopped and the woman said, 'I am sorry for Ludwig's manners. He will not harm you. It is that he is very protective of me.' Her English was good though underlain by a foreign accent. German probably but possibly Dutch or Danish, he was not sure.

'A very good protector,' he said.

'Yes,' she smiled. 'It is necessary, you know.'

'It certainly is these days. Lot of strange people about. Those gypsies, that caravan camp.' He nodded downstream.

'They are not gypsies. They are travellers, tinkers. The gypsy caravans are spotless. Also with beautiful decorations. The people are really clean. The women wash the clothes every day. You see it hanging up. I have nothing against the gypsies, the true Romany people. They live according to their culture. They are to be admired.'

She was evidently a woman with strongly held views. He changed the subject, spoke of the fine weather and she responded with the need for rain. He agreed. After that there was a hiatus which he broke by looking at his watch.

'Time's getting on. I have to reach the next bridge before turning.'

'So. Your discipline is good.' She smiled and once again he noticed how the smile transformed a rather serious face into one that was distinctly attractive.

'Habit more than discipline. I do this walk quite often. Two miles.'

'I too. Ludwig very much enjoys the towpath.' She hesitated, doubt in her eyes. 'But I have not seen you here.' The doubt was echoed in her voice.

'I have not been here long. Only a few weeks.'

'Ah, that explains. I have been in Europe these last weeks.' She jerked at the Alsatian's lead. 'Come, Ludwig. We go.' Suddenly animated, the dog got to its feet. She turned back to Barrett. 'Perhaps we meet again some time.'

'I hope so,' he said. 'It was good to talk with you.'

She nodded, smiled and walked away with the dog on a short lead. A minute or so later Barrett looked back. The Alsatian was once again off the lead, bounding ahead of her.

It had been a strange encounter and though it had lasted for so short a time he spent the rest of the walk thinking about the woman. He supposed that it was a matter of chemistry that he could feel so drawn to a complete stranger after the briefest of meetings, but it was undeniably so. Had she felt that too? There was no way of knowing. He now regretted having made the first move to resume walking. It would have been better manners to have left that decision to the lady. Had he done so he might have learnt something about her. Where she lived, for example. And they might well have exchanged names. Was she married? Almost certainly, unless widowed or divorced. Children? Probably, but they'd be late teenagers or older unless she'd married late in life.

There was little point in asking himself these questions. The important thing was to see her again and from what she'd said about Ludwig enjoying the towpath walks that should not be too difficult. Barrett had not particularly enjoyed Ludwig's company but he now felt better disposed towards the animal. It had, he reflected, been responsible for the first meeting and would, hopefully, provide the opportunity for the next one. In his mind he saw the Alsatian once again – big, powerful, battle marked, a V-like gap in the left ear, a long grey scar on the right flank – a vibrant beast straining at the lead which issued from the reel his mistress held so commandingly in her right hand.

A reel, he recalled, which had upon it diagonal stripes in red, white and green. Her national colours, perhaps. But she was certainly not Italian. What were the other countries with those colours? Hungary, Bulgaria? Others too that he could not recall. No, the diagonal stripes were no clue. Obviously the work of the manufacturer. A gimmick to improve sales.

Each day, week after week, Barrett walked the towpath, the colours of the trees and undergrowth changing as mid-autumn gave way to late, matching in a strange way the metamorphosis in his mind where cheerful optimism gave way to gloomy pessimism as the search for Ludwig's mistress failed to find her. At first he had simply repeated the pattern of the walk on which they had originally met, but later he varied the times and routes of the walks feeling certain that this tactic would succeed; by early winter it had not but he persevered; principally because he was determined to find her and, beyond that, because exercise was necessary and he found the walks stimulating. Whatever the weather there was constant life and movement on the Thames and along its banks. He never tired of watching the waterfowl and often took broken bread and biscuits to feed to them. He had taken to carrying binoculars and these too had heightened his interest in the waterfowl and other bird-life which abounded there. The craft on the river were another source of pleasure; motor-launches in an unending variety of size, shape and form, their occupants equally varied. In some, youngsters, cheerful and noisy, pop and rock often marking their passage with blazing sound; in others older people, the owners at the wheel grimly serious as if the responsibilities of command weighed heavily. There were countless skiffs and scullers, twos, fours, and eights, sometimes with coaches in skimmers bellowing instructions through loud speakers; the routine varying when the coaches cycled along the towpath, precariously it seemed to Barrett, their attention divided between retaining their balance and using their megaphones. At times he would watch canoeists at the weir, fearless, hardy young men who battled with the torrents, performing difficult manoeuvres, their frail craft often capsizing only to be swiftly righted, sometimes by what seemed a complete underwater roll.

On one occasion he was astonished to see, above the tree line in the direction of Heathrow, a distant aircraft performing loops and rolls and spectacular dives which seemed almost certain to end in disaster. It was only later when he had followed the towpath round to the left that he realized it was a miniature aeroplane, remote-controlled by two youths who, at that moment, manoeuvred the tiny craft back over the tops of the far trees to bring it skimming and whining down the river towards them. I'm getting old, he told himself, not to have spotted that earlier.

On these walks he always thought about those for whom he was searching – Ludwig and his mistress – always hoping that he would see them round the next bend. He fantasized about her life, where she lived, the things she might be doing, the chances of seeing her when shopping in Weybridge or Walton-on-Thames; sometimes his fantasies touched on her sex life and occasionally he would see himself involved, but always in what he regarded as an acceptable way. He was a puritan by instinct and felt that dwelling on such thoughts smacked of indecency and might somehow jeopardize his chances of seeing her again.

During those weeks of search he had changed the names by which he thought of her from 'Ludwig's Mistress' to 'Mrs Ludwig' and eventually, desiring something more personal, to 'Paula'. It seemed an appropriate name, one that went well with her personality, and he used it in his thoughts with pleasant feelings of familiarity. Sometimes there were false sightings which would raise his hopes; always the dog was an Alsatian and the person walking it a woman – on one occasion the animal, on close approach, turned out to be too small for Ludwig, on other occasions the damaged ear and scarred flank were missing. These false sightings, when his hopes were raised high for brief, heady moments only to be dashed minutes later, left Barrett in bitter frustration. The last time it happened he had shaken his head, calling aloud, 'Oh, for God's sake, Paula. When will I find you?' so that the lady with the Alsatian on a lead passing him at that moment looked at him in astonishment and walked quickly on.

While he was shaving one morning, something, a hunch, a gut feeling, told him that *this* was the day. He could not explain why he was so sure; perhaps it was that Paula was thinking of him, some sort of thought transference. On a few occasions in the past he had had that sort of experience when at sea. The other person involved had always been Margarita and when, later, they had been able to compare notes the evidence in favour of thought transference had seemed incontrovertible. Buoyed by these thoughts he whistled cheerfully as he shaved and showered, a prelude to the feelings of promise and wellbeing which were to be his throughout that morning as he went about his daily chores: writing a letter to his brother in Australia, taking his car to the garage for servicing, visiting the barber and shopping. The mood remained with him during lunch at The Anchor and afterwards when he set out to walk the towpath.

Determined to give his hunch the best of chances he began the walk an hour earlier than usual, following the route to the second bridge, the walk upon which he had originally met Paula and Ludwig. He had decided that he would, if necessary, walk the towpath two or three times that afternoon thus covering a wide span of time. It was cold now in the early days of winter, and where the trees had not already shed their leaves they were splashed with yellows, coppers and scarlets below a grey, wintry sky, its reflections an abstract painting on the wind-rippled surface of the river. The dank smell of decaying vegetation came from the undergrowth where mounds of windblown leaves had collected. A chill wind blew from the east and against it Barrett wore a thick sweater under his windcheater, a woollen scarf, a tweed hat and gauntlets.

Towards the end of his first walk to and from the second bridge the buoyant mood of certainty which had been with him through most of that day began to ebb, and doubts about his hunch began to assail him. Was it wish fulfilment that had made him so certain this would be the day? Was he about to fail yet once again? The hopelessness of his quest began to return as he came abreast of the small, private bridge which led to the house on D'Oyly Carte island; but he resolved nonetheless to continue the search. He would go on to the weir, a short distance ahead, turn there and set out again on the walk to the second bridge. He reached the bank opposite the weir, turned and started downstream again.

He had passed D'Oyly Carte island and was heading for the first bridge when he saw coming towards him something which made him tense and alert. A large Alsatian was casting left and right across the path, bounding into the undergrowth at times, then returning to the path and standing with ears alert facing the direction from which it had come. With trembling hands Barrett focused the binoculars, saw the heavily studded collar, the V-like gap in the left ear, the grey scar down the right flank. Without question this was Ludwig. His nerves stretched with anticipation and excitement, he trained the binoculars on the bend round which she would come. Long seconds passed before he saw the distant figure appear; a figure made larger, more ample, by winter clothing, her windcheater, scarf, soft hat and grey slacks very much what he was wearing. When she was still some distance away he began walking briskly towards her.

In those brief moments as they drew closer to each other he experienced a surge of emotion; would she remember him? Would he be able to establish some sort of friendship? Invite her to a meal? No, not at once. That would be too much, too soon. And there might be a husband. He didn't understand why he so often assumed there was not. Wishful thinking, he told himself. If they got talking and she learnt that he was a bachelor, alone and without friends in this area to which he had only recently come, she might, if only out of kindness, suggest something. Ask him to tea, or to join her on another walk with Ludwig.

The Alsatian was running back to her now, ears and tail laid low, so she must have called the dog though Barrett had not heard her with the wind blowing against the direction from which she was coming.

When Ludwig was still some distance away Barrett saw Paula stoop, clip a lead onto the Alsatian's collar. She jerked on it before continuing towards him, Ludwig in front, straining as always at the short lead. For the first time Barrett was able to see the reel she held and though no confirmation was needed he noted with relief the red, white and green diagonal stripes.

He stopped and watched, savouring the inner excitement at her approach. Moments later he could for the first time see the face under the brim of her hat – but it was not her face. It was the blue-stubbled face of a man with heavily lidded eyes and a generous jowl resting upon the scarf round his neck. Matted eyebrows, riding across the bridge of his nose, completed the picture of an implacably stern face.

Shocked, astonished and miserably disappointed, Barrett realized that this was the husband about whom he had thought so little. The hat, green and felt on closer inspection, with a feather in its corded band, was Tyrolean, distinctly Teutonic, decided Barrett. So Paula had not married an Englishman. That thought was at once abandoned for a more important one – the need to talk to her husband, a sure route to Paula.

Ludwig, now on a longer lead and some thirty or so paces away, was snuffling at the undergrowth to the right of the towpath. Barrett left the path and walked slowly towards the Alsatian. As he approached the animal it turned suddenly, the hair along its spine rose, it bared its teeth and snarled. The man holding the lead pulled on it, shouting, 'Heel, Ludwig. Heel,' in a throaty guttural as he began to reel in the lead. Ludwig obeyed the command, but glanced back several times at Barrett as if apportioning blame for the incident. Barrett had, in fact, approached Ludwig in the expectation of a hostile response. It would, he had felt, serve as an introduction to the man with whom he so urgently wished to speak.

With the Alsatian now at his heels on a short lead the man came on. He stopped a few yards from Barrett and stared fixedly at him. 'It is dangerous to interfere with a strange dog. An animal which does not know you.' It was a sternly delivered admonition, the man's hooded eyes bright with hostility.

Motivated by his desire to see Paula, Barrett determined to remain friendly. 'It is, I agree. But this is not my first encounter with Ludwig. We have met before.' Barrett smiled. 'Some time ago. Your wife was walking him on the towpath. She said he would not harm me.'

The stern eyes directed a long belligerent stare before shifting focus to the dog crouched at its owner's feet. With a hoarse, '*Komm, Ludwig,*' he jerked on the lead. 'We go.'

For Barrett the command had a chilling familiarity. He was pondering it when, with Ludwig at his heels, the man walked past him, staring ahead as if unaware of Barrett's presence. Without turning his head he called, 'I do not know what you talk about. My wife is already for many years dead.'

Coarsened by the harsh guttural of their utterance, the words seemed to Barrett to be pungent with threat and awful finality.

Watching the departing man, Ludwig once again foraging ahead on a long lead, Barrett's thoughts were confused. What was Paula to this person? Mistress, sister, housekeeper? Why had the man been so gratuitously rude, almost insulting? He could so easily have made a civilized reply, explained in a few words who Paula was: sister, friend, neighbour, whatever. Why the aggressively hostile response? Had he something to hide, was he incredibly jealous, the victim perhaps of absurd notions of infidelity?

A wild thought entered Barrett's mind. Perhaps Paula had been the man's mistress, killed by him in an act of catastrophic rage or jealousy. He was evidently a man with a grave personality problem, a psychotic of some sort.

Barrett asked himself these questions many times as he walked back to the weir, and the answers posed other questions; should he go to the police, tell them what had happened, mention his fears? But he had nothing to go on: no names or addresses, nothing specific. Two chance meetings on the towpath with the same Alsatian – once on a reel-lead with a foreign woman; once, weeks later, on the same lead with a foreign man. Two people about whom he had nothing but the most superficial knowledge; their appearance, their accents. Nothing more. As to Paula, how could he tell the police that he had woven an intricate fantasy around her; a fantasy of which even her name was part? The only facts, tenuous ones, his failure to find her during those weeks of search despite her remark that she often took Ludwig for walks along the towpath, and her last words to Barrett, 'Perhaps we meet again some time.'

Before reaching the flat he had made his decision – he would do nothing about what had happened, tell no one about Paula or Ludwig, or the blue-jowled man – just try to forget them, though that would take time. The decision saddened him. Paula – the woman who had for so long played a major role in the theatre of his mind – Paula had gone. Where, why? And now – who, what could take her place in his life, in his thoughts? Golf, bridge lessons at Adult Education?

Neither seemed in the least attractive now. Perhaps, in time. Perhaps.

THE CRY OF THE PEACOCK

Free for a moment from Mrs Menchip's attentions I looked up the long refectory table towards the President's end from which had come gentle laughter. From where I sat, midway down its considerable length, it had not been possible to hear what had been said nor to know by whom, but it did lead to my observing once again – over the glittering display of crystal and silver, splashed as if on some grand canvas with the colourful gowns of the ladies and the insignia of their cavaliers – the distinguished features of the delegate from Brazil, José Santos Cabral, beside him in subdued mauve, the neckline embroidered in silver, the ample figure of his lady. I had spoken briefly to Cabral during a session of the council but, other than that, did not know him.

Tall but stooped, with darkly circled eyes under a fine forehead, the white, wispish hair above it as appropriate as the blue-ribboned silver star which hung against his shirt front, this so evidently eminent man appeared to have about him an ineffable air of sadness, if not melancholy. Since I scarcely knew him this could be no more than my impression, the signals for which were the sad spaniel-like eyes, the drooping mouth and his unusually gentle and diffident manner.

My speculations about him were interrupted by the attentions of the wine waiter and, when his ministrations were done, by the weirdest of cries: shrill, harsh, eerie, which echoed through the great banqueting hall of the Castelho da Sāu Jorge as if some distant giant had scraped with an immense spoon upon a gargantuan plate.

'What on earth was that?' I asked of the affable lady on my right, Dora Menchip, the Israeli delegate. Her husband, a serious, frowning man who practised law in Tel Aviv, sat opposite her.

'It is the cry of a peacock,' she replied. 'You have seen the white peacocks in the gardens of the castle, yes?'

'No. Tonight is my first visit, I'm afraid.'

'After the dinner you should see. The walls of the castle are floodlit. You will see something of the gardens between the ramparts and the inner walls. They are very beautiful. Not only peacocks but flamingos, swans and ducks also. They swim in the waters of the moats, and nest in the reeds. I do not know what they do at night, but by day you will see them also on the lawns and by the fountains. They–'

'They'll be roosting at night,' cut in her husband with a scowl which suggested she had worked the subject long enough.

'If time permits I shall explore,' I said, so earning a grateful smile from Mrs Menchip before returning to my thoughts which were soon interrupted by the lady on my left.

'I could not help hearing that, Mr Loveday. But be prepared to be disappointed. Personally I feel that those who were responsible for the reconstruction of the castle were overenthusiastic. The gardens with their fountains, pools and waterfowl – and the benches and tables on the lawns for visitors – are rather out of character for a castle built by the Moors in the eleventh century, don't you think?'

'Twelfth century,' corrected Mr Menchip without looking up from his *sole bonne femme*. Mrs Fitch fixed him with an icy stare before turning back to me.

'I'll reserve judgement on that until I've seen the gardens, Mrs Fitch.' I did not care overmuch for Mrs Fitch's manner which tended to be adversarial. Mr Fitch, one of the Australian delegates, was a nice enough fellow who farmed crocodiles. A somewhat unlikely role, I thought, for the husband of such a lady.

This was my first attendance at such a function, the farewell banquet given by the host country to those attending the biennial assembly of the International Organization of Road and Motoring Associations. It had last met in Athens, before that in Paris, and two years hence it would meet in Buenos Aires – to it came the senior honorary officers and permanent officials of road and motoring organizations in many parts of the world. I happened to be an educationist by profession but I was also vice-chairman of a newly established motoring organization in an African country which had only recently achieved independence. Our chairman had been unable to attend and I was deputizing for him. For these reasons, and because I sensed disappointment that I was not black, I did not carry much weight in these august circles. I was, however, an interested observer.

The banquet proceeded at a leisurely but determined pace, the host President, the Portuguese Minister of Tourism, delivered an eloquent address, congratulating the assembly on its splendid achievements – I had thought them somewhat ephemeral – and doing so in three languages with the skill of a juggler keeping several hoops in the air at the same time.

IORAMA's President, a charming and thoroughly gracious lawyer from Brussels, launched into his reply on behalf of the delegates, quickly showing himself to be as deft a language juggler as our host. To see him better I turned in my chair and, when this posture became uncomfortable and the speech promised not to be brief, I turned back. Soon after doing this I saw a slight figure in a long, powder-blue chiffon gown standing behind José Cabral. The young woman, olive-skinned, her tightly drawn back hair as black as polished ebony, leant over Cabral's shoulder and held a sheet of white paper before his eyes. He appeared to consider it briefly, whereafter he turned, looked at her and gently, almost imperceptibly, shook his head. I had never seen such utter sadness in a man's eyes as I saw in Cabral's during that fleeting moment. With a sense of guilt, a feeling that I was intruding in something intensely personal, I was about to focus once again on the speaker when, to my astonishment, the figure in blue chiffon appeared to vanish. My first impression was that she must have fallen, but that would surely have been seen by Cabral, by some of the liveried waiters, of whom at least two stood close to where she had been, or by some of the guests seated near the Cabrals. But there was not the slightest indication that anything untoward had happened. I puzzled for a few bewildering moments about what I had seen and looked in vain for a door or other opening in the panelled wall behind the Cabrals. I began to wonder if . . . ?

The warm breath of Mrs Menchip whispering something into my ear halted my thoughts. '. . . speaks well,' she was saying, 'but too much.' With my eyes on the speaker I gave a slight nod of affirmation and at the same time resolved that I would, when the opportunity arose, ask Mrs Menchip if she had witnessed what I had. It occurred to me then that the wine water, whose attentions had been exemplary so far as I was concerned, had been required by Mrs Menchip to do no more than refill her wine glass with Perrier water. Although I felt reasonably sober, it was not in my nature to discount the possibility that alcohol had taken certain liberties with my vision, if not with other faculties. Certainly, at that time, no other explanation presented itself. If the stone-cold-sober Israeli delegate had seen the young woman in the blue chiffon gown, as no doubt she must have, she would probably be able to explain the strange phenomenon I had witnessed. By nature and training an empirical man, I looked forward to discussing the matter with her.

Loyal toasts having been drunk, the President announced that a video depicting the latest developments in traffic and parking control would shortly be shown in an adjoining room. For delegates' guests and others who so desired – his manner suggested their numbers would be few – it would be an opportunity to explore the castle and its precincts. The President looked at his wristwatch. 'But remember, carriages will be called at eleven o'clock. That will be in thirty minutes' time.' I liked the carriages bit. It sounded so much better than cars and coaches. Since I was no linguist I did not know if the same nuances applied when he repeated his announcement in Portuguese, French and German.

The delegates and their guests rose like a mounting wave which broke as they formed into little groups or went their separate ways. Mrs Menchip touched my arm. 'Now is your chance to see the gardens, Mr Loveday. It is unfortunate I cannot be with you, but I am on the executive.' She shrugged. 'For us the video is a must. But you can get a copy from IORAMA. I much recommend that you go to the ramparts overlooking the gardens.' She turned, pointed. 'Through that door, then through the great hall to the ramparts on the west side. The views from there are magnificent.' She laughed gaily. 'Most romantic at night. The lights of Lisbon. You will see. Now I must rush. My husband is frowning at me. He is very possessive.' She hurried away and with her went the opportunity to which I had been looking forward

– that of discussing with her the young woman in the blue chiffon gown. But at least she had made up my mind for me. It would be the ramparts above the gardens, not the video. As if to confirm the correctness of that decision I heard once more the weird cry of the peacocks.

On my way through the great hall I saw, well ahead of me, the tall stooping figure of José Santos Cabral. As I followed him out onto the terrace I wondered if I might not ask him about the young lady in blue. I soon decided, however, that it would be the height of bad taste for me to do so. I resolved then to put the matter from my mind for I realized it was fast becoming an obsession. Which was just as well for, as I passed him Cabral, who had stopped for a moment to light a cigar, gave no sign of recognition.

I went on across the stone paving of the terrace until I reached the western ramparts where I found a vantage point from which I could look down on the castle's gardens and the inner and outer walls. I was entranced. Behind me the floodlit castle with its rectangular, castellated towers stood massive and foreboding against the night sky, before me the gardens within the walls where dark laurels, tall cypresses and wind-bent olives shared the lawns with pools and fountains in a chiaroscuro of light and shade. The literature in my hotel room had dealt briefly with the history of Lisbon, the city of seven hills, with its Phoenician, Roman and Moorish origins. The early settlers had built primitive fortifications on the hill upon which the castle now stood – and here was I, Robert Loveday, middle-aged bachelor from Southern Africa, standing at its western ramparts contemplating not only the gardens but below and beyond them, to left and right, the lights of Lisbon spread like a magic, richly patterned carpet. It was bordered in the south by the broad reaches of the Tagus, the lights on its famous suspension bridge giving it the appearance of loops of brightly lit hammocks. Mrs Menchip was right, the views were indeed magnificent.

Looking down once more on the gardens, trying to reconcile the idyllic scene with the Phoenician sailors, the Roman and Moorish soldiers, the garrisons quartered on this hilltop in the dim, historical past, I was brought abruptly back to reality by the shrill cry of a peacock, nearer and more jarring than those I had heard before. And soon I saw its source – two white peacocks, their tail feathers spread like great white fans, were engaged in a mating ritual close to the tall statue of a knight in crusader's armour. There was little other bird-life to be seen but for a handful of ducks roosting beside a reed bed, their heads tucked back between their folded wings as if guarding against attack from the rear. My eyes were searching the darker areas where the flamingos and other species were probably roosting when I saw, dimly because it was partly in shadow, a seated figure before a music stand or easel. It became evident after some moments that this was an artist at work. A strange time to be painting, I thought, but from the angle at which he was seated it was evident that the castle was the subject. So this dimly seen, anonymous artist was painting a nocturne – perhaps another Whistler at work – and what a challenging subject, the floodlit castle with its arboreal surround seen from the outer reaches of the garden.

It was a warm, moonless night in early October, fanned by a gentle breeze coming up from the Tagus, a breeze which brought with it the faint and distant clamour of Alfama, the ancient village within the outer walls where *fado* music and muted shouts and laughter suggested the night was still young. All this, the magic of the night, clothed my senses with wonderful feelings of tranquillity, of wellbeing and wonderment that I should be at this place at this time.

My reverie was rudely interrupted by the cry of a peacock and I realized at that moment what a jarring, eerie sound it was. Inwardly I cursed it for destroying the serenity which had been mine only moments before. Once again I focused on the garden, saw the wretched white peacocks displaying with absurd conceit their fan-like tail feathers, beyond them the faint outline of the artist at work in the shadows. I was wondering how much was already on the canvas, when, quite suddenly, the seated figure stood, moved away from the easel and stepped out from the shadows. I saw then, with some surprise, that it was a woman. Surprise, I suppose, because I had assumed that the artist was a man. She began walking slowly towards the moat which ran along the foot of the ramparts where I stood. As she drew nearer I saw that she had on a pleated smock of the sort that artists wear; I saw, too, that she was young, olive-skinned, her shining black-as-ebony hair drawn tightly back from her forehead. With an overwhelming sense of *déjà vu* I realized that this was the woman I had seen at the banquet in a blue chiffon gown. So there was no mystery, she had slipped away to change, not vanished mysteriously. But there was still much to be explained. Why had she appeared so briefly halfway through the dinner? What was on the sheet of paper she had held before Cabral and which had apparently so saddened him? Was it not odd to have changed her apparel and begun painting at such a late hour? And, finally, could my eyes have so deceived me that the vanishing act I thought I had witnessed was simply an illusion?

It might have been but what was happening now, down in the garden below me, was not. The young woman in the artist's smock was closer now, walking towards the moat, heading to the left of where I stood. She had a small sheet of paper in one hand, a handkerchief in the other. My attention was diverted for a moment by a strange sound on my left – something between a gasp and a cry. It seemed quite close. I looked that way, thinking somebody might be in trouble, and saw the tall stooping figure of Cabral, the blue ribbon with its silver star and the glow of his cigar clearly visible despite the thirty or forty metres between us. As I turned back to watch the young woman – she was now quite close to the moat – I saw her stop, throw back her head and extend her arms in a strange gesture – of what? Supplication? Entreaty? Despair? Whatever it may have been, her arms were extended towards Cabral for I turned in time to see him slowly shake his head, drop the cigar and hold his open hands over his eyes. In that dim light it was a weird scene, as charged with impassioned emotion as one from Mozart's *Don Giovanni*, and once again I felt embarrassed that I should be intruding, however innocently, on something so manifestly personal to José Cabral and the young woman, whoever she might be. Nevertheless, curiosity persuaded me to look down into the garden once more for what I privately resolved would be the last time. I did so – but she had vanished. I use that word because 'gone' would not describe what had happened. Five, perhaps ten seconds before she had been on the lawn close to the moat. She could not possibly have moved out of sight in that brief moment. She could not have fallen into the moat, there was not a ripple on its surface and there had been no sound of a splash. She had done precisely what I had seen her do at the banquet, vanished, and once again I was mystified. There had been nothing unusual about her appearance, nothing unsubstantial, transparent or apparition-like – on the contrary, the very flesh and blood of young womanhood. For some time my eyes searched that part of the garden where she had been standing, but to no avail.

I looked at my watch, conscious of the President's warning – the half-hour was almost up – and began to make my way back into the castle soon to find, as on the outward journey, that José Cabral was again ahead of me.

The entrance hall before the main portal was filled with departing guests when eventually I arrived there and I was delighted to see among them my neighbour at dinner, Dora Menchip. Her serious and possessive husband was at her side. I was determined to question her about the incident at dinner. If she had seen what I had it would confirm that my experiences that night were neither mental nor hallucinatory aberrations. It had become important to me, perhaps to the point of an obsession, that any suggestion that I had been suffering from either should be dismissed.

The Menchips were on the far side of the hall and I lost no time in making my way towards them. En route I was buttonholed by Donald Fitch, the crocodile farmer. His breath and jovial shining features were testimony to the excellence of our host's wines and the industry of the waiters who served them.

'Hi, Mr Loveday. Howya doin', cobber?' was his cheerful greeting. 'Great stuff, that video. Unbelievable what those goddam Yanks are up to in California. Some of them multilevel interchanges. Jesus, they make the limeys' Spaghetti Junction look like a lumpa rat bait.'

'Yes, they do,' I lied. 'And a perfectly splendid dinner. Now, if you'll – '

'I'll say.' He held up an admonitory finger. 'But – '

'Sorry, old chap, I'm wanted over there. See you later, I hope.' I hurried on through the throng of people and finally reached the

Menchips. 'So glad to see you,' I said. 'There's something I must ask you.'

Mrs Menchip gave me a warm smile, her husband scowled down at the mosaic inlays on which he stood.

'And what is that, Mr Loveday?' she enquired.

'At dinner tonight, about halfway through, during the President's speech, who was the young lady in a pale blue gown who appeared suddenly behind José Cabral and his wife, leant over between them and showed him a sheet of paper and then suddenly vanished? I mean quite literally vanished.'

Mrs Menchip looked at me in surprise. 'José Cabral is a bachelor. Do you mean the rather plump lady in mauve and silver?'

'Yes, I do.'

'That is his sister. She is always with him at official functions – and when he travels. But I saw no young lady in a light blue frock.' She shook her head. 'I think you must be mistaken, Mr Loveday. Throughout that speech I was watching the top end of the table and I would surely have seen such an unusual incident – I mean a young woman doing that while the President was speaking. Yes, I would have most certainly seen that. Wouldn't I, Maurice?' she appealed to her husband.

'Yes, she would have,' said Mr Menchip, looking at me with the sort of tight-lipped doubt which I presumed he affected when discussing litigious matters with his clients.

'And Cabral is no ladies' man,' continued Mrs Menchip. 'Certainly not since that tragedy. You know the story do you, Mr Loveday?' Her expression suggested that she hoped I did not.

'No. Until this assembly I had not even heard of him.'

Mrs Menchip looked relieved. I think she was looking forward to telling me the story. 'It was a great tragedy, you know. A sort of Shakespearian tragedy. It was, of course, many – '

'Get on with it, Dora,' prompted her husband. 'They've begun calling coaches.' As if in affirmation of this a disembodied voice from somewhere ahead called, 'Coach for the Tivoli Hotel,' and a number of people began to detach themselves from the throng and move towards the portal.

'As I was saying,' repeated Mrs Menchip with a defiant glare at her husband. 'It was of course many years ago. José Cabral was a counsellor in the Brazilian Embassy in Lisbon. At a diplomatic dinner here, in the Castelho da Sãu Jorge, he met and fell in love with a beautiful young woman, Felicia Gomes. She was then studying art in Paris but was here on vacation. It was a truly romantic affair. He was somewhat older than Felicia. But it made no difference, they were madly in love. A year later his tour of duty here was ended, they became engaged and he returned to Brazil. They had agreed that – '

'Coach for the Hotel Avenida Palace,' announced the disembodied voice.

'That's us, Dora. You'll have to finish the story some other time. Sorry, Mr Loveday, but we really have to go now.'

'That's very rude, Maurice. I'm going to finish the story. You go on ahead. I won't be more than a minute. Go on. I'll join you.' She swished him away with a flourish of her hands.

With a final scowl Mr Menchip moved off to join the little group making for the portal.

'Terrible man. But I love him.' Mrs Menchip smiled sweetly. 'Now I'll really have to hurry, Mr Loveday. Where was I? Oh yes. Before José left for Brazil they had agreed that as soon as she completed her art course she would make the liner voyage to Rio where he was to meet her.'

'Come on, Dora. The coach is waiting for us,' shouted Mr Menchip from the portal. 'We're delaying it.'

Mrs Menchip snorted, hissed, 'Damn the coach', then waved to her husband. 'Right, Maurice. I'm on my way.' To me she said, 'A day or so before Felicia Gomes finished the art course José cabled her to say she must fly, not come by sea. He would tell her why when she arrived. She did not like flying but she replied that – '

Once again the sound of Mr Menchip's angry voice rumbled across the entrance hall. 'Dora. Come at once, please.'

Mrs Menchip pulled her shawl about her shoulders, shook her head defiantly. 'Sorry, but I just have to go now.' As she moved away she called to me over her shoulder. 'The plane in which Felicia was travelling crashed in the ocean. There were no survivors. José Cabral had dreamt that the ship she'd booked on sank in a gale and she'd drowned.' Mrs Menchip was moving away again but I just caught the words, 'That was why he sent that cable.'

NIGHTMARE

Donovan Bates, late-thirtyish, confident, assertive, capable (and ruthless, his divorced wife might have added), was driving along a country road in Wiltshire on a windy rain-drenched night, his dark eyes, set deep in his rugged, half-bearded face, searching the road ahead, his mind busy with the events of the day.

For him it had been a long one. Leaving London early that morning, he had driven to Bristol where he spent the day at one of his company's factories discussing delivery date problems for an important new client in Düsseldorf. It had been a frustrating, disappointing day.

Leaving Bristol in late afternoon he had driven deep into the Wiltshire countryside to his widowed mother's cottage. Despite failing health she had stubbornly refused to move into a home where she would, in her son's view, have received the care and assistance she so evidently needed. But she was a determined old lady and nothing he had been able to say could change her mind. The inability of the factory to meet the Düsseldorf delivery dates, and the refusal of his mother to do the sensible thing, were two problems which bounced about his mind like tennis balls hit against a brick wall.

After an early supper with his mother, it was in fact rather more of a high tea, he had kissed her goodbye with a mixture of affection and irritation, got into his car and set off along minor country roads making for the A-road which would take him to the junction with the M4 near Swindon.

It was some time later, when rounding a bend, that he was flagged down by a waving torch. In his headlights he saw a tall figure, the dark, white-banded, peaked cap and yellow waterproof. He braked hard and pulled to the side of the road. The tall figure came to the driver's window and trained the torch beam onto Bates's face, before switching it off. 'Sorry. Just wanted to see if you looked okay.' It was a woman's voice. 'I'm in trouble. My car's broken down and I have to get to Amberyot by eight.'

'Where is your car?' It was a gruff, challenging response. He hadn't seen any car parked along the road, and he disliked having a torch shone in his face.

'It's about half a mile up that side road just before the bend.'

He'd seen the side road, and Amberyot was only about three miles ahead. He was about to tell her to get in when a car passed, flashed its lights and hooted derisively.

'What's all that about?' she asked.

'Nothing. Just yobs commenting on the man-picks-up-girl scenario. Get in. I'll drop you off at Amberyot.'

'Oh, great,' she said. 'Thanks a lot.' She walked round to the near side of the car, opened the passenger door and stood there for a moment, pulling off the yellow raincoat.

'It's very wet. I'll put it on the floor in the back. Don't want to spoil your beautiful upholstery.'

She folded the raincoat, opened the rear door, put the coat in the back, closed the door and came to the passenger seat. During that time she had been illuminated by the car's interior lighting and he had an impression of high cheekbones, slanting eyes and a generous mouth. She was colourfully dressed – red slacks, light blue jersey with a bold floral pattern, and a white scarf with red polka dots. The dark peaked cap's white band was patterned like a chessboard.

He engaged gear, pulled into the road and accelerated.

'Thought you were a policeman,' he said. 'The cap and the yellow oilskin.'

She laughed. 'Good protection for a woman walking alone at night. Would you have stopped if you hadn't thought it was the police?'

'Don't know. But it's just occurred to me – those yobs must have thought you were nicking me.'

'Yah. I s'pose so.'

'What about your car?'

'Bernard will come out and fix it. He runs the filling station in Amberyot. Opposite the pub. Knows Bernice's weaknesses.'

'Who's she?'

'My clapped out little Renault.'

During the rest of the journey they chatted briefly, exchanged names – hers was Gwyneth Evans which accorded with the lilting accent. 'But they call me Gwyn.'

'Donovan Bates,' he said. 'They call me Don – and a few other things. You live in these parts?'

'Yes. On the farm where I work. A couple of miles from where Bernice broke down.'

'You farm, do you?'

'No. Farming's too physical for me. Plodding round in wellies, cleaning cow-stalls. Not my thing. I keep the books, look after the office. And you?'

'Foreign sales. Industrial machinery.'

'You've got foreign languages?'

'Yes. French and German. And I get along in Spanish and Italian.'

'You must be very – ' The sentence was broken by a series of sneezes. She scrabbled in her shoulder-bag. 'Oh, dear,' she said nasally. 'Have you any tissues? Mine are in Bernice.'

'Maybe. Try the glove box.'

She struggled with the latch lock. 'Can't get it open.'

'Squeeze the two ends towards each other.'

She tried again and it opened. 'Silly me,' she said, then, after a brief search, 'No luck. None here.' For good measure she sneezed again.

He took a handkerchief from the breast pocket of his jacket. 'Use this. It's clean.' He passed it to her.

She took it. 'Are you sure? It's such a good one. Pity to spoil it.'

'Use it,' he said brusquely. 'That's what it's for.'

She blew her nose with noisy thoroughness, after which there was more small talk; she was to meet an old friend in the village, at The Shorn Ram. 'Poor dear, she has problems.'

'Who hasn't?' he said.

'But for you, I'd have been terribly late. And she'd have worried herself sick. She's like that.'

'Most people are. Problems make worries.'

The rain stopped and a few minutes later the lights of Amberyot showed up ahead, the neon signs of the filling station dominating the more modest illuminations of The Shorn Ram where he stopped the car. She got out, left her shoulder-bag and torch on the seat, opened the rear door, took out the yellow plastic raincoat, put it over her arm and came back to the open door. He waited, impatiently because he was tired and late, while she searched the pockets of the raincoat.

'Bloody hell,' she complained. 'Sure I had it in this coat.'

'What?'

'Bernice's key. Must be in my bag. Sorry, I won't be a sec.' She opened the bag. 'Can't see a thing. Looks like a jumble sale. D'you mind holding this. Shine it into the bag.' She passed him the torch and he did as directed. She dug like a terrier, gave a squeak of triumph, and produced the key. 'Sorry to have been such a nuisance.' Her smile revealed rows of splendid teeth, as rigid and regular as a white-uniformed guard of honour. 'It really has been smashing of you. Thanks a lot.'

'Forget it,' he said. 'It was nothing.'

'Your handkerchief.' She held it up. 'I'll post it. Washed and ironed. Got a card? For your address.'

'Keep it,' he said, engaging gear. 'Bye now. Take care.' He swung the car out onto the road, kicked down the accelerator and swept away with a plaintiff squeak of tyres. He was irritated. It had taken the best part of five minutes to get rid of the woman. It was late, he still had a long way to go, and he was beginning to feel the effects of a disappointing and worrying day.

By the time he reached the block of flats in Hampstead it was close to midnight. He took the lift to the fourth floor – the top floor – walked down the passageway and let himself into the flat he shared with Giselle who taught at a language school. They had lived together for almost a year, had much in common, and the relationship was proving a good one. She had gone to visit her family who lived near Montpellier and was due back in a week. He missed Giselle. It would be great to have her back.

He hung up his raincoat, went through to the bedroom, put his briefcase in a cupboard, took off his jacket and tie and went through to the living-room where he poured himself a whisky and soda. Before closing the curtains of the picture window which overlooked the Heath, he stood for a moment contemplating the view which had never ceased to please him; at all times and in all seasons it seemed to massage his senses, to impart those emotions of wellbeing and discovery which often befall big city dwellers when they find themselves in the country. How fortunate, he thought, to live in London with over four hundred acres of country outside your window. It was not an original thought but it was one in which he indulged every time he looked out over Hampstead Heath.

Before going to sleep that night he thought briefly of the woman to whom he had given a lift to Amberyot. She had been pleasant enough, not bad to look at, but he was glad he'd not given her his address. That sort of thing could lead to complications. She might have written or phoned on posting the handkerchief; that could have upset Giselle. His last thought before falling asleep was to remind himself to substitute the Düsseldorf papers in his briefcase with those for Copenhagen. He had already faxed the results of the Bristol discussions to his office in the City.

Donovan Bates left Gatwick for Copenhagen at eight-thirty next morning. On arrival he took a taxi into the city where he booked in at the Angleterre. A tight schedule kept him busy for the next two days and time passed quickly. On the third morning he got up early and worked at figures for the Danish contract. After breakfast he went to reception, asked them to call him a taxi and said he'd be waiting in the lounge off the foyer.

He idled away the time by paging through a copy of the *Daily Express* which he found on the table beside the chair he had taken. Though there were both TV and radio in his bedroom he had done no more than listen briefly to the BBC World Service in the mornings while shaving and dressing. But for that he was out of touch with UK news and though the paper was a day or two old he was interested in the financial news. He glanced through that, was turning to the sports pages, when a headline on an inner page caught his eye: *AMBERYOT MURDER*, beneath it in smaller type, *Missing Woman's Body Found.* Having so recently passed through that village he began reading the report with more than ordinary interest.

The body of Gwyneth Evans had been found in the woods about a mile from The Shorn Ram where she had last been seen. She had been strangled but there were no signs of sexual assault. There followed a description: age, appearance and the clothes she had been wearing. Even if her name had not been mentioned, he would have been in no doubt as to who she was. The report concluded with the customary appeal to anyone who had been in the area at the time to contact the police if they had information which might be helpful.

The report shocked Donovan Bates in a way which no other report of that sort had ever done. It was no longer impersonal, distant, of no significance, just another murder. On the contrary this report was intensely personal – he knew the victim, had been with her shortly before her death; his emotions were those of personal involvement. Why would anyone want to murder a decent, sensible, straightforward person like Gwyneth Evans? What sort of man would have strangled her, and for what reason? Bates was asking himself these questions when a page came to tell him that the taxi was waiting.

During the journey to the factory on the outskirts of the city, Donovan Bates's attempts to concentrate on the presentation he would shortly be making were constantly frustrated by recollections of the murder report. Increasingly he felt the burden of personal involvement, and his first instinct was to phone the police as soon as he got back to the hotel. What he could tell them might well provide a vital clue: that she was meeting a woman friend who had problems, that her car had broken down on a side road a few miles from Amberyot, that she had intended asking Bernard at the filling station to go out and fix it – these seemingly ordinary facts might provide a missing piece in the jigsaw puzzle the police would be working on.

By the time the taxi arrived at the factory he had made up his mind; yes, definitely, he would phone the police as soon as he got back to the hotel. He would say that he had read the report in the *Daily Express* late that afternoon.

It was while returning to the Angleterre in a car driven by one of the factory's Danish executives that Donovan Bates had second thoughts about phoning the police. It's something I'll have to think about very carefully when I get back to the hotel, he told himself. I can't possibly concentrate on the problem with this guy firing questions at me as if he were hosting a quiz show.

When they got to the Angleterre Bates suggested a drink, hoping fervently that the Dane would graciously refuse, whereas he graciously accepted. Indeed, he did not leave until they'd had the second drink the Dane had insisted upon. 'You have this one with me. A man cannot stand on one leg, yes?' It was past seven when he finally left.

Bates went up to his room, took off his jacket and tie and settled himself in a deep chair, his outstretched legs resting on a stool. The presentation had been successful, there were still a number of contractual points to be settled, but he'd been assured that the deal was on course. Next, the design people would have to come over and do their stuff. The satisfaction which would normally have been his was, however, overshadowed by the problem which had nagged at him all day. Indeed, it had resulted in his refusal of the Executive Director (Planning)'s invitation to dinner that night, the sort of client invitation one just didn't refuse when a large order was at stake – but he'd done so, 'with the very deepest of regrets. Afraid I'm not feeling very fit. Upset stomach. Probably something I ate last night.' It was untrue, of course, but it sufficed, and he thought the Danish director's, 'I am sorry to hear that,' was said with faintly concealed pleasure.

But thoughts of the Danish contract were soon pushed aside. His initial reaction to the Amberyot murder – to phone the police without delay – had given way to worrying thoughts about the possible consequences.

Like it or not he was involved. At first this had seemed absurd. He'd been with the woman for ten minutes at the most, and then only because he'd played the Good Samaritan. But, and it was a big but, for those ten minutes she had been in his car, talking to him. He must have been one of the few people to have been with her so shortly before she had gone missing. The information he could give the police might seem trivial to him, but it could well be vital to them.

There was in his mind, however, a growing fear – if he phoned the police would he not be inviting trouble, placing himself in a potentially dangerous situation? They might well have doubts about his story, subject him to a damaging interrogation, treat him as a suspect. Who could vouch for his account of what had happened other than the dead woman? Absolutely no one, he had to admit, and in his mind the words reverberated like distant echoes in a cavern. On the other hand if he failed to phone the police, might not that failure implicate him? No, he decided – he'd been in Denmark when the media carried the story that she'd gone missing and, later, reported her murder. He would, if necessary, be able to say that he'd been out of touch with UK domestic news, which was true but for his chance reading of the *Daily Express*. When he returned in three days' time, the story would probably be stale news. In any event they might well have found the murderer by then, or at least know who he was. It seemed to Bates, on balance, that his most sensible course would be to forget that he'd ever read the story.

But during the course of a virtually sleepless night he found that it was quite impossible to forget the murder story – the horror of it, and his personal involvement, assumed proportions so frightening that he could not stop tossing and turning in bed and getting up at times to pace the room in an effort to calm his nerves.

At dinner that night he had realized it would be wise to consider seriously what evidence there might be to link him with Gwyneth Evans's murder. While his first instinct had been to shrug it off as a non-sequitur because he'd had nothing whatever to do with her murder, certain realities soon asserted themselves. While guilt had to be proved, so, though less frequently, had innocence, and that could well apply in his case, however bizarre that eventuality might seem.

So it was in the course of that long and restless night that he examined the evidence against himself. Again and again he went over the short time he had spent in the woman's company, reliving mentally every second of it, and the result was disturbing. Disturbing because as the night went on he was able to recall a number of things which might well implicate him – things which he'd overlooked during the course of a busy day; a day during which he'd sensed a problem but been unable to put his mind to it.

First of these was the car which had hooted as it passed while Gwyneth Evans was standing at the driver's window of his car. What was the hooting about? Derision, amusement at the man-picks-up-girl scenario? Annoyance that he had not pulled the Rover further off the country road, or that the woman should have been at the near-side window in the interests of road safety? Or had the driver thought, as Bates had done, that the figure in the yellow raincoat and dark peaked cap with chequered band was a policeman? Something like that, but whatever it was, the driver, and passengers if any, had seen the incident.

By the time a maid had brought him morning tea an exhausted Donovan Bates had thought of other clues, other evidence against him. Fingerprints? Yes, hers. On the Rover's door handles, perhaps on the sill of the window next to the front passenger seat. And on the front of the glove box. More disturbing, perhaps, was the handkerchief he'd given her. Neither his name nor his initials were on it, but his laundry mark was. That would be enough for the police. Then, with the chilling recollection which follows a nightmare, he remembered her torch. Its plastic surface would have upon it *his* fingerprints. There were no signs of sexual assault, the *Daily Express* had reported. So there was no possibility of genetic fingerprinting to prove his innocence. The web of evidence against him was tightly woven. Worry gave way to fear, irrational and consuming, to a sense of guilt for a crime he had not committed.

He arrived back in England sick in mind and body, the problem and his irresolution having grown larger and more frightening with each day that passed. How could he possibly go to the police now? With such a substantial body of evidence against him how could he remotely hope to establish his innocence? During the long and restless hours of night his imagination now dwelt not so much with what had happened as with what lay ahead. The pictures which projected themselves upon the screen of his mind made of his bed a torture chamber; sweating, he would leave it at intervals to move about the flat but the images of fear would not let him rest – they were too strong, too sharply delineated: his arrest, the interrogation, the trial. The feebleness of his defence, the hostile faces, one of them, perhaps, Giselle's. The press and other media reports as the trial progressed. What would his mother be thinking, his friends, his business associates, the members of his squash and golf clubs? *Always thought he was a bit odd, a bit of a loner. You never know with that type. Tended to keep things to himself. Bloody shame for poor Giselle. He must have been crazy. Some sort of sexual hang-up, I dare say. Or the woman knew something he didn't want out.*

And then the finale, the judge grave, eyes as cold and sharp as broken ice, the thin colourless lips mouthing the deadly ritual: *For a crime so motiveless, so callous, so heinous, the taking of a defenceless young woman's life, there can be only one appropriate punishment. Donovan Bates, I sentence you to life imprisonment.*

Once back in London he had made a point of scanning through several newspapers each day looking for reports on the Amberyot murder, and of course he listened avidly to home news on TV and radio for the same purpose. But to no avail. Presumably there was nothing fresh to report and he was dismayed; unless the police found the killer he, Donovan Bates, would continue to be the prime suspect.

At his office in the City his condition had been noticed. Charles Sims, head of his division and a good friend, and Josephine, his secretary, had shown both curiosity and concern.

'Is all well with you, Donovan?' Sims's face had screwed up into a mark of interrogation.

'Yes, Charles. Why?'

'You look bloody awful. What's the trouble? Have you seen a doctor?'

'I'm okay, thanks.'

'Are you sure? It's being talked about, Don.'

'What d'you mean?'

'The way you look. Josephine's worried about you too.'

'Very considerate of her. But it's none of her business.'

'That's not fair. She's concerned. So am I. What the hell's gone wrong, Don?'

'Nothing really. I'm under pressure, I suppose. My mother's health is deteriorating. She has cancer, you know. And she's living on her own and won't go into a home where she'd get the care and attention she needs. She's incredibly obstinate. And there's the Düsseldorf contract. That's going totally and unbelievably wrong, as you well know, Charles. These things get a man down, interfere with sleep. The mental and physical batteries run down, don't get charged if you can't sleep. That's what's wrong. Nothing more.'

Sims shook his head. 'You're a worrier, Don. That's your trouble. You always have been. Of course your mother's health is a problem, but don't forget she has a right to deal with the situation the way she wants to. You worrying yourself sick about her is not going to help her, or you. Same with the Düsseldorf contract. So, it's going off the rails, but that's not remotely your fault so for chrissake stop worrying about it. We need you here, Don. Need you fit. So, get your act together. Would you like a break? Get away somewhere? Giselle's back this weekend, isn't she?'

'Yes, she is. But I don't want a break, thanks all the same.'

Donovan Bates knew that a break wouldn't do any good. The problem would go with him, be worse than at work because he'd have more time to think. But he couldn't tell that to Charles.

A day or so later, having trimmed his beard, he went to the window overlooking the street for no particular reason other than observance of a long-established ritual: shower, rub-down, trim beard, move to window, look down on life in the street below, at the ordinary, reassuring things. The red milk float passing lazily by, its passage marked by frequent stops and the darting figure of the milkman, bottles in hand. The hurrying, purposeful stride of those who had to be early at work, cars like Matchbox toys sliding by, cyclists crouching low in the saddle on the uphill slope, sitting back relaxed on the downhill, elderly ladies exercising their dogs, waiting patiently at lampposts, lead in hand, while their charges raised hairy legs.

For Donovan Bates there was on this occasion, however, the jarring note of a police car which came slowly up the hill. As he watched, it stopped opposite a block of flats lower down on the far side of the road. A following car parked immediately behind it, both vehicles on a double-yellow line. Two men in uniform got out of the police car at much the same time that two men in windcheaters, blue jeans and what had been white shoes, got out of the car behind. Both parties crossed the street, there was a brief consultation between them, after which the officers in uniform came up the street, followed at some distance by the two men in plain clothes. To Bates, watching the scene with rising tension and a quickening heartbeat, there was not the slightest doubt that the latter were detectives. He drew back from the window as the posse approached, but continued watching through a slit between the gathered curtain and the windowframe.

As the two uniformed men walked slowly up the pavement, evidently in no hurry, the detectives keeping well back, Bates watched and waited, dry mouthed, for what he knew must come. He had gone through the mental torture of this scene so often that the only differences now were matters of detail. He knew that the police would come abreast of the building, turn right, look up at the front door to check the number was right before mounting the steps and entering the building. The janitor's hours were 8.30 to 5.30 so they would go straight to the lift. When they'd done all those things, and he'd heard the distant clang of the lift gates, he went through to the living-room and flopped into an easy chair. Trembling, sweating, he waited for the sound of lift gates at the far end of the landing on his floor. Fear had done its work, he was no longer capable of critical, analytical thought. What was about to happen to him was monstrous, surrealistic; he was caught up in the theatre of *Grand Guignol* and there was no way he could alter the script.

It's not, he told himself, my character, my upbringing, my intelligence, diligence, whatever, which decides these things – there was the metallic rattle of lift gates at the far end of the landing, after that the sound of footsteps, faint at first but growing slowly louder, the firm, well-shod steps of policemen. The rhythm of his heartbeats faltered, began jumping like terrified mice, breathing became more difficult, noisier, until he was panting – he returned to his thoughts, these things were decided by chance: random, unrelated, uncontrollable, so able to destroy you. The footsteps were close now, heavy, implacable. They stopped outside his front door, and he waited in an agony of apprehension for the ring of the bell, his thoughts a jumble of recollection: Gwyneth Evans standing in the rain at the Rover's window, the censorious hooting of the passing motorist, chatting to Gwyneth on the way to Amberyot, dropping her at The Shorn Ram, holding her torch, giving her his handkerchief, Gwyneth no doubt telling her waiting friend why she was late, describing as women do the man who'd given her a lift.

These were among the reasons why the police whose muffled voices he could now hear, were at the front door. Ring, ring – for chrissake ring, he pleaded. Get it over – he pressed balled fists to his eyes. But the bell didn't ring. Instead there were voices and muffled laughter. Laughter, by God! Laughter about what?

The heavy, deliberate footsteps sounded again, going on down the passage, away from the lift, growing fainter until he could hear them no longer. Was this a ruse? Were the white-shod detectives still there? There'd be no telltale footsteps from those shoes. What was happening? He didn't know, and he suddenly realized that he no longer cared. Drained now of all emotion he went through to the kitchen, began making a cup of coffee. Obedient to habit, he switched on the radio, was aware of the newscaster's voice without listening to it until, as if a bomb had exploded, the words 'Amberyot murder' hit his consciousness – the disembodied voice was saying something about a police spokesman at Devizes. '. . . The man who has been helping with enquiries, an unemployed farm labourer of no fixed abode, has now been formally charged with the murder of Gwyneth Evans and will appear in . . .'

There came from Donovan Bates a strange sound, something between a strangled cry and a hoarse laugh. The mug of coffee spilled onto the kitchen table, leaving pools of dark liquid like the formless splashes of contemporary art. He went to the bedroom, threw himself onto the bed, tears running down his cheeks.

'Thank God. Oh, thank God,' he sobbed, turning his face into the pillows. Later he sat up, dried his eyes and went to a mirror. He shook his head at what he saw. 'You'll never be the same,' he told himself. 'Never be what you were before.' He thought of the man in jail in Devizes, sharing with him the mental torture suffered and still to be endured.

Innocent or guilty the horror had to be the same. He may well be innocent, reflected Bates, caught like me in a web of chance. Whether he is guilty or I am innocent is not the issue. If they'd not got him it could well have been me. Innocent or guilty you have to suffer. You can never go back to what you were before.

Relief, yes, but at what price? All confidence gone, in its place, pervading everything, the threat. Somewhere out there, something unknown, beyond control, all powerful – chance, waiting to destroy you.

TEA AT THE RITZ

After lunch at their club in St James's two men sat in the lounge talking, at times about current events, at others ruminating about times long gone. Their conversation was quiet, leisurely and intermittent, the frequent silences in no sense embarrassing for their friendship extended over rather more than thirty years.

Tom Bagshot and Henry Bowlby were both in late middle age, the former rather more so than the latter. Tom Bagshot was a big, heavily jowled man, his drooping moustache as dark and extravagant as his eyebrows, the fiery cheeks beneath them telling of high blood pressure. He dressed carelessly, the collar creased, the tie ill-knotted, the blue suit under pressure everywhere, the waistcoat straining at its buttons confirming that the fight against appetite had long since been lost. A more or less permanent scowl did him less than justice for he was a genial man.

Bowlby on the other hand was tall, slim and well dressed, his clothes, elegantly worn, spoke of good taste and an excellent tailor. A smooth oval face and friendly enquiring eyes made him look rather younger than he was despite partial baldness.

Able to dredge through the events of a long-standing friendship they were much at ease together although at times they might have seemed irritable and contradictory to the uninformed observer. True to the pattern of old friends, they were well aware of each other's shortcomings upon which, at what seemed appropriate moments, they did not hesitate to remark. Both men were comfortably off and comparatively idle having inherited the wealth of their more industrious forebears.

Bowlby looked at his watch. 'H'm. Time's getting on.'

'It always does. Third time you've looked at your watch in as many minutes. Catching a train?' Bagshot brushed his moustache with a large forefinger.

'No. I have to see my tailor.'

'I used to do that sort of thing. Ready-mades now. Much less fuss.'

Bowlby nodded understanding. 'Yes. Yours look like that. Pre-Thatcher vintage, I'd say. They don't seem to have kept up with growth.'

Bagshot ignored the thrust. 'It's not late. Can't your tailor wait?'

'Afraid not. I've a busy afternoon. My tailor, then tea at The Ritz.'

'Really.' Bagshot's eyebrows arched incredulously. 'Tea at The Ritz. Aunt, niece?'

'A lady,' said Bowlby casually.

'Do I know her?'

'I think not.'

'Then you've just met her. Otherwise you'd have told me all by now.' Bagshot lifted *The Times* from the table beside him, began unfolding it.

'Would I, Tom?'

'Yes, you always do. And tea at The Ritz. This has to be something rather special. Not really your line of country. Who is she and where did you find her?' He lowered *The Times*, looked over the top of it. 'Let's have the story. I can see you're bursting to tell it.'

'One doesn't discuss ladies in one's club, Tom.'

'Doesn't one? You and I quite often do.' Bagshot looked round the room. 'When we know we can't be overheard.'

'I met her in New Bond Street, actually.'

'Pick up, was it?'

'I suppose you could call it that. She tripped and fell. Scattered her shopping, handbag, the lot. I picked her up, collected the bits and pieces and returned them to her. She was badly shaken but very brave about it.'

Bagshot's index finger was again busy with his moustache. 'Age, looks?' he enquired in a bored but dutiful tone. 'Marital state?'

'Late twenties, early thirties, I'd say. One doesn't ask a distressed young lady if she's married, divorced, shacked up or single.'

'No. But married ladies usually wear wedding rings. I suppose you didn't look.' Bagshot rearranged himself in the armchair. A large and more than ample man, he found the operation was difficult, involving grunts and heavy breathing. 'And looks?' he persisted.

'Most attractive. Lovely eyes, nose and mouth, the rest to match. Super smile. Like when she thanked me for all I'd done when I put her in the taxi.'

'To take her where?'

'Haven't a clue, Tom. Possibly Kensington.'

Bagshot frowned, shook his head in weary disbelief. 'Surely you heard her tell the cab driver. Or weren't you listening? You never were too bright. So how did this tea at The Ritz thing happen?'

'We had a brief chat before the taxi arrived. When she said she couldn't thank me enough I suggested tea at The Ritz as my reward. She said she couldn't make it that afternoon so we settled for this afternoon. I asked her where she lived and she said in the country. In Town for a few days. Staying with an aunt in Kensington.'

'Truly romantic, Henry. Like the twenties. When did you last have tea at The Ritz?'

Bowlby shook his head, narrowed his eyes. 'Long time ago. Can't really remember. Why?'

'Packed with tourists, I'm told. Lots of Americans, jeans and T-shirts, cameras. Japs, too, of course. You'll be photographed. English gentleman taking tea with English lady. Be sold as a tourist souvenir in Tokyo.'

'She seemed to like the idea.'

Bagshot produced a leather cigar case, said, 'Really,' took out a cigar and went through the ritual of preparing and lighting it. Bowlby leant forward, lowered his voice.

'Actually, there's a slight problem. I'm rather counting on you to help, Tom.'

Bagshot grunted. 'There usually is with you.' He returned the cigar to his mouth. 'Well, let's have it.'

Bowlby launched into a lengthy explanation. He had an important dinner that night. There would be a number of City people there according to his stockbroker whose guest he would be, and an excellent guest speaker, some undersecretary or other. He couldn't quite remember who.

Bagshot snorted. 'My dear Henry, you do drop yourself in it, don't you? I can't think of anything more dreadful than that sort of dinner except perhaps tea at The Ritz. But what's the problem?'

Henry's problem, as it happened, took rather a long time to explain. He began by saying that it was a question of where he should change that night. When Bagshot suggested that he should change where he always did when in Town, at the club, Bowlby said that that wouldn't really do. When asked why he became clammish but under pressure confessed that it concerned Lucinda.

Bagshot's dark, doggy eyebrows lifted. 'Lucinda? Lucinda who?'

'That I prefer not to disclose. I saw her name on an envelope when I picked up her things.' Bowlby had a mental image of the filigreed silver pillbox. Very important to his plans, that pillbox.

'I see. Well, continue with the drama. The unnamed lady and your problem.'

'Actually, Tom, I was thinking of your flat in Chelsea. I mean, if I could change there it would simplify things. And I know you're off to Midhurst this afternoon, so if – '

'I am but Margaret isn't. Forget it, Henry. She thinks you're a bad influence.' He leant back, blew a cloud of smoke at the ceiling. 'And how would changing in our flat have simplified things?'

Bowlby explained that he had found Lucinda extremely attractive. He was, he reminded Bagshot, off to Scotland for three weeks; leaving tomorrow. If he had somewhere to change other than the club he thought he might –

'Oh God! Not that again,' interrupted Bagshot. 'Aren't you getting on a bit for that sort of thing? And if you must, what's wrong with a hotel room. Tea and crumpet at The Ritz. Ha-ha-ha.' Bagshot's head went back, stretching his jowl alarmingly.

'I think that's in rather bad taste, Tom. This is a serious problem in human relations.'

'Rubbish! You're close to sixty. A randy old bachelor, that's the problem.'

'I do dislike your language, Tom. You've coarsened in recent years. And I'm disappointed. I thought you would help. Lucinda likes me. One can tell when the chemistry is right. I just feel that I should get to know her better before we go our separate ways.'

'You mean get her into bed.'

'Not at all. Simply be with her somewhere where we can talk meaningfully. Develop a friendship in a way one can't in public.'

Bagshot shook his head. 'Rubbish.' He raised *The Times* again, a gesture which irritated Bowlby who gazed rather helplessly at a portrait of the Duke of Wellington, wishing that he had the Iron Duke's resolve. He cleared his throat, returned to the business in hand.

'Seen your friend Lucky Lasby lately?'

From behind *The Times* Bagshot growled, 'No. He's in Paris.' Bowlby said nothing, biding his time. A few days earlier Bagshot had told him he'd turned down an invitation to accompany Lasby on a short visit to Paris. 'Like the food, can't stand the people,' he'd said.

Bowlby, who was playing his hand carefully, knew that Bagshot, a close friend of Lasby's, occasionally used the fax in Lasby's West End apartment for messages to and from brokers in New York and Frankfurt. He knew, too, that Bagshot had a key to the apartment so that he could get to the fax when Lasby was out of Town.

'Tom,' he said gently, 'if Lasby's in Paris, any chance of changing in his apartment in Larnchester Mansions? I gather you have a key.'

Bagshot lowered *The Times*. 'I have, and there isn't.'

Moved possibly by Bowlby's mortified sigh and almost whispered 'Oh, well, if one's oldest friend won't help . . .', Bagshot relented. With some effort, accompanied by more heavy breathing, he rummaged in a waistcoat pocket and produced a key. 'You can have it for a couple of hours but, as far as I'm concerned, solely for the purpose of changing. No funny business. Is that understood?'

'But of course, my dear chap. No option. Got this damned dinner, haven't I? But many thanks for your help, Tom. Most kind of you.'

Bagshot grunted.

'Tell me, Tom, you know Lucky Lasby well. What sort of chap is he?'

'I like him. A lot of people don't. Much younger than us. Still plays polo. Used to be good. He's an old gambling chum of mine. We've put in a good deal of time together at the Claremont. Mostly baccarat. He had a lot of luck at that a few years ago. That's where the "Lucky" comes from.'

'What does he do for a living?'

'Soldiering. He's in the Blues. And he plays the market.'

'Married? Family in the country?'

'Neither. He has this apartment in Larnchester Mansions, and a place in the country where his brother and sister-in-law live. The brother is his bailiff. Lasby's not the marrying sort. Fairly uncomplicated life, really.'

Bowlby stood up, straightened his tie, looked at his watch. 'Must go now, old boy. Most grateful.' He held up the key, grinned cheerfully. 'I'll return it tomorrow. Leave it in an envelope on the club noticeboard. Bye now.'

'Bye, Henry. Take care.' Bagshot once again opened *The Times*.

They met in the foyer of The Ritz soon after four that afternoon, Lucinda looking summery and beautiful in a flowered dress and a wide-brimmed straw hat from under the brim of which she smiled at Henry in the most engaging fashion.

'Sorry I'm late,' was her breathless greeting. 'The traffic was unbelievable.'

Henry laughed. 'Five minutes is scarcely late for a lady. Let's find our table. I've been warned that tea at The Ritz is rather different from what it was.'

She gave him a quick sideways glance, giggled. 'So have I. My aunt was horrified. Said I should have insisted on Fortnum's. But I'm sure we shall enjoy it.'

'I'm sure I shall. It's the company that counts.'

'Very gallant of you.' She hesitated, laughed nervously. 'Do you realize that I don't even know your name?'

'Henry Bowlby. And you are Lucinda Elliot. Just one moment.' They had reached the booking table outside the entrance to the dining-room. He spoke to the receptionist. She consulted her book, gave him a number and before long they were shown to their table.

Lucinda looked round the elegantly luxurious Palm Court, gave him a huge smile. 'It's gorgeous, isn't it?' she said. 'Heavenly décor. Makes me feel I'm wrapped in pink silk with gilded ribbons tied in lovely bows, reflected again and again in those fabulous mirrors. How could my dear aunt prefer Fortnum's? I don't remember it being like this when last I came, all those years ago.'

'Glad you like it. Very different from what I remember. I think we went up some stairs in those days.' He looked round at other tables from which there came the steady buzz of human bees. 'It's full all right. But they look pretty reasonable. I don't see the T-shirts, denims and trainers my friend Tom Bagshot spoke of. I expect he was pulling my leg.'

'I suppose so.' She looked thoughtful. 'How did you get a table at such short notice? My aunt says one has to book at least a fortnight in advance.'

Bowlby grinned. 'Influence. My sister's. She knows somebody who knows somebody who's a VIP in this neck of the woods.'

'Lucky man, aren't you?'

A waitress came, they ordered tea, Lapsang Souchong at Lucinda's request, cakes were chosen and she began pouring the tea.

'Tell me,' she said, 'how on earth did you know my name?'

'Ah, bit of detective work that.'

'But seriously. How did you know?'

'Among the things you scattered was a postmarked envelope addressed to Lucinda Elliot. By the way, I should have asked. Hope you're none the worse for that fall. It looked a nasty one.'

'It was rather. But I've recovered. A few bruises. Otherwise I'm fine.'

While the conversation progressed in formal and predictable fashion Bowlby glanced occasionally at those at tables in his line of sight and concluded that Tom Bagshot was right in at least one respect – there were clearly some tourists and there were cameras, though none in use so far as he could see. There was perhaps a certain informality in the dress of a number of guests but, on the other hand, the décor seemed more lavish, the atmosphere in some ways more formal, than on the occasion of his last visit; which was not surprising since it had been many years earlier. He remarked upon this to Lucinda who pointed out that much else had changed during that time: the sixties had, she said, seen the last of many rather stupid social shibboleths, made people free to be themselves, to do their thing the way they wanted to, to enjoy life and not be bound by conventions which they felt were senseless.

Delighted that the conversation was now heading in such promising directions, and entirely on her initiative, Bowlby was enthusiastic with his, 'How right you are, Lucinda,' and as this was the first time he had used her name he experienced a delicious sense of familiarity which he hoped was reciprocated by the owner of the blue eyes which regarded him so seriously from under the brim of the straw hat. Encouraged by this, and aware that most people liked talking about themselves, he began questioning her. She lived in Somerset, near Montacute, she told him. Loved country life, came to Town occasionally on shopping expeditions and for the theatre, opera and ballet; and of course to see friends. She almost always stayed with her aunt in Kensington, who was a darling. From time to time he prompted her: was she married, were there children, what were her interests, did she ride to hounds, was she a keen gardener, when would she be returning to Montacute . . . ?

No, she was not married, but had been. It had not worked well so they'd parted, amicably and without regrets. There were no children so it had not been difficult. No, she didn't ride to hounds and didn't like the idea of blood sports.

She then questioned him along much the same lines, to find that he too was divorced, had two daughters, both now married, one living in Canada, the other in France. He, too, lived in the country and did not ride to hounds; shooting, fishing, golf and bridge were his leisure pursuits. Was he retired? No, not really; he explained that there was nothing to retire from other than farming which he'd done for a few years before getting bored with it. That had been a long time ago. Yes, he came to Town occasionally, not very often now, stayed at his club usually but sometimes, like now, at Larnchester Mansions in the apartment of an old friend. Bowlby was rather pleased with the way he'd got that in.

She looked up quickly, frowning. 'How very interesting. Larnchester Mansions – sounds faintly familiar. Rather grand, are they not, and much sought after, I gather.' Her stare softened into a quizzical smile. 'Is your "old friend" a lady?'

'Good heavens, no,' protested Bowlby. 'Tom's anything but that.'

'I was teasing.' She laughed or, as Bowlby would have put it, tinkled. He was beginning to adore the tinkle, a truly melodious sound somewhere between a tiny laugh and a small chuckle. He looked at his watch – 5.35. There wasn't all that much time left. He turned to her. 'By the way, there's something I'd very nearly forgotten. Your pillbox.'

'What on earth do you mean?' Her eyebrows lifted into little arches.

'It was among the things I picked up yesterday. Found it in my pocket last night.'

While he spoke she was fidgeting through her handbag. She looked up, smiled. 'Yes, it's missing. I keep a few Disprins in it. Haven't opened it for ages. But I'm so glad you've got it. I'd hate to lose it. Belonged to my mother.'

There followed a discussion about getting it back to her. She was off to Somerset the next morning, he to Scotland. Would he be sweet and post it to her? He suggested that he had a better idea – they could take a taxi to Larnchester Mansions and pick it up there. He would, he explained, have asked her to dinner but he had to attend one in the City. 'Something I can't back out of,' he said sadly. She shrugged her shoulders, smiled and told him that she, too, was booked for dinner. In Kensington with friends of her aunt.

'So, come along with me in the taxi. It'll take ten or fifteen minutes at most and then it can take you on to Kensington.'

She regarded him doubtfully, as if seeking to read his mind. But soon the frown disappeared and the blue eyes twinkled. 'Yes, Henry. Good idea. It'll save time, won't it?'

Once again he experienced that strange thrill of familiarity for this was the first time she had used his name. The bill settled, they made their way out, Bowlby giving one last look at those around him while silently thanking The Ritz for the tea which had so splendidly advanced his plans. Aloud, he said, 'Wasn't too awful, was it?'

'No, Henry, it wasn't. On the contrary, it was a simply splendid tea.'

During the short taxi journey conversation was once again formal and brief, each busy with their thoughts, Bowlby congratulating himself upon his foresight in having, earlier that afternoon, made a short visit to Lasby's apartment where he had left a small suitcase containing the clothes into which he was to change for dinner that night. In it was Lucinda's pillbox, in a sense the key to his endeavours concerning her.

'Well, here we are,' announced Bowlby, as the taxi came to a stop. A commissionaire opened the door and helped Lucinda out. Bowlby paid the cab driver and followed. Once in the foyer he turned to her with a sympathetic smile. 'Well, that didn't take long, did it?' She agreed, and he wondered if she'd noticed that he'd not told the cab driver to wait. He led the way to a lift. They had it to themselves for which he was silently thankful as he pressed the button for the third floor. Arrived there, he led the way down a corridor, turned right at its end and stopped eventually at door number 18 which he unlocked.

'Come in,' he said, flourishing an arm. 'Tom Bagshot's pied-à-terre.' They went through another door into a large, club-like room. Bowlby flourished another arm. 'Here we are, my dear. Make yourself comfortable while I hunt for the pillbox. It's in my suitcase.'

She moved unhesitatingly towards a large leather armchair and sat down, her hands clasped behind her head. 'This room', she announced authoritatively, 'is one that I like although it is so much a man's room. Such a weird mixture. Half what I suppose one would call a large study, with its oriental rugs, leather upholstery, attractive mahogany bits and pieces, and all those mannish things – cutlasses and sabres and their scabbards on the walls, regimental photos, hunting prints. And that awful lion – I couldn't live with that.'

Bowlby looked at the lion or, more correctly, at its skin which lay on the floor beneath the window seat, the glassy eyes in the stuffed head glaring ferociously at nothing, the red-gummed, sabre-toothed mouth savagely agape.

'He must like living with it,' said Bowlby in tones of mild reproof. 'And fortunately you don't have to.'

'H'm,' she said, looking at him with an enigmatic smile. 'You mustn't take me too seriously, Henry – I was being feminist. Daring to criticize male taste.'

'And why not?' conceded Henry.

'And if I may dare to finish my criticism – the room is also half I don't know what . . . those office things, I mean.' She nodded towards the far side of the room where telephones, a fax machine and other office equipment stood on a big leather-topped table, beside it a filing cabinet.

'Tom Bagshot plays the market, has quite a portfolio, you know. He needs those things. Rather likes having them around.' Bowlby's tone was again mildly censorious.

'Of course,' said Lucinda contritely. 'But your friend Bagshot must surely be a soldier. Very much a traditional one, I'd say.'

Bowlby looked up from the suitcase he had opened on the floor. 'It *is* a man's room. He *was* a soldier, long ago.' He let loose a small cry of triumph, closed the suitcase and walked across to where she sat.

'Hold out your hand, Lucinda, and shut your eyes.'

'Not some horrid trick, I hope.'

'Now would I trick you, Lucinda?' He smiled abashed reproach. 'Close your eyes.'

She closed her eyes and put out her hand. He pressed the silver pillbox into it. 'Now open your eyes.'

'Haven't played that game since I was very small. But how glad I am to see this.' She held it up before her eyes. 'And in future, Henry, please don't pocket things belonging to ladies who fall down in the street.'

He made a face, said, 'What base ingratitude,' and sat down on the settee beyond the coffee table.

Lucinda indulged in another slow look round the room. 'Your Tom Bagshot must be a keen polo player.' She pointed to the mantelpiece where a number of silver-framed photos of mounted polo players and games in progress stood in close company.

'He used to play when he was younger. Still a keen follower.' Bowlby was chiding himself for not having put the photos away in a drawer during his earlier visit, when she got up and walked across to inspect them more closely.

'They all seem to be of the same man. Your friend Bagshot presumably. Good-looking, isn't he?' She pointed to one of a player standing at the head of his pony.

'Yes, I suppose you could say that.' Bowlby was not happy about the direction in which the conversation was heading. He had told her that it was Bagshot's apartment simply because it had sounded rather better than saying that he'd been lent the key by a friend of the man who owned it. He now regretted that deception and decided to change the subject.

'Let's have a drink,' he suggested, pointing to the silver tray with soda siphon and glasses which stood on a table beneath a corner-cabinet the contents of which he'd examined earlier that day. She looked at her watch, then at him. 'D'you think we should? I mustn't be too late. I adore my dear aunt but she's awfully old-fashioned and fussy about punctuality.'

He sensed that she thought the idea of a drink was not a bad one. 'Don't you think we should celebrate the return of the pillbox? After all, it's rather an important event.'

She agreed and he poured the drinks, hers a dry vermouth, his a whisky and soda.

In the event they had several drinks and gathered a good deal of what she laughingly referred to as 'flying speed' by which time, after an unconvincing refusal, she accepted his invitation to inspect Tom Bagshot's apartment. 'It's rather nicely done,' explained Bowlby. 'Some well-known interior designer. I forget his name.'

Emboldened by a new-found confidence, bolstered by Lasby's whisky, Bowlby led the way with almost proprietorial zeal; first to the dining-room, then the kitchen, then back through the living-room to the bedroom and, finally, to the ornate bathroom where he responded to a sudden urge to embrace his attractive companion who responded with a whispered, 'Oh, Henry!' Encouraged by this he repeated the treatment more resolutely, eliciting on this occasion a response so warm that he suggested she might care to return to the bedroom and try the three-quarter bed for size. After the slightest of hesitations she accepted this proposal with a flash of her blue eyes and a maidenly giggle. Bowlby later emerged from the bathroom with a towel round his waist to find her tucked in the large bed looking, he thought, particularly attractive in the half-light she had contrived by drawing the curtains and switching off all but a discreetly screened bedside reading-lamp. He lost no time in joining her.

Later, deeply content, he lay back in the comfortable bed pleasantly aware of the warm, lithe body beside him. He was, however, aroused from this subliminal state by a shriek from its owner who with sudden violence sat upright. 'My goodness, Henry. Just look at the time.' She pointed to the digital clock which blinked its red message on the bedside table. 'I must fly,' she added, leaping out of bed.

'What a pity.' He sighed. 'I was rather hoping there might be time to go round the course again.'

'You're boasting, Henry.' She flashed him a smile as she slipped into her panties and bra with the speed and assuredness of long practice.

He lay watching her for a few moments before getting out of bed, rewinding the towel round his waist and making for the bathroom. 'I must put something on,' he called over his shoulder. 'Won't keep you a moment.'

Lucinda, now all but fully dressed, was putting on her shoes. 'Can't possibly wait for you, Henry. Must dash now.' She dazzled him with another brilliant smile. 'But thank you for a gorgeous tea at The Ritz. Couldn't have enjoyed it more.' She slung her handbag strap over a shoulder, stopped for a moment at the door and called to him. 'Be a darling, Henry, and straighten the bed before you leave. Must rush. I'll let myself out.'

He was protesting that he'd be ready in no time when he heard her open the front door and close it behind her. Swearing loudly he switched on the shower, adjusted the temperature, got under it and returned to his thoughts. They had failed to exchange addresses or telephone numbers, though fortunately he had seen the envelope with her name and the Kensington address – her aunt's address no doubt.

Determined to see Lucinda again he resolved to lose no time in tracking her down through that address. It shouldn't be difficult, might even be done by telephone if she and her aunt had the same surnames. At this point it occured to him that here, too, was a problem. He didn't know Lucinda's maiden name. To add to his troubles the soap slipped out of his hand and he had to scramble for it on the shower floor, banging his head on a tap in the process. Returning to the vertical and his problem he decided he would have to call on the aunt. He would say that he had mislaid her niece's address. Developing this theme he came up against another problem; a mental image of the envelope revealed an ugly truth: he could not recall the Kensington address. It had been *something* Mansions, but the something eluded him. So did the street name of which he had not the slightest recollection. Thus he was left with an enigma . . . Lucinda's aunt lived in *something* Mansions, somewhere in Kensington. This, he sadly acknowledged, was no address at all. Nor had Lucinda got his address; they'd just not got round to that subject, and he'd not even given her the name of his club; so the situation was pretty hopeless. Devastated at the prospect of never seeing her again, he switched off the shower and began towelling himself down with a fury that somehow gave him comfort. That done he hung the towel on the heated towel rail where he had found it and went down the passage to the bedroom.

To his astonishment he was not alone; a maid was making the bed. She looked up, and gave a squeak of dismay. Bowlby hurried back to the bathroom where he grabbed the towel and once more put it round his waist before returning to the bedroom where he'd left the evening clothes into which he was to change. The maid was still busy with the bed. She saw him, looked away. 'Sorry sir,' she said. 'I didn't know anybody was here. The Major usually tells me if he's expecting guests.' Bowlby was wondering how best to deal with that information when she added, 'I thought those belonged to the Major.' She pointed to the trouser-press over which Bowlby had draped his evening clothes. Beside it stood his small suitcase.

With the more ludicrous parts of his anatomy now covered, Bowlby's confidence had returned and he launched into a brief explanation. He and the Major were old friends. He'd been lent the key so that he could change for dinner, which was what he'd been doing when she arrived. At this point he looked at the bed. 'Had a rest before changing. Tired after a busy day,' he added with sudden hindsight. 'I had every intention of making up the bed myself. Sorry to have bothered you.' He smiled with all the charm he could muster.

'It's no trouble, sir,' she insisted, saying she would come back later to finish the room. That would not be necessary, he said. He would wait in the living-room until she had finished. With a small chuckle she said, 'The Major won't have it called the living-room. He calls it his study. Very fussy he is about that.' Another light laugh emphasized the point.

'Yes, of course. I'd forgotten that. He always talks about his study.' Bowlby felt that Tom Bagshot had somehow let him down, should have warned him about this quirk of Lasby's. Taking with him a few essential items of clothing and a comb, he left the bedroom.

Once again in the living-room, he slipped on a vest and underpants and combed his hair before sitting down in an armchair. He was about to pull on his socks when the door from the lobby opened and a man came in – a man, noted Bowlby, with a long, weathered face, fair hair and military moustache, the protuberant eyes somewhat indeterminate in colour. Of average height and slight build he wore his clothes with casual elegance. He appeared to be in his early forties. The protruding eyes seemed to grow larger as he shut the door firmly and strode into the room, his inquisitorial stare directed at Bowlby who found its persistence and the accompanying silence unnerving.

Responding to a compulsive desire to break the silence Bowlby said, 'Hullo. Can I help you?'

'You certainly can,' replied the stranger.

'May I ask in what way?'

'I want an explanation.' The large eyes were faintly bloodshot. 'And it better be a bloody good one.'

Offended by this outburst Bowlby abandoned his attempt to pull on a sock. 'What sort of explanation?'

'Who you are and what're you doing here?'

'Henry Bowlby. I'm changing for a City dinner. And who, may I enquire, are you?'

'Never mind that. This happens to be my apartment. How did you get in?'

Bowlby's right hand plucked at his forehead like a harpist at her strings as he strove to conceal his alarm. Aware that there was a limit to this ploy he once more concentrated on pulling on a sock. The man who's stare so disconcerted him bore little resemblance to the photograph of the man standing beside a polo pony. Was this intruder a well-dressed, well-spoken con man who knew that the owner of the flat was abroad; tipped off by the maid perhaps? The situation looked as though it might become pretty rough; it would require careful handling. Bowlby looked up, sock in hand.

'Are you Major Augustus Lasby?' he demanded.

'I am – how did you get in?'

'To confirm that you are Major Lasby tell me your nickname. The one your close friends use.' Bowlby felt that if the stranger could not answer that correctly he'd have called his bluff. A pretty shrewd question, he decided.

The man came closer, the glare from the bulging eyes a shade more menacing. 'You're in no position to cross-examine me, my friend. I'm about to call the police. Now.' He held up an admonitory finger. 'How did you . . . ?' The door from the bedroom opened and the maid came in.

'Good evening, sir.' She looked surprised. 'I thought you were in Paris.'

'I was. I am now here.'

'I see, sir.'

'Any messages?'

'They're on your table, sir. With the letters. Miss Tandy did the fax and answerphone up to midday yesterday. Before she left for Bournemouth. Will that be all, sir?'

'Yes it will.' Lasby scowled.

With a timid sideways glance at Bowlby she left the room.

Lasby's eyebrows lifted ominously as he glared at the other man. 'Been having it off with Frieda, have you?'

'I resent that remark,' protested Bowlby. 'Of course I haven't.'

Lasby flustered him with another long, silent stare before saying, 'You're in no position to resent anything. You still haven't explained how you got in. How the hell did you? Frieda, was it?'

'No it wasn't. It was Tom Bagshot. He said I could use it to change for a dinner in the City. Gave me the key. Said you were in Paris, that you were an old friend and that you wouldn't mind.'

Shaking his head Lasby went across to the leather-topped table and glanced at the neatly stacked letters and messages. 'Tom's got a bloody nerve, hasn't he?' He ran a hand over his smooth hair, sighed.

Bowlby reflected that it was most unfortunate that Lasby should have returned from Paris a day early. It was evident that, in the circumstances, the less said the better since Lasby was clearly in a foul mood. While another broody silence descended upon the room Bowlby was thinking that it would have been a lot worse if the maid had not done the bed. He'd not intended to tackle that until he'd finished dressing. A covert glance at the small table beneath the corner-cabinet further reassured him – the silver salver was empty. The maid had removed the glasses which he and Lucinda had so recently used. Bless dear Frieda, he thought; but I wonder what she made of *two* glasses, one still half-full of vermouth? As if reading his thoughts Lasby had gone across to the corner-cabinet. He turned to Bowlby. 'Care for a drink?'

Anxious to please, Bowlby said, 'Yes. A small one. I've got this confounded dinner.'

'Nonsense, my dear boy. Flying speed's what you need for that sort of torture.'

Bowlby winced. The phrase was all too familiar and reminded him that he'd already acquired rather a lot of that condition. He had visions of arriving at the dinner in an aggravated state of insobriety, and wondered if he could miss it without mortally offending his stockbroker. It was a decision he would have to make later.

'Soda or water?' came from Lasby.

'Soda, please. A good squirt.'

'Prefer water meself. And not too much of that. Soda murders Scotch. Makes a sissy drink of it.'

Unwilling to take up the challenge, Bowlby said nothing. Lasby brought the drinks across and lowered himself onto the settee. They drank in silence, almost as if unaware of each other's presence, until at last Lasby said, 'Afraid you'll have to clear off, old boy. Once you've got into your glad rags. I'm expecting a visitor.'

'But of course. I'll get on with changing right away.' Bowlby put his half-finished drink on the salver and began levering himself out of the armchair.

'Oh, sit down,' said Lasby irritably. 'You don't have to bolt. Finish your drink. As long as you're gone by eight.'

'I'll be gone long before that. This dinner, you know.' There followed another long silence, now one of so many that Bowlby regarded them as a Lasby peculiarity. They were, however, less dangerous than conversation so he said nothing. Later, another drink was poured, Bowlby protesting that this must really be his last, and a small one at that. He wished fervently that he could explain that it would be his fifth in less than an hour. He chided himself for not refusing the drink but, anxious not to upset his host who appeared dangerously unpredictable, he had lacked the courage to do so. That apart, he felt a little alcoholic stimulation was no bad thing in the difficult situation in which he now found himself.

With both men once again seated, glasses in hand, silence returned and for some time each man was alone with his thoughts, Lasby staring gloomily at the contents of his glass which he held up to the light, frowning as if somehow concerned at what he saw there. Presently, without looking up, he said, 'I suppose Tom told you I was resigning?'

'No. He did mention something about litigation. Feared your luck might be running out. Said he hoped you'd stay in Town and not back off into the country.'

'Did he tell you what the litigation's about?'

'No, he didn't.'

Lasby's eyebrows signalled doubt. 'Funny. Tom's a bit of an old woman when it comes to that sort of thing.' He shook his head and renewed his inspection of the yellow liquid in his glass before draining it. The ensuing silence, as had all the others, lay like a blanket over the faint snarl and rumble of traffic in the street below. At length Lasby sighed deeply. 'So unfair. That bloody woman. She's determined to take me to the cleaners. They all have an eye to the money, you know. The more beautiful and innocent they look the more lethal they can be.'

Bowlby, beset with his own more immediate problems, made no attempt to get involved in Lasby's, other than to remark that women could be difficult. This appeared to irritate Lasby who said that Bowlby couldn't have had much experience of the opposite sex if he'd found them no more than difficult. 'Bloody predators, old boy. That's what they are,' he growled in a voice hoarse with venom.

Bowlby nodded assent. He was anxious to finish dressing, to pack his things and go, and so conclude an embarrassing situation. On the other hand it was still too early to leave for the dinner, so there was little point in hurrying.

'It's not only the money. It's having to resign,' continued Lasby's complaining voice. 'I mean – that bloody woman. How could she be such a bitch?'

Since Bowlby had no idea who the woman was or what she'd done, and the questions were clearly rhetorical, he made no attempt to intervene and instead emptied his glass before putting it back on the salver.

He was about to announce his intention to continue dressing when there was a knock on the door from the lobby. Lasby shouted, 'Come in,' the door opened and a woman stood in the doorway, her eyes wide with surprise. Lasby sprang up, took her by the arm, closed the door and pulled her into the room where he embraced her warmly. 'Lucinda, my darling. What a lovely surprise.' His eyes shone with affection. 'But why are you here? I'm supposed to be in Paris. Our date is for tomorrow.'

He took her hand, led her over to the settee. She ignored Bowlby and he, accepting the clue, looked away. She was frowning at Lasby.

'Are you sure?'

'Absolutely.'

She scrambled furiously in her handbag, produced a diary, flicked through its pages. She looked up, made a face. 'Oh, dear. You're right, Augustus. It is tomorrow. How very stupid of me.'

'No problem, my dear. I'm expecting a visitor shortly. Geoffrey Fell, my solicitor. Said he'd pop in and bring me up to date. We'll sort that out later. In the meantime let me introduce you to this oddly clad gentleman. Henry Bowlby – Lucinda Elliot.' He waved a hand in either direction. 'He's a friend of Tom Bagshot. Tom said he could change here for some dinner the poor chap has on tonight. Tom gave him a key.'

'I see.' Her tone was dubious as she continued to ignore Bowlby. 'Sorry I interrupted . . . ' She shrugged. ' . . . the changing for dinner.'

Sensing that she suspected an unsavoury relationship, Lasby hastened to explain: he and Bowlby had met for the first time about half an hour earlier. He had come straight from Heathrow to find Bowlby in the flat. He looked to that gentleman for confirmation.

Aware that the situation and his appearance verged on the ridiculous, Bowlby managed a self-conscious, 'Yes. No more than half an hour, I'd say.'

She looked at Bowlby for the first time. 'I'm sorry if I sounded unfriendly, but I was somewhat surprised.' She glanced at Lasby. 'You see, I know most of Augustus's close friends, and well . . . your state of undress. I'm sure you understand, Mr Bowlby.'

'Yes, of course I do. But please call me Henry.'

Outwardly calm, Bowlby was asking himself what on earth she was up to, and what her relationship with Lasby was. Evidently very close, he decided. And she was certainly no stranger to the apartment – obviously had a key. Very odd, very devious. Pretending that it was all new to her, asking questions about the photographs and so forth. I daresay she took some of them, he said to himself. Accepting my story that the apartment was Bagshot's, making an absolute bloody fool of me. Not at all the sort of person I thought she was. But she can't be the woman who's involved in litigation with him. He obviously adores her.

Lucinda for her part was silently thanking the Almighty that Augustus had not arrived half an hour earlier, for she had every intention of being the second Mrs Augustus Lasby. That he should have returned from Paris a day early was totally unfair and absolutely shattering.

'Let's have a drink', that gentleman was saying, 'before we set Henry on his way. He looks as though he could do with one.' With a cackling chuckle he made for the corner-cabinet and began pouring the drinks. That Lasby made it a vermouth for Lucinda without consulting her confirmed Bowlby's belief that they were intimates.

Lasby was bringing over the salver of filled glasses when there was a knock on the door which led to the lobby. He called, 'Come in,' the door opened and Frieda, the maid, entered the room. Glancing up from his task of avoiding spillings Lasby smiled. 'Hullo, Frieda, what's the problem?'

'This, sir.' She held up an earring, her face a study in blankness. 'I found it in your bed when I was straightening it this evening.'

Bowlby felt the chill thrust of a dagger in the region of his stomach. The earring was Lucinda's. He had admired it over tea at The Ritz –

green and blue butterflies set in silver. He realized that he must have dislodged it when nuzzling her ear during the delightful interlude in bed. With a flash of intuition he realized that her unexpected return had almost certainly been for the purpose of retrieving it. She'd probably become aware of its loss while in the taxi on the way home. While Bowlby was tussling with these thoughts, Lasby had taken the earring from the maid.

'My present on your last birthday, Lucinda.' He smiled happily. 'I see you're wearing the matching brooch. Lucky that Frieda found this.' He dangled the earring.

'Yes, it was lucky,' agreed Lucinda in a small voice.

'Lucky Lasby's luck rubbing off on you, what?' Grinning, he put a hand on her shoulder. Moments later his expression became suddenly grim, he folded his arms across his chest, bowed his head and stared at the pattern on the Persian rug beneath his feet as if seeking there the answer to whatever troubled him.

Lucinda's thoughts were chaotic. My God, she asked herself, oh, my God, what's coming next? Frieda is supposed to be in Nottingham visiting her bed-ridden mother – not due back until tomorrow – she knows damn well the earring's mine – so what is this? Jealousy, revenge for some slight, real or imaginary? Whatever it is it's totally unbelievable. My God! What a wretched, scheming, unscrupulous bitch she's turning out to be.

Lasby appeared to be coming out of his trance. He coughed, glared at the maid. 'Tell me, Frieda. Why were you making my bed this evening? I haven't slept in it for days.'

Please God, let her say she was changing the linen for his return, prayed Lucinda.

'It was untidy, sir. Been slept in since I did the room this morning.'

'Any idea by whom?' Lasby's voice rasped like a steel file.

The maid avoided his challenging stare, gazed at her feet. 'Perhaps this gentleman, sir.' With averted eyes she nodded in Bowlby's direction. 'He was in the bathroom when I came in shortly before seven this evening to tidy and dust.' She took a deep breath, her voice dropped to little more than a whisper and her eyes all but closed. 'That was just after I saw Mrs Elliot leave the apartment. I didn't know there was anyone else there until,' she hesitated, nodded again in Bowlby's direction, 'until this gentleman came through from the bathroom.'

PHILEMON'S TANK

For Philemon Molefe, January was an important month, not only because it was the first of the year but because his birthday fell during it. On what day was far from certain – his mother could not recall the exact date nor could his father who had several wives and regarded the matter as unimportant. But Philemon was a serious young man and though illiterate had in his eighteenth year, when applying for a pass at the Government pass office in Middelburg, decided that his date of birth was 15 January 1918. Since the registration of births and deaths in the remote reaches of the Transvaal where Philemon's family lived was not in those days taken overseriously by the authorities concerned, his assumption went unchallenged. For his part Philemon felt secure in the knowledge that at least the month and year were correct for his mother had assured him that it had been in the first month of the year in which the Kaiser War had ended.

It was against this background then that he celebrated his twentieth birthday on 15 January 1938 on the Andrews' estate, Magalies View, where he worked as a labourer, helping to build a shed, planting trees and making a rock-pool for Madam's new water garden. It was fed by a borehole at the back of the main house on the twenty-five-acre estate which lay to the northwest of Witkoppen, some 17 miles from Johannesburg, and facing the distant ranges of the Magaliesberg mountains.

Philemon's twentieth birthday was a memorable one for reasons which he explained to Nathan that evening as they sat round an open fire beside their tent watching two mutton chops sizzling and spitting like fighting cats.

'Madam give me the chops, also one poun' cash, when she say,

"Happy birthday, Philemon". She must know this from my passbook, you see. She is very good woman, this Madam. She say, "You and Nathan have done good job on rock-pool so the chops are for both, but the cash is birthday *bonsela*, so only for you, Philemon." 'That is what she say.'

Nathan's grunt could have registered disapproval or disenchanted acceptance. Philemon took it to be the latter and decided not to mention the tank just yet as that might be too much for Nathan. Instead he dwelt on the fact that he and Nathan, temporary labourers on the estate for the last eight months and engaged only for the purposes of tree planting, building a new garden shed and completing the rock-pool in the water garden, had that morning been told by Titus, the head gardener, that their services would no longer be required after the end of the month.

'You see, Nathan, these are good people. To get two weeks' notice is very special. We are only temporary workers and such people have no rights to notice. This you must know.'

With a click of disapproval Nathan shook his head and turned the chops with a piece of fencing-wire. 'This is not good. For me two weeks' pay instead of notice is better. Then you can look for other job still with money in the pocket.'

'You want too much, Nathan. Is not possible like that. Anyway, other job does not worry me. I am going home to the kraal to see my parents. I hope to take them some gifts for they have been good to me.'

'What gifts are these, Philemon?'

'Some time I tell you. Now I make plans.'

Nathan turned a flaring chop from one side to the other, skewered it with the wire and transferred it to Philomen's tin plate upon which there lay a large lump of *putu*, or mealie meal as the white people called it. 'You always making plans, Philemon, but nothing comes. Will be same next time. You shall see.'

Philemon smiled to himself and changed the subject to the excellence of Madam's mutton chops.

Snug under the blankets in their tent that night Philemon thought about the tank and developed the project which had been in his mind since early that morning when Esau, the stableboy, had broken the momentous news: the old corrugated-iron tank on the roof of the stables was to be replaced in a day or so by a new and larger one. The old tank had a few rusty patches and a slight leak in one of its seams but nothing, in Philemon's view, which was really serious. He fell asleep thinking about the tank.

Next morning after a cursory wash from a bucket of cold water he slipped on shirt and shorts and made for the stables. There he carried out a more detailed examination of the tank until Esau arrived on the scene and reminded him that it was near to seven o'clock and he'd better get on with his breakfast of coffee and brown bread and jam.

Breakfast finished, he and Nathan cleaned their plates and mugs, stowed them away in the tent, and went across to the big shed behind the stables where they kept their picks and shovels. As was usual at this time they said little to each other having done their talking at breakfast. Nathan was first to leave the shed, Philemon dallying so that he might have yet another look at the tank. With the early-morning sun gleaming on its corrugated flanks it looked to him like a giant golden honey-pot of the sort he had seen in shop windows, a truly beautiful object which he greatly desired. For Philemon this was the moment of truth – there was nothing in his life just now which was quite as important as the tank.

With pick and shovel over his shoulder he was leaving for the work-site when he saw Baas Andrews coming up the path from the main house. He stepped aside as the white man approached.

'Morning, Philemon.'

'Good morning, my Baas.'

'Madam tells me you were twenty yesterday.'

Smiling bashfully, Philemon nodded, then, summoning all his courage, he burst out with what was so much on his mind.

'My Baas, when the new tank comes what is for the old tank?'

The white man looked towards the blue ranges of the Magaliesberg as if the answer might lie there. Rubbing his chin, he turned to Philemon with a puzzled frown. 'The truck that brings the new one will take away the old one. Why?'

'My Baas, I would be very happy to have the old tank.' Philemon's voice had become husky, and he looked at the ground rather than at the white man who was staring at him in amazement.

'For Pete's sake, Philemon. What for?'

'To take to my father's kraal, my Baas. When I go home after finish of the month.'

The white man shook his head, smiled. 'You people never cease to amaze me. How the hell do you think you can take that bloody great tank back to your kraal, more than a hundred miles away?'

'I have plan, sir. I can do it.'

'What's the plan, my boy?'

'My Baas, I have friends. They will help me.'

'With transport, you mean?'

'Yes, my Baas. In such a way. The old tank can be very good for my father's kraal. He will be too happy to have such a tank, for when the rain come.'

Mr Andrews shook his head, looked at his watch. 'It's getting late. You'd better be getting on with your work.'

'Yes, my Baas. I go now.' Philemon began to move off down the path.

'And you can have the tank,' the white man called after him.

Two long nights of worrying, and long and involved discussions with Nathan, were necessary to bring Philemon's plans to some sort of fruition. The first hurdle had been overcome. The tank was his, but time was limited. The old tank had been replaced by the new one on the very day that Baas Andrews had said he could have it. Now it stood, forlorn and undignified, on a patch of veld grass behind the stables. There were just twelve days left before Philemon's notice expired when he would have to leave Magalies View.

Since the tree planting was not yet finished everything to do with the tank had to be attended to during his time off – except, of course, thinking about his plan; something which seldom ceased but for sleep. The Ndebeli tribal kraal where his family lived was in the Transvaal highveld between Vaalplaas and Verena, some distance from the road down to the Wilge River. With Nathan's help – he was semiliterate – and the map in the *AA Handbook* which they borrowed from the

Madam's car, the distance from Magalies View to the kraal was about 120 miles. It could have been less but Philemon wanted to avoid main roads and travel on country roads and tracks wherever possible. He hoped to average about 17 miles a day, thus completing the journey within eight days if all went according to plan.

The first problem Philemon had to tackle was the law. Previous encounters with the police, principally in connection with the pass laws, but once for a traffic offence, riding Nathan's bicycle at night without a light – it was on a remote country track across the veld near Magalies View – had made him wary of the law; it was important therefore to make sure that his plan would not bring him into conflict with it.

Fortunately Nathan had a friend, Ezekiel, who worked as teaboy and cleaner in the offices of a firm of Johannesburg lawyers. At Philemon's request Nathan invited Ezekiel to spend an evening with them at Magalies View promising *maningi nyama na tshwala* – plenty of meat and beer.

Ezekiel duly came and in the course of a pleasant evening round the open fire Philemon outlined his plan. After discussing certain of its details Ezekiel confessed that it was somewhat unusual. He did not himself know how it stood with the law but he undertook to discuss the matter with James Gollop, a law student employed by Corker, Brunson & Chad as a junior. 'This young white man is very clever with the law,' explained Ezekiel. 'Also is good friend to Africans. I will ask him to say for sure if this plan can be okay with the law. In some days you will hear from me about this.'

Disappointed that Ezekiel had not himself been able to settle the legal problem, Philemon decided to press on with other aspects of the project while awaiting Ezekiel's report-back on the views of James Gollop. That evening he borrowed Nathan's bicycle and rode across the veld – this time with a light – to visit another friend, Lucas, who worked on a smallholding. His employer, Baas Visser, kept a small herd of donkeys which were used for various purposes. Some were hired out for children's rides at fêtes and birthday parties, others were sold to private buyers of whom there were few. From time to time an old one was sold to a country butcher who would slaughter the animal and sell its meat to Africans or as animal feed to a private zoo. The going rate for a donkey was a pound, for an old one, ten shillings. All this was known to Philemon through his friend Lucas to whom he confided his wish to buy a donkey, for collection in about ten days' time.

'I have not much money,' he told Lucas. 'My wages is only two poun' ten for month, but I want donkey not too old, also not too expensive. I must feed donkey and this can be more money.'

'Let donkey eat veld grass. This cost nothing.'

'Some place is no veld grass, then I must give food.'

Lucas disappeared into the darkness, returning later to report that Baas Visser wanted one pound for Koko, a middle-aged donkey. 'Very strong, very good worker,' stressed Lucas. Philemon offered twelve and sixpence, Lucas again disappeared to return with shining eyes. 'Baas Visser can take fifteen shilling. Otherwise no deal. He say this is giveaway for such a donkey as Koko.'

'Why is name Koko? In Fanagalo this word mean grandparent. Must be old donkey.'

'Koko is young grandparent. You are my friend, Philemon. Koko is very strong donkey. For fifteen shilling you make good bargain. For this you can be sure.' So hands were slapped to settle the deal, and Philemon handed over seven and sixpence, the balance to be paid on delivery in ten days' time. He rode back to Magalies View in the darkness singing an old tribal song his mother had taught him. It was a happy song – about a young shepherd boy taking home to his mother fresh guinea fowl eggs he has found in the long grass while tending the cattle. 'What I take back to my parents' kraal shall be better than eggs of guinea fowl,' murmured Philemon. He had a mental picture of handing over the tank and Koko to his astonished and delighted parents.

In the days that followed or, more correctly, the late afternoons and nights, Philemon made further progress with his plans: from Wiseboy, who worked at the local garage, he purchased from the scrap-heap at the back of the premises an old exhaust pipe for five shillings. With flanges at both ends and some eight feet in length it was exactly what he needed.

Shortly before noon the next day Baas Andrews came down to the new area below the rock-pool where they were planting the last batch of oaks, planes and sycamores. He checked the new holes to see if drainage stones, compost and manure were in place. To Titus, the head gardener, he said, 'Yah, it seems okay.' He glanced at Nathan and Philemon, digging nearby, their faces and bare chests wet with sweat. It was mid-summer, and a fiery sun beat down from a cloudless sky.

'These boys working hard, Titus?'

'Very hard, my Baas. They are good workers.'

The white man gave them an approving look. 'Yes, I can see.'

This was the opportunity Philemon had been seeking. He determined to use it. As his employer started off towards the rock-pool he quickly overtook him. 'My Baas, pliz can I ask you?'

'Yes. What is it, my boy?'

'About tank, my Baas.'

Baas Andrews grinned. 'Oh, the tank. What's the problem?'

Philemon explained. He had to make certain things for the tank. Could he have some of the bitumen-treated split poles left over from when they built the new garden shed? Also the old hose, lying with the split poles behind the stables and –

'Christ, you don't want much, do you? So what's the "and"?'

Philemon saw that the white man's face showed amusement, not anger, so he pressed on. 'My Baas, I must make things for the tank. I have no tools or the vice. If I can use workshop . . . ' He paused, breathless, 'then can make things.'

'H'm. What sort of tools?'

'The saw, the hammer, also the chisel, my Baas. And some nails and screws. Not much, my Baas. Just few things. Also pliers perhaps.' Philemon looked at his feet rather than face the white man's penetrating stare which could be like the glint of a thrown assegai.

'Okay, Philemon. You can have the split poles and the old hose-pipe, and you can use the workshop. You were handy with tools when we built the garden shed. But only outside working hours. And mind you don't bugger up my tools. They cost money.'

Philemon grinned. 'The Baas is too kind. The Lord will make good reward.'

'Hope you're right. Now get on with your work. Titus doesn't look too pleased.'

Philemon lost no time in rejoining Nathan and getting on with the digging. Titus was not angry. He had heard the conversation and had been told a little about the tank project by its new owner. He regarded the whole thing as a harmless joke but admired Philemon's tenacity even if he did laugh at his eccentricity.

For Philemon, assisted at times by Nathan, the next week was one of considerable activity at the end of each working day. Late into the nights the workshop lights were on and from it, and behind it where the tank now lay on its side, came an endless cacophony of hammering, sawing, and drum-like metallic noises; added to these were the sounds of voices, sometimes raised in annoyance, at others quietly earnest – occasionally there were outbursts of laughter, not infrequently uproarious.

One evening Baas Andrews dropped in to see how things were going. Philemon showed him the work being done on the tank, explained the reasons for it and the ultimate goal. At this the white man exploded with laughter.

'You can't be serious, man. You'll never make it. What d'you think the police are going to say?'

'My Baas, I have friend in lawyer's office. He send message that plan is okay for law. Has already send me Baasie Gollop's words in letter. This letter can be here tomorrow.'

Baas Andrews turned his head slowly from side to side, lit a cigarette and drew on it deeply before exhaling little puffs of blue smoke through his nostrils. The Baas makes like railway-engine leaving station, thought Philemon.

'You'll never make it, my boy. But full marks for trying. And that old rubber hose you want. What's that for?'

'For same like tyres, my Baas. In two, three days we finish. Then Baas shall see how this can work.'

With another shake of his head and a smile of puzzled amusement the white man said, 'Let me see that letter from your lawyer friend when it comes.'

Late in the afternoon of 30 January Lucas arrived at Maglies View with Koko on a rope lead. It was the first time Philemon had seen Koko. The day he'd bought him the donkey had been busy at a children's birthday party in the Saxonwold and he'd had to take Lucas's word for it that Koko was a fine strong donkey. Now Philemon examined his teeth, checked his flanks, and trotted him on the lead. He decided that Koko, though not young – indeed, if anything, a trifle on the old side – was strong, healthy and not a bad buy. Encouraged by this, he handed Lucas the outstanding balance of seven shillings and sixpence and asked him to convey his thanks to Baas Visser. He then led Koko to the paddock at the back of the stables, where he tethered him for the night near the all-but-completed tank.

A day or so previously the letter from Ezekiel, with James Gollop's opinion, had arrived and that evening, sitting round the open fire outside their tent, Nathan had read it to Philemon.

> *Tell your friend,* wrote James Gollop, *that I have studied the relevant Provincial ordinances and can find nothing in them which makes illegal that which he has in mind. The definition of a wheeled vehicle does not specify how many wheels it must have. There are references to the means of propulsion, motor vehicles, animal-drawn vehicles, bicycles and so forth, but nothing, as far as I can see, which excludes the vehicle Philemon has in mind. It must, however, during the hours of darkness, exhibit a light visible to oncoming traffic, and I would suggest that he also fits two red reflectors at the rear of the vehicle, one at each extremity. As far as I can see it does not require to be registered or licensed. This, presumably, because those drafting the legislation were unlikely to have envisaged such an unusual vehicle. Please wish your friend* hamba gahle *on my behalf. I shall be interested to learn, in due course, how the journey goes.*

'This is what James Gollop say, Philemon. Now we shall talk of it and I will explain,' said Nathan. 'Because he is clever university man, he use plenty big, too-hard words. But I can tell you what such things mean.'

By the time they had finished discussing, dissecting and interpreting the letter it was well past midnight.

Philemon awoke next morning in a state of excited anticipation for this was not only his last day at Magalies View but the day upon which he and the tank would leave for his family's kraal in the Loskop district. Titus had, in a moment of indulgence, said that he and Nathan need only work for that morning. Philemon was delighted. He had planned to set out on the journey after work that evening. Since there were certain last-minute things to be done that would have meant getting away between seven and eight which would have been on the late side. As it was he now had the whole afternoon free in which to attend to all sorts of details and, best of all, there would be time for a trial run round the drive with Koko, inspanned for the first time. That morning Philemon worked like a man inspired, singing many of the songs of the Ndebeli tribe, mostly those about the land and the work which had to be done upon it as the seasons chased each other through the years.

During the afternoon many things happened. His first task was to fit to the tank the two-tiered, split-pole frame that had taken so much time to build. With Nathan's assistance the frame was lifted into position above the tank – now lying upon its side – and gently lowered into position, the holes in the two V-shaped frame supports fitting over the axle housing which projected from each side of the tank. A strong galvanized wire was then slid through the hollow inner axle and bent ninety degrees to the vertical where it was secured to the frame on either side. The hollow axle casing was the old exhaust pipe Philemon had found in the scrap-heap behind the garage. The inner axle which rotated within it was a length of galvanized-iron water piping left over from Madam's water garden. Both axles had been well treated with black axle grease before insertion. Holes to take the axle had been made in each end of the tank. When Nathan questioned the wisdom of this Philemon had observed, 'Is not problem. Abram Dhlomo come every month from Loskop to fix things at the kraal. He is plumber and good with soldering iron. He will fix holes.'

Perhaps the most difficult part of the work on the tank had been the fitting of two X-shaped braces of split poles inside the tank ends to strengthen them against the axle load, the axle itself passing through them at the junction of the Xs. Philemon had had to climb into the tank through its manhole and work there by lamplight, setting up the split poles and other materials passed to him by Nathan.

Before fitting the frame, several lengths of old garden hose had been passed round the tank at its centre and at each end. Securely fastened with baling-wire, and lying within the tank's corrugations, these were the tyres Philemon had had in mind when asking Baas Andrews about the old hose-pipe.

There remained only the fitting of the shafts for Koko and the preparation of his simple rope harness. When that had been done, Koko was inspanned for the first time and with Philemon leading him on a single rope bridle, Koko and the tank – known to the Africans on the estate as *lo makulu sondo*, the donkey tank – set out on their first journey: from behind the stables to the drive where the servants had gathered to witness the trials. Baas Andrews was still at his office in Johannesburg and Madam was playing tennis at the Country Club, so the occasion was an uninhibited one. There was much amusement: whistles, catcalls, cries of encouragement and derision, and repeated exclamations of surprise and admiration for the way in which Koko and the tank performed. No one it seemed, save Nathan, had thought that Philemon's crazy idea would work so well in practice.

Having completed two circuits of the drive Philemon led Koko and the tank back to the paddock behind the stables where he unharnessed the donkey and rewarded him with a feed of oats from the nosebag Nathan had made as a parting gift.

For a number of reasons Philemon had decided that he and Koko would set out on their journey at six o'clock that evening. High summer would give them daylight for the first hour or so, the traffic would be light and chances of encounters with the police, an ever present fear, should be less. He would outspan for the night at eleven o'clock, or earlier if he and/or Koko showed signs of exhaustion. Another reason was that by six o'clock Baas Andrews and Madam would both be home and he felt it was important they should witness the departure since they had done so much to make it possible. Only that morning, before leaving for his office, the Baas had given him back James Gollop's letter together with one signed by himself saying that he had given the tank to Philemon who had his authority to take it by road to his father's kraal in the Loskop district. He concluded this *To Whom Concerned* letter with: *Legal opinion has been obtained and confirms that Philemon's journey with the tank is not in breach of any of the provisions of the Provincial Road and Traffic Ordinances. I trust that every assistance will be given to this hard-working young man to complete his enterprising journey successfully.*

Baas Andrews had also made him a present of a large bag of oats for Koko and Madam had given him an old overcoat and a thick jersey, garments from the wardrobes of her sons who were away at university in the Cape. 'The nights can be cold in the highveld,' she'd said. 'Even in mid-summer.'

The last hour before departure was spent loading the frame with equipment and personal items. A few large things like the bag of oats, the sack containing Philemon's few pieces of clothing, his colourful African blanket and the overcoat, were laid across the split poles on top of the frame but everything else was hung on its rear cross-members – *everything else* was not inconsiderable: a bag of old tools: hammer, saw, pliers, spanner and hatchet – bought for a few shillings from his garage friend, Wiseboy – two canvas water bags, coils of spare wire, of old hose-piping and rope. A bag containing a billycan, a tin plate, a kitchen knife, wire fork, spoon and a tin bowl. Another bag filled with bread, mealie meal, tins of sardines, corned beef, condensed milk, and small packets of coffee and sugar – almost all of which were presents from Madam. Also hung on the back rail was the hurricane lamp and two metal cans, one with paraffin for the lamp, the other filled with axle grease.

Including Koko, Philemon's costs so far were five pounds, seventeen and ninepence. A major item had been the cost of new trousers he had bought for Nathan in recognition of his invaluable assistance. Titus had given him a sheath knife.

The departure from Magalies View soon after six o'clock that evening went well. Baas Andrews and Madam were there with the Boulters, their nearest neighbours. The white people stood on the oval lawn outside the front door of the main house, while the servants and their friends lined the drive. Lead in hand, ahead of Koko harnessed between the shafts, stood Philemon. Nathan, wearing the new trousers and a red band round his forehead, brought up the rear.

Baas Andrews made a brief speech, congratulating Philemon on his skill and enterprise in building *lo bongolo ngola* – the donkey wagon – and wishing him and Koko a successful journey. The onlookers clapped, there were shouts of '*Hamba gahle*' – go well – Philemon saluted the Andrews', pulled on Koko's lead with a '*Tina hamba*' – we go – which Koko evidently did not understand for he made no effort to move, swishing his tail and tossing his head to dislodge flies. Nathan at once ran forward, put his shoulder against Koko's buttock and shoved. Koko turned his head, looked at Nathan with what seemed mild surprise, before breaking into a slow walk, the tank rumbling and groaning after him. There were renewed cheers from the onlookers who fell in behind the tank and followed it down the drive. The happy cortège passed through the gates and set off down the dirt road. They had not gone far when a group of piccanins emerged from a clump of thorn bushes in the veld below Magalies View and took station ahead of the procession. Prancing, clapping and whistling to the strains of penny whistles and cow-hide drums they stayed with Philemon and the tank until they reached the Witkoppen road, by which time members of the original cortège had left to go home.

It had been a fine occasion, decided Philemon. One which had given him great pleasure and renewed confidence in his ability to succeed in the difficult task ahead.

Soon after eleven o'clock that night he decided that it was time to outspan and rest. They had followed the road to the north by way of Leeukop and Kyalami and were now passing through sparsely populated highveld where there was little to be seen other than the distant flicker of lights from smallholdings, many of them well back from the road. The journey had been comparatively trouble free.

Darkness had fallen not long after sunset when he'd lit the hurricane lamp and hung it from the pole which stood mast-like at the front of the frame, not far from Koko's tail. The traffic had been light, mostly cars, sometimes a wagon or cyclist. A number of cars had hooted, some drivers had shouted, why and about what he'd no idea, and an African cyclist had stopped to ask him where he was taking the donkey-roller. Twice in the last hour or so Koko had shown signs of tiring. On each of them Philemon had stopped, given him water and handsful of sliced carrots and a rest of ten minutes or so. When eventually Philemon decided that they'd had enough he led Koko into a roadside clearing and there, under a clump of blue gums, unharnessed and tethered him to the trunk of a nearby tree. He watered him from the tin bowl and gave him the nosebag well filled with oats.

It was a dark night with a clouded sky which shut out the moon and the stars, while a chilling wind from the southeast made it colder than Philemon had expected. He feared it might rain if the wind dropped and the temperature rose.

Using a fireplace of large stones left by previous travellers, and dried twigs and branches from the trees and bushes round the clearing, he lit a fire, made coffee and had a meal of bread and sardines. Afterwards, sitting on his haunches beside the glowing embers, he thought of many things. First, of Koko for whom he had a growing affection. The donkey was old but big and strong and, unlike some donkeys, willing. Next, his thoughts turned to the tank. It made more noise than he'd expected – a rumbling, groaning, squealing noise, as if there were pigs and goats in it being taken to market. On the down-slopes – they'd not been too steep – the simple wooden lever on the front of the frame acted as a brake when he pulled it forward so that the other end pressed against the tank. On the up-slopes, near Leeukop one had been steep, he'd used the harness he'd made for himself: a breastplate of canvas from which two lengths of rope led to the shaft ends, the breastplate held in place by an apron-like loop which Philemon slipped over his head. Even with the pull of his twelve stone added to Koko's rather greater one, the steep slope had been hard work. The only mechanical problem had been a loose hose end. With light from the hurricane lamp and wire and pliers he had soon dealt with this.

Philemon's thoughts moved on from the present to the future, to the kraal in the Loskop district where not only his family but Sozana would be waiting for him. He hoped to be there in seven or eight days' time if all went well. Sozana and her family would think well of him for making such a difficult journey and for bringing such fine gifts. In time, when he had enough cattle of his own to give to Sozana's father as *lobola* for his daughter's hand in marriage, he would stop working for the white people. He and Sozana would make a life of their own with children and cattle, some poultry and cash crops at the Ndebeli kraal. That was where he belonged and that was the life he wished to live, the life that his forebears had lived before the white people had come and made things difficult.

The smell of wood smoke, the warmth from the glowing embers, had made him drowsy and he was ready for sleep. He stood up and listened for a moment to the night sounds of the veld, the click-click of crickets, the croaking of frogs in a nearby culvert, the constant *kie-weeet* of plovers, and the distant barking of a dog coming down on the wind like the staccato plucking of a banjo.

After checking that all was well with Koko he took a small roll of canvas from the top of the frame, unfolded it on the ground beside the tank, laid the old overcoat over it, wrapped himself in the colourful Basuto blanket and laid himself down to sleep, the jersey Madam had given him his pillow.

It was not the sunrise that woke him next morning but a plaintive neighing by Koko. He jumped up, went to the donkey and found the tether wound round his legs.

'You are strong donkey, Koko, but not clever,' he admonished him. 'Tonight I make the rope not so long. Now I think you like breakfast, is right?' Having given him water and the nosebag of oats, Philemon gathered more tinder for the fire, lit it and set about preparing his breakfast of *putu* and strong coffee. That done he put away the canvas groundsheet, the blanket and overcoat, and harnessed Koko for the day's journey. Before leaving the clearing he doused the fire with handfuls of soil.

Taking Koko's lead he said, 'Come on, old donkey, *tina hamba* – we go,' and they rumbled out of the clearing onto the road. He knew from the map Nathan had made for him, with place names in large block letters, that he must go past Halfway House, look for the signpost

OLIFANTSFONTEIN and follow it to the right. That meant crossing the busy Jo'burg-Pretoria road which he expected to reach before noon. He had no watch but, like most kraal dwellers, he got a fair idea of the time from the sun and moon and the behaviour of animals.

It was too early for traffic on the Jo'burg-Pretoria road and though he had to travel a short distance along it before he came to the Olifantsfontein sign there were no problems.

Travelling now on a minor country road, his confidence returned. 'Is good, Koko, on small road.' He patted the donkey's neck. 'We outspan just now and make rest, okay?' But he had spoken too soon. Not long after they'd rounded a bend lined with long grass, acacias and *withaak* thorn bushes, Philemon heard behind him the deep-throated and unmistakable rumble of a Harley-Davidson motorcycle, standard equipment of the Provincial traffic police. He turned as it came round the bend in a cloud of red dust and bore down upon them like some fearsome predator before overtaking and coming to a stop a short distance ahead. A very large man in uniform, a khaki shirt with sergeant's stripes, riding-breeches, peaked cap and highly polished leggings, dismounted and came towards them. He wore dark glasses over a sun-reddened face, the principal features of which were a walrus moustache and a heavy jowl. For Philemon, the black handle of a large calibre revolver poking out of the leather holster hanging at the sergeant's side completed this fearsome picture of the law.

The sergeant walked past Philemon and the donkey in silence, then round the tank, examining the paraphernalia hanging from the frame. He took off his cap and scratched his head before taking a good look through the tank's manhole. Putting on his cap he turned back to Philemon.

'Your passbook,' he demanded in a voice as big and deep as himself. Philemon produced it, the sergeant examined it, returned it to him. 'Now my boy,' he said, 'what are you doing on a public highway with this tank and the donkey?' He spoke in Afrikaans, a language with which Philemon was barely familiar, his life having been spent at the kraal but for the time working in Johannesburg.

Speaking English, a nervous Philemon explained, produced Baas

Andrews' letter and James Gollop's, the latter, typed on the letterhead of Corker, Brunson & Chad, looking authoritative and official.

The sergeant again took off his cap and scratched his head. He looked at the letters, then at Philemon. Replacing his cap he spent some time reading the letters before handing them back. 'You kaffirs.' He shook his head severely. 'The things you get up to. Man, I just can't believe it. Bladdy old water tank pulled by bladdy old donkey on a public bladdy road. And you get your *rooinek* baas and his *rooinek* lawyers to give you these bladdy letters. I mean, what's the good of bladdy road laws if you kaffirs can bugger them up like this? *Allemagtig! Ek weet nie.*' He took off the dark sunglasses and with a khaki handkerchief wiped pools of perspiration from beneath his eyes. Philemon saw then that instead of the anger he had expected to see in them there was something more like amusement.

'Okay, my boy. So now you can go.' The sergeant replaced the sunglasses. 'But *pas op* – look out. If you make trouble for the traffic, you'll make plenty bladdy trouble for yourself. Understand?'

'Yes, my Baas. Thank you, sir.'

The sergeant went back to his Harley-Davidson, the engine came to life with a throaty roar, and man and machine were soon lost to sight in a cloud of red dust.

'Is bes' luck for us,' Philemon confided to Koko. 'Sergeant is big government man. Can make plenty trouble. But this one is good man, Koko. He know from letters we mus' be okay. So we go now. By an' by we come to good place. Then we make outspan an' you shall eat veld grass.'

The rest of the day was uneventful but for the now customary demonstrations of interest by other road users: much hooting and shouting, mostly good-natured, gestures of derision or appreciation – Philemon's limited knowledge of body language making it difficult to know which – and, when anywhere near native kraals, the inevitable retinue of joyous, prancing piccanins. On two occasions passing cars stopped ahead of him, people got out with cameras and took photographs – they were, they said, tourists from overseas – and, having questioned him about Koko, the tank and his journey, they tipped him, got into their cars and drove off.

Philemon showed Koko the two shining shillings which lay in the palm of his hand. 'You see, Koko, this is plenty money. This peoples make picture of you, also of tank. They will not stop to make picture of me. So this money is for you and tank. Now I give you carrot. Tank cannot eat so I say thank you tank.' Philemon took a carrot from the bag on the frame, gave it to the donkey, took its lead and they resumed their journey.

The country began to change as they got further away from the Witwatersrand. Now, rolling landscapes of maize rode the contours like green-striped seas from which rose *koppies* clothed in veld grass and thorn bush, their slopes strewn with great boulders, their summits sometimes crowned with granite outcrops which shimmered mirage-like in the summer sun.

That night they outspanned in a small clearing beside a railway line. All was well until soon after midnight when a thunderstorm burst upon them, rain, hail and lightning lashing the landscape with sudden fury, the noise of it drowning Philemon's, 'Will stop soon, Koko,' as he scrambled through the manhole into the tank where he remained curled up until the storm had passed. He found the tethered Koko calm and untroubled, munching veld grass.

But for the roar and clatter of an occasional train the rest of the night passed without incident.

As the days followed each other Philemon and Koko made steady progress to the northeast, passing through Kaalfontein, Bapsfontein, Rooikoppies and other *dorps*, crossing the main road from Pretoria to the Kruger Park at Bronkhorstspruit, then heading northeast again on the road which led through Vaalplaas and Verena to Loskop. Philemon had established a routine of sorts, averaging fifteen or so miles a day in two stages – one in the morning, beginning at about six and finishing between ten and eleven, another in late afternoon from five to ten or eleven at night. In the periods between, he and Koko fed and rested in that order, both remaining remarkably fit. It should not be thought, however, that all had gone smoothly: on the contrary there had been a number of incidents and problems. On one occasion an infuriated farmer on whose land he had outspanned in the belief that it belonged to the roads people, had threatened to *sjambok* him and shoot the donkey – Philemon had compounded his crime by lighting a fire, and the farmer, kicking it out in his rage, set his trouser ends alight. Philemon showed great presence of mind in dousing the flames with a water bag. But for this he might have been in the most serious trouble. Even so, the farmer made him pack up and leave that night, late though it was.

On another occasion he was involved in a frightening row with an overtaking motorist who all but ran into the tank from behind. Getting out of his car, he abused, pushed and finally struck Philemon, complaining that he should have had a proper red light at the back of the tank. Philemon protested, point out that there were two red reflectors there in addition to the all round light of the hurricane lamp. He ended with, 'Sorry, my Baas, but you can see tank show more light than ox wagon.'

That this was undeniably so seemed only to further inflame the white man. Aiming a kick which Philemon adroitly dodged, his attacker roared, 'I don't take cheek from any bloody kaffir.'

What might have been a dangerous situation was averted by the arrival of a car which stopped and from which stepped a large, bearded man who wanted to know what the trouble was. To Philemon's surprise his violent, abusive assailant became suddenly meek, treating the bearded man with exaggerated respect and launching into a rambling explanation which the newcomer interrupted with, 'You've been drinking again, Jannie. Get back into your car and sleep there until daylight.' The bearded man watched him go, after which he questioned Philemon about the tank, Koko and his destination. Philemon once again produced the letters, the bearded man read them in the light of the car's headlamps. Handing them back he said, 'Right, my boy, you can go now.' He hesitated, smiled. '*Hamba gahle.*'

Philemon, Koko and the tank rumbled off into the night, the twinkling hurricane lamp marking their passage. The bearded man went to the car where Philemon's assailant sat crumpled in the front seat. 'Listen, Jannie. You leave that young kaffir alone. You didn't see his light because you were drunk. Now get into the back seat and sleep it off, or you'll be appearing in my court again. And you won't get off so lightly next time. Understand?' Jannie's mumbling reply as he moved into the back seat, suggested that he did.

The bearded man got back into his car, started the engine and drove off. In no time he had passed the hurricane lamp, giving three short toots as he did so. Philemon waved, and when the dust had settled, he spoke to Koko.

'The one with beard is good man, Koko. The other is *skellum*, drink too much. But if I hit white man is very bad. I can be long time in jail. So I mus' do nothing, Koko, because I am black man. Can be better to be donkey sometimes.'

There had been another brush with authority. This time a policeman in a *dorp* who objected to the noise the tank was making. 'You get all the bladdy dogs barking while people try to sleep. This is no good, understand?' Philemon apologized, said he would put more grease on the axle and also make Koko travel more slowly. The policeman stayed for a moment, watched Philemon open the can and begin stuffing black grease into the tubular axle. Then he got onto his bike and pedalled away, grumbling about what the kaffirs would be up to next.

Philemon told Koko there was no doubt the tank had been making too much noise. He had delayed greasing the axle because it was a messy job and he wanted to get clear of the *dorp* first. When he had finished the task and got the tank moving again, he once more confided his thoughts to Koko. 'This policeman is good man. Not make trouble. He can see we are okay. Also he want to get home quick.'

Near Vaalplaas, where the road descended steeply, the slope had become too much for the split-pole brake. Philemon had quickly swung Koko and the tank round to face up the hill. He had then put two large stones under the tank on the downhill side, reversed Koko's position between the shafts so that the donkey was facing the tank, and reharnessed him. With the rope-bridle now round his hindquarters Koko's weight acted as an additional brake when they resumed the descent.

There had of course been mechanical troubles. Most common of these, the ends of hoses which served as tyres breaking loose and flapping alarmingly. Philemon would tie them back with baling-wire but it was a difficult time-consuming operation. Occasionally nuts on the shaft bolts would work loose and need tightening – eventually he bound the nuts to the bolts with baling-wire and this solved that problem. Most difficult was the heavy wire which anchored the axle assembly to the frame. In spite of the axle grease which he applied liberally, friction at the axle extremities cut into the wire which he had to replace, a task which took him the best part of two hours.

Water was another problem, the two water bags frequently needing replenishment. Sometimes he did this from streams under causeways, but more often by asking at the back door of *dorp* houses for permission to draw water from a garden tap – front doors were out of bounds to kaffirs.

By the afternoon of the seventh day Philemon was in familiar country, one in which he had spent the first eighteen years of his life, and this made him a very happy young man. The terrain, the rock-strewn hills and valleys, the winding country roads and farm tracks, the swathes of veld grass rippling in the wind as if at the command of some unseen drill sergeant; the mottled browns, whites and blacks of grazing cattle, challenging splashes of colour on the rural landscape; shiny cacti bearing prickly pears, sharing rocky outcrops with trailing bushes of wild figs, the fruits of both prized by the people of the kraal; an intensely blue sky strewn with cottonwool clouds floating like yachts on an azure sea; the smell of hot earth, of cow dung; the mauve ridges of distant mountains – these things stirred Philemon's senses, feeding his nostalgia for the country of his youth.

Earlier that day he had reached Susterstroom, a small *dorp* where he turned south, following a minor road which led eventually to the Wilge River. Some distance down it he turned north and travelled along a farm road. It ran along a ridge below which, on the eastern side, the Wilge River snaked its way down towards the great mine where the Cullinan diamond was found and where, over the years, many of Philemon's forebears had worked. On the western side of the ridge the high land fell away into a hollow between the hills not far from where Philemon outspanned for what would be their last night on the road.

He chose a small clearing on the Wilge River side, set among thorn bushes and wattle trees, and well off the road. Here he unharnessed Koko and as a special treat, a reward for the donkey's hard work, so soon to finish – Philemon hoped to reach the kraal towards noon the next day – he led him across the road and down the slope behind the ridge of rocks to a small stream fed by a spring where, years before, Philemon had bathed in its tingling cold waters on a steaming day in mid-summer. There he tethered Koko, tying the rope lead round the trunk of a cabbage tree, so the donkey could both stand in the stream and graze on the lush green grass along its banks.

'I come back for you, Koko, when I finish my *skaf.*' *Skaf* in this instance was *putu*, coffee, and the last tin of meat Mrs Andrews had given him.

Later, sitting by the embers of the fire on which he'd cooked his meal, Philemon sat thinking. Tomorrow was the great day, the homecoming after an absence of two years. He recalled with pride what he had achieved: the long journey from Magalies View, the difficulties he had overcome, the fine gifts he would be giving to his parents, the tank and Koko; the money in his pocket, savings from his work at the Andrews', the copper bangles for Sozana, the excitement of seeing her, his parents and friends again, the stories he would have to tell them.

It was a fine night, the moon riding high, the only sounds the mournful wail of jackals and nearer at hand the squeaky-pump cries of bush partridges, over it all the smell of woodsmoke. Crossing the road on his way to fetch Koko, he realized that it would soon be midnight – the final leg of the journey would begin at about six o'clock in the morning. Ahead of him the rim of the hill was marked by jagged rocks from which cacti grew, their large succulent leaves silhouetted against the skyline, standing upon each other like limbless acrobats. He made his way across the ridge, between the rocks and cacti, and stopped for a moment to look down on the stream below. There, bathed in moonlight, he saw Koko. The donkey was not only standing in the little stream but frolicking, splashing the silvery water with his head and forefeet while neighing with pleasure, pausing at times to munch at the moist grass overhanging the banks. Philemon watched in wonder for some moments before clapping his hands and breaking into loud laughter. 'You are strange donkey, Koko, but I like you too much,' he shouted, adding, 'You are hard worker and also clever.'

Leading Koko back over the ridge Philemon reflected upon his relationship with the donkey. During the course of their strange journey a companionship had grown up between them which was to the young man a very real one. As the journey progressed he felt increasingly that Koko understood what was said to him. Why, otherwise, did the donkey so often prick his ears and nod his head in apparent understanding when spoken to, or stamp a foot and throw his head when admonished?

Philemon was happy to think that though he was giving Koko to his father, they would continue to be together at the kraal. That was important to him in a way he could not really explain. Perhaps it was because he would be able to ensure that Koko was well looked after.

These thoughts were in his mind when they reached the clearing and he set about tethering the donkey to the foot of a bush which stood between the dying fire and the tank. Philemon had knelt to pass the rope halter round the stem of the thorn bush when Koko neighed loudly, jerked the rope out of his master's hand and moved violently backwards, his hindquarters striking the tank a massive blow which pushed it over the edge of the clearing onto the steep slope which ran down to the Wilge River. Astonished at Koko's behaviour which he attributed to an excess of high spirits brought on by the frolics in the stream and the full moon, Philemon failed to react in time to restrain the tank which had begun to roll down the steep slope. Instead he recovered Koko's lead and clung to it while he watched with growing horror as the tank gathered speed, crashing down the hillside, its twin shafts pointing skywards like speeding goal posts. In the moonlight every detail of its rampaging journey was only too visible as it crashed into and over rocks which littered the hillside, the sound of these impacts reverberating through the still night air like the beats of a giant metal drum, the tank shedding parts of its whole at each impact until there was soon no sign of the wooden frame, nor of the paraphernalia which had hung from it.

Watching with quickening heartbeats, Philemon saw that there was worse to come when, two-thirds of the way down the long slope, the tank struck a boulder which altered its course to the right, so bringing a lone farmhouse into its wild line of descent. Philemon froze with fear when the implications of this became apparent; as in a nightmare he saw himself being sentenced – to death if someone were killed, or to years in jail if they were not. But he was utterly powerless. The tank was now close on a mile away.

The only thing left to him was to pray to his ancestors that the worst might not happen, not that there was time for prayer, it was all happening rather too fast for that. But the very thought of his ancestors evidently did the trick for when the tank was within a short distance of the farmhouse it struck another, somewhat smaller, rock which deflected its lethal course. As it was it sped past the farmhouse, crashing through fencing into a small shed from which what looked like sheets of crumpled white and brown paper fluttered into the air. The tank, having presumably achieved its terminal velocity, continued down the slope until, with a spectacular bound, it crashed into the Wilge River which must instantly have invaded its now many apertures for it sank almost immediately, so far as Philemon could see, without a trace.

Working fast, he packed his overcoat, the Basuto blanket, canvas groundsheet and bag of cooking utensils, and tied them onto Koko's back. Having doused the fire and removed all traces of his stay, he left the clearing with Koko on the lead and set off along the track which would in time take them to the kraal.

He had not seen any lights go on in the farmhouse and wondered hopefully if the noise of the tank's descent had failed to wake its occupants. He doubted if there were any clues among the debris on the hillside which might incriminate him – the tank, fortunately had disappeared. The only things he possessed which gave his name and other details were his passbook and the two letters. These were stowed away safely in his back trouser pocket.

'This is very bad thing you have done,' he told Koko. 'The tank is finished, the hard work of Nathan and myself is for nothing, also the long journey we make. The tank smashes the farmer's fences and henhouse, also perhaps some hens. Now we have no rest after such long day. We must go fast to be very far from this place when the sun comes.' To mark his displeasure, Philemon spat into the veld grass. 'I am not pleased with you, Koko.'

The donkey shook its head, neighed defiantly; or was it pleasure in the knowledge that it could now walk free?

CONDUCT UNBECOMING

From the Barents Sea a long finger of dark water, the Kola Inlet, pierces Russia's Arctic coast; along the inlet lie the naval bases of Polyarnoe and Vaenga Bay, below them the port of Murmansk, the destination of the twenty-seven weather-beaten, snow-encrusted merchant ships which had formed the core of convoy RA 127 and which now steamed slowly down the Kola Inlet having shed their escorts. Though it was close to noon, they were no more than dim shapes in the brief twilight of what passed for morning in the Arctic winter.

But for two destroyers, a sloop and a frigate, which were still carrying out an antisubmarine sweep in the waters outside the entrance to the inlet, the remainder of the twenty-five strong escort force had entered and, after oiling from the tanker in Vaenga Bay, had gone to their assigned berths; the escort carrier and the cruiser to anchorages in the bay, the destroyers to the wooden jetties at Polyarnoe.

For a few days ships and their men would be rested in this Arctic outpost, enfolded in a gloomy synthesis of snow and ice, dark forbidding mountains, endless night and fearful cold. The voyage from Loch Ewe to the Kola Inlet had exacted its toll of men and ships. The weather had been appalling, and the action fierce in the later stages of the voyage when the convoy was attacked by enemy aircraft and submarines. The ships and their crews, tired and battered, were sorely in need of rest and recreation but Polyarnoe, with its lack of amenities, its bleak terrain scattered with cheerless, thrown-together structures of red brick and scattered wooden hutments, had little to offer. The men would kick a football about on snow-laden ice, there would be intership visits, small children wrapped in furs and looking like agile bears would come skiing down to the ships to wave and laugh and smile with the sailors who would throw them Mars bars, the daily *nutty ration* provided by a thoughtful Admiralty.

Among the destroyers lying alongside in Polyarnoe were several V&W escort destroyers, old stagers from the 1914–1918 war, among them HMS *Witherston*, a veteran of Russian convoys. Her captain, Lieutenant Commander H. H. Skape was a 'dugout', an officer on the retired list who had been called up for active service when war broke out. He had under his command a ship's company of close on two hundred men, many of whom had seen much action after several years of war.

Witherston was an unhappy ship and had become more so in recent times. Loyal to the ship and their shipmates, the crew in general did not discuss this but coteries of officers in the wardroom and men on the messdecks did, and it was evident from their mutterings that all was not well in *Witherston*. Those outside the coteries sensed this, suspected the reasons for it, but in the main believed that war-weariness and taut nerves had much to do with it.

To compound this, and hanging over the ship like a dark and menacing cloud, was the knowledge that the respite in Polyarnoe was brief, that the battle with the weather and the enemy would be joined again in a few days when a convoy of empty merchant ships would have to be escorted back to the Clyde. The gauntlets of the U-boat patrol lines outside the Kola Inlet, and between Bear Island and the North Cape, and enemy air attack and Arctic gales, would again have to be run. It could be more difficult this time than on the outward journey because the Germans now knew that British warships were in the Kola Inlet and would shortly put to sea with a homeward-bound convoy.

A game of darts was in progress in one corner of the wardroom, in another several officers, drinks in hand, had gathered round the Charley Noble, the ancient but efficient heater resplendent with highly polished copper chimney. Ian McPhee, the engineer officer, and

George Watts, the warrant gunner, were at the wardroom dining-table discussing some technical matter.

The officers round the Charley Noble had a number of things in common; they were in their early or mid-twenties, they were RNVR lieutenants though of different seniorities, and they had spent most of the war at sea.

They had something else in common, a dislike bordering on contempt for their Captain to whom, among themselves, they referred as 'Skape', rather than the more customary 'Old Man'. They were talking to each other in low voices, aware that John Lawson, the First Lieutenant, or Number One as he was known, was within earshot though busy with a darts match against Calthorpe, a midshipman.

The gloomy mutterings round the Charley Noble had become more explicit, grown louder. Clifford Bailey, the senior RNVR, remarked with some emphasis, 'I think he's mentally sick. Some sort of psychopath.'

'I'd say just plain mad,' came from Philip Martin, the navigating officer, a quiet, thoughtful young man with a scarred forehead and nervous, restless hands.

'I'm thinking you're all too kind,' said Brandon Evans in his Welsh singsong. 'In my book the man's a raving bloody lunatic. I mean that row on the bridge yesterday with the yeoman. It was unbelievable. Shouting and ranting at Rutter, and him quiet and dignified and in the right all the time. I wonder the man did not strike him.' The Welshman shook his head in disbelief before lighting a cigarette.

O'Donovan, the A/S officer, a large, muscular young man with a face old before its time, said, 'I would have and bugger the consequences.'

'It's easy enough to say that. But Harry Rutter isn't a call-up. He's regular navy and he has a wife and kids to worry about. He's not going to throw away all that it's taken to get to yeoman of signals because of an insulting, dugout shit like Skape.' O'Donovan looked across to the hatch to the wardroom pantry. 'Scarpio,' he called. The Maltese messman appeared in the wardroom moments later. The Irishman held out his glass. 'The other half, Scarpio, me boyo.' The rest of the group had the same idea and Scarpio went off with the empty glasses. The temporary silence which followed amplified the background noises which gave the ship life: the circulating pumps, ventilating fans, the generators and, from time to time, the shrill blast of a bosun's pipe followed by a routine order over the ship's broadcast.

'Now where were we?' O'Donovan's prominent eyebrows furrowed. 'Ah yes. The yeoman's problem. But of course Skape knows all that. Knows that Rutter has to take it. Like he *thinks* we have to take it. He's a vicious, cunning little bastard. Concentrates on finding fault, real or imaginary, then letting fly because he knows, or thinks he knows, that we have to take it. But he's wrong there, me boyos. I for one, don't intend to take it. I believe – '

'That will do, O'Donovan,' interrupted the First Lieutenant who had left the dartboard and was standing behind the armchair in which the Irishman was sitting.

The latter turned to face Lawson. 'What will do, Number One?'

'Criticism of the Captain, whatever one's private view, is not permissible in the wardroom. It is bad for discipline, is an act of disloyalty, and as such it is,' Lawson hesitated, 'conduct unbecoming.'

'Unbecoming what?' challenged Brandon Evans.

'An officer and a gentleman,' said the First Lieutenant defining his creed. A brief argument in low key followed, Bailey pointing out that the situation was going from bad to worse, that they could not take much more before breaking point was reached.

The First Lieutenant shook his head. 'I look to you as officers to ensure that there is no breaking point. Just grin and bear it, like the weather. And never forget that the Captain has much less sleep and is under far greater stress than any of us, however frightened, worried and tired we may be. At sea he leads a far more uncomfortable and lonely life than we do, lived out between the bridge and his sea-cabin, that wretched little dog-box with nothing but a red light too dim to read by. While we're at sea he's stuck in the same Arctic clothing – can't afford to take it off in case there's an action alarm or other emergency. Remember these things and make allowances.'

Tight-lipped and grim the First Lieutenant left the wardroom followed by Ian McPhee, the RNR engineer lieutenant, who had in a strong and resolute Glaswegian accent expressed support for Lawson's views. Shortly afterwards he was followed by the warrant gunner. 'Like a division in the House of Commons,' suggested Bailey, 'but with no surprises.'

Lawson's strictures had, however, put something of a damper on conversation about the Captain. Those gathered round the Charley Noble became unusually quiet and soon found reasons to go their separate ways. They had, nevertheless, agreed to meet in Bailey's cabin that night at eleven.

The afternoon, dark and little different from night, lay heavily upon Polyarnoe, the blackout imposed on ships and shore compounding the gloom. The frontline and enemy-held airfields in Finland were less than a hundred miles from the Kola Inlet. For *Witherston* the afternoon had been uneventful until, in its late stages, Kieran O'Donovan who was duty officer, was sent for by the Captain.

On arrival in the Captain's day-cabin he found the First Lieutenant already there. He knew Lawson well enough to sense that he was unhappy and embarrassed, and if this were not warning enough, Skape's face certainly was. It was a long, narrow face, deeply lined, with dark hooded eyes and the flattened nose of a professional boxer. To O'Donovan, who knew them well, the signals of suppressed fury were clear enough; the facial muscles flexing, the protruding blood vessels on either side of the forehead pulsing like stricken earthworms, the eyes averted and partially closed, the fingers of one hand tapping on the desk at which he sat.

'You are officer of the day, O'Donovan?'

'Yes, sir. I am.'

'I take it you've been on the iron deck at times?'

'Yes, sir, I have.'

'Have you seen the gangway sentry?'

'Yes, sir, I have.'

'Noticed anything odd about his uniform?' With that question Skape looked up for the first time, his eyes on the middle buttons of O'Donovan's reefer.

'No, sir. He's wearing a watchcoat and Arctic seaboots.'

'Anything odd about the watchcoat?' Skape's voice had risen to a higher pitch, the fingers to a faster tapping. Lawson, reading the symptoms, frowned, shifted his weight uneasily.

'Nothing in particular, sir.'

Skape sat bolt upright. 'Nothing in particular.' The noise that came from his throat was half shout, half squeak as if his voice had broken. 'His watchcoat is not only grubby and paint-stained but it is secured with a length of spunyarn round his waist. My standing orders stress that gangway sentries shall at all times be properly dressed, particularly in foreign ports.'

O'Donovan's expression had hardened. 'The outside temperature is well below freezing, sir. It is snowing and the wind is biting. I imagine the spunyarn is intended to tighten the watchcoat round his body and keep the wind out.' It was said with defiance. Lawson assumed that Skape realized this, for the expected explosion hadn't materialized. Instead the Captain stared at O'Donovan with the surprised expression of a newsreader whose script had been removed. His tone dropped to a lower key. 'You may have noticed, O'Donovan, that the Russian sentries on duty ashore – *communist* sentries – are smartly turned out though the battlefront is just over the Finnish border. They have precisely the same weather to cope with as our gangway sentries. Now, can you explain why a sentry on duty on the upper deck of a British warship should look dirty and scruffy?'

The young Irishman said nothing, looked straight ahead, his eyes on the bulkhead behind Skape.

'I thought you might not be able to answer that, O'Donovan. One doesn't expect much from the boglands of the unhappy isle, the playgrounds of your gun-happy Eire friends, and of course you *are* RNVR. But surely to God you could make some effort to behave like a naval officer. You really must try to – '

O'Donovan turned on his heel and walked out of the cabin, slamming the door behind him. Skape leapt to his feet, his face contorted with anger. 'Did you see that, Number One?' he shrilled, the hooded eyes blinking, an arm outstretched towards the door. 'He walked out while I was addressing him. Slammed the door. You saw that, didn't you?' he challenged.

'Yes, sir. I think your remarks about Ireland upset him.'

'What? Because I spoke the truth? Not a word of what I said was anything but the truth. Now was it?'

Lawson was silent. The Captain had gone too far. Even he now probably realized that he would be unable to take any disciplinary action against O'Donovan having spoken to him in such insulting fashion.

Skape began walking the length of the day-cabin. After a turn or two he stopped, spoke without looking at Lawson. 'I shall decide later what to do about that young man's insulting behaviour. Yes, I shall certainly do that.' He waved a dismissive hand in Lawson's direction. 'And now you may go, Number One. But don't forget what you have just witnessed.' There was a hoarse rattle in Skape's throat as if dice were being thrown there.

The First Lieutenant left the cabin.

Late that night the four RNVR officers met in Bailey's cabin in conspiratorial mood. Each brought a tumbler the purpose of which was apparent when O'Donovan arrived with a bottle of Irish malt whiskey. Though there had been no discussion on the point it was sensed that he was leader, the man to whom they should look for a solution to their problem. They had come from their cabins in the officers' flat in tiptoed silence, opening and closing doors with equal discretion. Bailey's cabin, though furthest from the closed door to Skape's quarters, was close enough to make silence imperative if the Captain, a notoriously light sleeper, was not to know about the meeting.

Having poured the malt whiskey, O'Donovan opened the proceedings with an account of his latest brush with the Captain. 'I walked out on the bastard. Couldn't take any more of his insults. I just wish he'd try some tough action against me. Arrest or confinement to my cabin pending his report to Captain D. But he daren't do anything like that with Number One having been a witness. So he's up a gum-tree.'

In the general, more or less whispered discussion which followed, examples of Skape's behaviour were cited: outbursts on the bridge, in the wardroom, stoppages of leave for petty misdemeanours, placing RNVR officers on a watch-on-watch basis – four hours on, four hours off – for such offences as failing to sight something before he did, allowing the ship to get out of station while investigating an asdic contact – as if it were possible not to – humiliating RNVR officers in front of the men, frequent and heavily sarcastic references to the unreliability of 'wavy-navy' officers. Brandon Evans reminded them of a recent outburst on the bridge when Skape had said, 'I suppose one shouldn't expect too much from clerks and sales assistants, but surely to God even those pin-headed occupations leave you with a smattering of common sense?'

Since the Captain was a 'dugout' who, after retiring as a lieutenant, had worked in the personnel department of a minor local authority, that sort of sarcasm was particularly resented.

With the second round of Irish whiskey the discussion livened up and moved on to the subject of what should be done about Skape's behaviour. It was agreed that whatever action was decided upon could no longer be delayed. Bailey explained: 'We've reached breaking point. The return journey begins in a few days' time. Then another ten or twelve days at sea, depending on the weather.' He paused, looked at the tired faces, studies of baffled concern in the feeble light of the cabin. In the sudden silence the squeak of circulating pumps and the whirr of generators grew larger. The slow footsteps of the gangway sentry on the deck above sounded like the muffled beat of a funeral drum. From somewhere in the distance came the faint sounds of gunfire. 'You know what sort of behaviour we can expect from Skape,' continued Bailey in a low, deep voice. 'What worries me rigid is that one of us is going to let go – clobber him, or tell him to get stuffed. It could well be you, Kieran. You've a . . . well, let's say a short fuse.' He smiled sadly. 'Though we've all been tempted to have a go. But I don't have to tell you what will happen if we do.'

O'Donovan drained his tumbler. 'That's why we've got to act now. Agree to do something decisive. To prevent anything like that happening.'

'Indeed, and it's easier said than done.' Brandon Evans stubbed out his third cigarette. 'But I agree that we can all be in some danger if the man goes over the top, so to speak.'

'Or into the drink,' said O'Donovan. 'Wouldn't give much for his chances if he was down on the iron deck on a dirty night. If a sea didn't take him there's a few on board who'd be happy to help the little bastard over the side.'

'Steady there.' Bailey shook his head in mock disapproval. 'Remember what Number One said about conduct unbecoming – '

There was a chorus of ' – an officer and a gentleman.'

'Holy Mother, what's that little shit Skape then?' O'Donovan ran a hand through a mop of unruly black hair. That and a hirsute chest had earned him the name Tarzan on the messdecks. He held up a hand. 'Wait a moment. Those words of mine hold the germ of an idea.'

'What words?' asked Martin quietly. 'Destroyer captains, including ours, don't go down to the iron deck at sea. They remain on the bridge or in the chartroom or their sea-cabins.' Martin blinked, ran a hand across his eyes.

'Right. But they do go down to the captain's heads to crap, don't they? Especially ours with his morbid concern and preoccupation with the state of his bowels. Unless there's an action alarm or some other sort of hassle he goes down to his heads soon after watches change at midnight. That takes him down two ladders to the iron deck, whatever the weather, on every, repeat *every*, night at sea. So, me boyos, we – '

'You can't be serious,' interrupted Bailey. 'About ditching him, I mean.'

'I bloody well am. Screaming gale, thundering seas, night as black as Africa – bang, slap, shove and into the drink topples our nasty, crazy friend. Unloved, unmourned I have to say, but not a soul the wiser.' O'Donovan's rhetoric was legend in the wardroom.

'That was a bit noisy, Kieran.' Bailey's hands signalled diminuendo. 'Keep your voice down.'

In a high-pitched, low-key whisper Brandon Evans hissed, 'You're daft, Kieran. Why, man, that's murder, it is. We'd never get away with it, I'd say.'

There were murmurs of support for the Welshman. The last of the Irish malt was poured, Bailey accepted a cigarette from Evans who was lighting his fourth or fifth and the discussion continued in a low key but without any sort of practical solution to their problem. Tired, worried and disconsolate, they were about to call it a day when O'Donovan once more took the stage.

'Look,' he said, 'I've an idea I want to work on. Just give me a little time. I reckon that what I have in mind can be made foolproof. Let me work on it.' He tapped his forehead. 'Tell you more same time tomorrow.'

'You won't, you know. We've got those Russian submariners coming to dinner tomorrow night. It'll be some party. Those boys don't go home early when there's gin and whisky around.' Bailey blew more smoke into the smoke-filled cabin.

Philip Martin complained, 'Do you people have to go on smoking?' He fanned at the smoke with a folded periodical. 'The smell in this cabin is appalling. Cigarette smoke, body odour and Irish whiskey. No wonder we can't think straight.'

Kieran O'Donovan hauled his big bulk upright. 'I can. Tell you more night after next.'

Clifford Bailey was straightening the crumpled quilt of his bunk where Martin and Evans had been sitting. Over his shoulder he said, 'We've only four days left before we sail.'

'I know,' replied O'Donovan. 'That's why you must give me a chance. If we don't get rid of this little sod pretty quick something really serious is going to happen. I for one will not take any more without losing my cool. In here, just talking about it, that may sound fanciful but up there, on the bridge,' he gestured with an extended thumb, 'in a screaming gale with that impossible little shit shouting insults at you, it's no way fanciful. If we hit him or tell him to get stuffed, KR&AI take over: court martial offences: insubordination in the face of the enemy, striking the Captain. Holy Jesus! There's a firing squad or a long jail term at the end of that lot. So why risk it if there's an alternative? A safe and easy one, the way I'm – '

He was interrupted by the sound of a door opening and shutting in the passageway, followed by footsteps, a ragged cough and the faint clanging of steel. Bailey held a finger to his lips. Moments later he said, 'Okay, relax. It was the gunner going up for something. I'd know that cough anywhere.'

Before leaving the cabin they had agreed on the need for absolute secrecy, and the futility of asking Number One to come in on whatever course was decided upon. They all liked and respected him but they decided it was safer to keep things to themselves. Apart from John Lawson's known views on discipline he was RN, a career officer, as was George Watts, the warrant gunner. Ian McPhee, the engineer officer, a cautious, highly conservative Scot, was RNR and a good deal older than the RNVRs.

'Can't expect any of them to get involved,' said Bailey. 'All right for us. Our careers are in civvy street. If things go on at the present rate, and Skape continues with his bullying and insulting some of us won't have careers anywhere.' On this sober note the meeting broke up and they went off to their cabins.

On the following night seven Russian officers from the Polyarnoe submarine base were piped aboard and greeted at the gangway by the First Lieutenant and Clifford Bailey who led them down to the wardroom where they were seen to be pink-faced and fair-haired, but for a small thickset lieutenant whose features were oriental. One of them, Ivan Ivanovitch, large, cheerful and deep of voice, had a smattering of English, but none of *Witherston*'s officers spoke Russian. Despite this the party soon got into its stride, Scarpio's generous tots of gin and whisky breaking down barriers. His attempts to communicate with the Russians in debased Italian caused some amusement but evoked little comprehension.

Dinner was a splendid success, the Russians repeatedly praising the food and wine with extravagant gestures and fine-sounding phrases. Ivan Ivanovitch repeatedly fell back on *excellentissimo* which he correctly assumed his hosts would understand. Dinner concluded with a speech of thanks by the senior Russian officer, to which John Lawson replied. Though they understood not a word, *Witherston*'s officers applauded the Russian speech, the Russians returning the compliment with enthusiasm when Lawson spoke.

The serious business of dinner completed, the party moved to the starboard side of the wardroom where the Russians were introduced to 'evolutions', a series of rumbustious games such as Priests of the Parish, Pass the Body and several more. Since these were strenuous and many of the participants unlikely at that stage to have impressed a traffic officer, the proceedings were noisy, cheers, shouts and uproarious laughter the order of the night. Skape had given permission for the party, and as there were two water-tight bulkheads between his cabin and the wardroom he was well insulated from the noise. Such wardroom parties, cheerful and boisterous, were a time-honoured tradition in the Royal Navy – in wartime, for evident reasons, they tended to be a little more cheerful and boisterous.

The 'evolutions' were in full swing when Scarpio, grave faced, came up to the First Lieutenant. 'Message from the Captain, sir,' he said in a low voice. 'Wants to see you in his cabin immediately.'

Lawson knocked on the door, heard Skape's, 'Come', and entered the cabin to find the Captain pacing it. He was still wearing a snow-flecked duffle coat, the hood thrown back. He was a gaunt man of less than average height and when talking to Lawson, a tall man, he would raise himself on his heels. When angry, as he now was, he forgot that ploy and instead glared at a point some inches below Lawson's chin. 'Break up that wardroom party, Number One,' his voice quivered with emotion. 'And get those bloody communists off my ship.'

The First Lieutenant could scarcely believe what he had heard. 'May I ask why, sir?'

'You will hear why shortly. In the meantime carry out my orders. As soon as your *guests* have gone you are to muster the RNVR officers on the quarterdeck. Report to me when that has been done.'

'What am I to tell our guests, sir?'

'Say there's an emergency. Anything you like but get them off my ship.'

'You said the RNVR officers are to muster, sir. *All* our officers are entertaining the Russians.'

Skape glared at the top buttons of the First Lieutenant's reefer. 'You heard my orders. Get on with them.'

The First Lieutenant turned on his heel and left the cabin, his face grim with anger. He recalled the Captain's snow-flecked duffle coat. He'd obviously been snooping on and around the quarterdeck, listening in through ventilators and otherwise to what was going on in the wardroom. Lawson wondered if Skape was not, as Clifford Bailey had recently suggested, a psychopath.

Back in the wardroom Lawson took the engineer officer aside and told him briefly what had happened. 'I have to make a credible excuse', he said. 'So act out the part, Chiefy.' Lawson then called for silence. 'I am extremely sorry, gentlemen, but there is an emergency. We have been ordered to land all guests and prepare for sea.' The engineer officer hurried out of the wardroom muttering, 'I'll have to see about steam,' while Bailey tried to explain to Ivan Ivanovitch what the First Lieutenant had said. The message got through eventually, Ivan addressed his comrades, there were cries of dismay, heads were shaken, thumbs-up signs given, glasses drained, and the Russians, escorted by Lawson and Bailey, went on deck, shook hands with their hosts and stepped down the gangway. Snow was falling heavily as they crunched off into the bitter night singing – as only Russians can – a rousing Cossack song.

Shortly afterwards Lawson reported to the Captain that the RNVR officers were mustered on the quarterdeck. Skape, his face moist with perspiration, was already in his duffle coat despite the heat given out by the steam radiators in the day-cabin.

He and Lawson had gone down the passageway, climbed the steel ladder to the lobby, and were about to step out onto the iron deck, when three piercing blasts sounded almost on top of them. Skape jumped, squeaked, 'God, what was that?'

'Destroyer going astern, sir. *Voracious*. She's come in from a sweep over the Skolpen Bank. I think you must have seen the recall signal this afternoon, sir.' Skape grunted.

They left the lobby and stepped out into the dark, wintry night, the snow crunching under their feet, Skape leading. He stopped. 'Where are they?' He coughed bronchially.

'Just forward of the screen, sir. There's a muffled deck-light there.'

Skape peered at the four shapes lined up in front of the screen. Silhouetted by the feeble glow of the deck-light behind them, it was not possible to see their faces. 'I thought I had made it clear to you,' he paused, 'to you *gentlemen* . . . ' a longer pause, this time for the roar of aircraft passing overhead. When they'd gone, he continued, '. . . made it clear a long time ago that as naval officers you are well below par. That I attributed to skimped training and limited experience. In the light of your conduct tonight I must amend that judgement because you have shown yourselves to be a bunch of drunken, brawling louts.' With his hands plunged into the pockets of his duffle coat, Skape swayed slightly as he spoke, the dim glow of the deck-light making a cartoon of the deeply furrowed face with its sunken, pouched eyes and flattened nose. 'What do you think your Russian *friends* think of you? More important, what d'you think *my* ship's company think of you – the sailors on the messdecks, the petty officers in their mess? They will get blow-by-blow accounts from the wardroom stewards. Personally, I'm thoroughly ashamed of you. When I gave permission for you to entertain Russian naval officers – communists – in *my* ship, I presumed you would behave like officers and gentlemen, that your behaviour would conform to the high standards of the Royal Navy. You have done neither of those things.'

As senior RNVR officer, Bailey tried to explain. 'The party was no different from any of the wardroom parties we've had in the past in this ship, or any other destroyer parties we've been to here or on the Clyde, or in Derry or St John's. And all our officers took part, not just the RNVRs, sir.'

A deep voice, O'Donovan's, broke in. 'The Russians are our allies, sir. Not our enemies. They are fighting with us, not . . . '

Skape's face puckered with fury. 'Don't any of you people bloody well dare to talk to me like that.' His voice had risen to a near scream. 'Keep your mouths shut or I'll have you put under arrest for insubordination.' He must have realized that he had, perhaps, gone too far for his tone changed, became mildly conciliatory. 'As it is I intend to do no more than stop your leave when we get back to the Clyde. But there will be no more wardroom parties, Number One, until such time as I decide otherwise.' Skape coughed noisily before stumping back over the snow-covered deck to the lobby.

Soon after the Captain's harangue the four RNVRs had gathered in the dark, stuffy atmosphere of Brandon Evans's cabin. Suffering still from rage and impotence at Skape's impossible behaviour, tired by the long day and their activities and imbibitions at the wardroom party, they were in a dangerous mood. The cabin's deck-head light was off, the only luminant the shielded bunk-light. O'Donovan was the last to come in. He threw his cap onto the bunk, addressed no one in particular. 'That's it. As far as I'm concerned that's enough. Skape's got to go.' The normally deep voice had become a loud whisper.

'Go where?' Philip Martin enquired.

'Over the side.'

'And how indeed will that happen?' Brandon Evans lit a cigarette and blew smoke into the already smoke-fouled atmosphere. His cabin had been chosen for the meeting because it was furthest from the Captain's.

'A combination of primeval darkness, gale-force winds and seas, Skape's habitual midnight crap, his arrival on the iron deck at the same moment as us and a giant sea, *Witherston*'s violent roll to starboard, poor brave Skape swept against the guardrail, our valiant but fruitless attempt to save him. Tragic, but Arctic gales can be like that. They are dangerous meteorological phenomena. Finally let me say that the method I'll be detailing to you tomorrow night is safe – *dead* safe.' O'Donovan grinned, ran a hand through his thick head of hair and yawned. 'God, I'm tired.'

'Who is *our*?' asked Clifford Bailey, leaning his back against the closed door.

'I'm one, one of you lot will be the other. That is, down on the iron deck. But we'll all four be involved one way or another since we're permanently lumbered with the first and middle watches. Skape's punitive measure, you'll recall. There's a certain poetic justice about that, I'd say.'

Unlike the gathering in Bailey's cabin the night before there were no rumbles of dissent, no sense of disapproval of the plan Kieran O'Donovan evidently had in mind. Instead there was in the brief silence which followed an unspoken sense of resolve, an iron acceptance of a way out, however drastic. These were young men under intense pressure, living in an unreal and dangerous milieu, accustomed to death and destruction, and old before their time. Driven by grim circumstance, they were determined to rid themselves in their own way of a bullying, domineering tyrant since naval discipline and the customs of the Royal Navy offered them no foreseeable relief from an intolerable situation.

Bailey went back to his cabin and, moments later, crossed the passageway to the First Lieutenant's. He found Lawson at his desk reading.

Bailey wasted no time. 'It just can't go on, Number One. Something's going to give. That behaviour is unforgivable. Breaking up the wardroom party, having us muster on deck – and why only the RNVRs? You and McPhee and the gunner and the midshipman were just as much involved in the party as we were. We've at least another fifteen days before we get back to the Clyde. Something will have to be done now. If it's not, the consequences can be bloody serious. Possibly for all of us.'

'Is that a threat?' Lawson put down the book he'd been reading.

'Of course not. It's a warning – and a cry for help.'

'I know he's become . . . well . . . difficult. He's got an obsession about RNVRs. Absolutely unjustified. Don't ask me why.' Lawson shook his head. 'Some incident, some time. I don't know. Something buried deep in his mind. But I'm not prepared to be a party to any conspiracy – nor to countenance one – against my commanding officer, however difficult he may be. When we get back to the Clyde I may be able to have a private word with Captain D. He's a very decent, understanding man.' The First Lieutenant ran a hand over his forehead, sighed deeply. 'I'm sure you appreciate that I can't throw away my career by reporting secretly and adversely on my commanding officer.'

Bailey laughed mirthlessly. 'Not even if he's a raging lunatic?'

'He isn't one. But he does make life difficult for some . . . ' Lawson shrugged his shoulders.

'For a lot of people, including the coxswain and the yeoman. This is an unhappy ship, Number One. You know that and you know why. Can't you reason with Skape? Point out that the situation is explosive? That things may happen which will be as damaging to him as to those who do them?'

'I don't know what you're driving at, what you have in mind. I am limited in what I can do. Not only by KR&AI,' he tapped the book he'd been reading, *Kings Regulations and Admiralty Instructions*, 'but by the

Customs of the Service. We are all limited by them.' The First Lieutenant looked very much more than his twenty-five years.

There was a momentary silence but for the crackling of the cabin's steam radiator and the distant sound of a ship's siren. Bailey looked puzzled, defeated. 'All I can tell you, Number One, is that there are some officers who are no longer prepared to take his behaviour. His effort tonight has brought matters to a head. The journey back to the Clyde begins in two or three days' time. You know what it's going to be like. Bloody awful weather, air and submarine attacks more than likely, everybody under exceptional pressure. We expect and accept that. But we're no longer prepared to be goaded, bullied and insulted, particularly in front of the men. Nor will we take any more vicious or stupid punishments, like putting us on a watch-and-watch basis, or this blanket stoppage of leave – for RNVR officers only – because we have a perfectly normal wardroom party. Skape's round the bend. He's become a dangerous man. Unless action is taken now, before we sail, something pretty grim can happen.'

The First Lieutenant directed a puzzled frown at Bailey. 'You are the senior RNVR officer on board. I look to you to see that nothing unpleasant does happen.'

'Unpleasant! For God's sake, Number One. This isn't a prep school outing.' Bailey shook his head and left the cabin. Lawson put his elbows on the desk and his face in his hands. He and Bailey had served together for more than a year; they liked and respected each other, but the problem confronting the First Lieutenant was beyond his experience. Other than waiting for an opportunity to discuss it with Captain D when they got back to the Clyde, he had no idea how to deal with it. But he was desperately worried.

As was his custom after rows with his officers, Skape did not appear in the wardroom next day for breakfast or lunch. Instead he took those meals in his large and comfortable day-cabin. At 0900 that morning he had sent for the First Lieutenant. Later, in the wardroom before lunch, Lawson gave no indication of what they had discussed though it was known he had been with the Captain for some time.

At noon the ship's motorboat was called alongside. Dimly seen in the half-light, the First Lieutenant, the warrant gunner who was duty officer, the coxswain and the chief boatswain's mate stood at the salute as the Captain was piped over the side. To the leading seaman who was coxswain of the motorboat, Skape gave the order, 'Flagship, starboard gangway, Bennet.' It was typical of Skape to have added the entirely superfluous 'starboard gangway'. The flagship, HMS *Launcher*, the escort carrier flying the flag of the Vice-Admiral commanding RA 127, was at anchor in Vaenga Bay. Commanding officers of HM ships always used the flagship's starboard gangway, a naval custom since the days of Nelson.

There was some curiosity in *Witherston*'s wardroom as to the purpose of Skape's visit to the flagship since no signal requesting his presence there had been received. It was, however, assumed that it was to attend a convoy conference for the return journey to the Clyde, possibly arranged at the Loch Ewe conference before RA 127 sailed for Murmansk. A conference for the return journey was unusual, most eventualities having been discussed at Loch Ewe.

At 1705 Ernest Kyle, the petty officer telegraphist, knocked on the open door of the First Lieutenant's cabin. 'Signal from *Launcher*, sir.' He passed the clipboard to Lawson who thought the eagerness in his manner suggested a message of unusual importance.

Headed, *To Witherston, repeat SBNO Polyarnoe, FOIC Greenock, from Launcher*, it read: *Lt Cdr HH Skape to Launcher for special duties stop Lt JR Lawson to assume temporary command Witherston TOO 1703.*

A few minutes later a messenger brought a letter to the First Lieutenant. 'Come by hand, sir. *Launcher*'s motorboat. Cox'n says he has to wait alongside for gear to take back to the flagship.' The letter addressed to Lawson and marked *Personal and Confidential*, was from the Vice-Admiral's chief staff officer. It confirmed the earlier signal and requested Lawson to have Lieutenant-Commander Skape's clothing and personal effects packed and placed in *Launcher*'s motorboat *with the utmost despatch*, which was naval parlance for 'and do it bloody quick'. The letter continued in more personal vein:

For your personal and confidential information I should add that our

Surgeon Commander reports that Lt-Com. Skape has suffered a severe neurological breakdown due to exceptional stress over a considerable period of time. He is urgently in need of rest and treatment and will be remaining in Launcher *for these purposes and for passage to the Clyde and subsequent hospitalization.*

Congratulations on your appointment to temporary command. I have every confidence that the experience will prove invaluable. Please destroy this letter and treat its contents as strictly confidential.

Yours sincerely,
Tom Webster

The First Lieutenant sighed deeply, tore the letter into small pieces and dropped them into the wastepaper basket. Poor devil, he thought, recalling events earlier that morning. Soon after breakfast a messenger had informed him that the Captain wished to see him immediately. Sensing that this was something to do with the events of the previous night, and uneasy about the form it might take, Lawson had gone to the day-cabin. There he had found Skape sitting at his desk, head and shoulders sprawled across it as if in a state of collapse. When Lawson coughed, Skape had looked up and the younger man had been shocked by what he saw; the Captain's habitual scowl had gone, the hooded eyes were bloodshot and his cheeks were wet with tears.

'My nerves have gone . . . gone to pieces, Number One.' The Captain's voice was broken, something between a croak and a gurgle. 'I can't take any more,' he sobbed. 'Nearly two years on these . . . it's too much . . . no one should have . . . be forced to suffer that.' The sobbing became more pronounced. 'Sleep's impossible . . . never get a hot meal up there . . . in that dreadful sea-cabin . . . gale after gale . . . bridge voice-pipe just above the pillow, six inches from my ear . . . it's never silent . . . never-ending reports . . . from the officers of the watch . . . and every other Tom, Dick and Harry . . . lookouts reporting . . . wheel and engine orders . . . chat on the bridge . . . in the wheel-house . . . asdic reports . . . those never-ending pings. I hear them all the time . . . all the time . . . they're driving me mad . . . red alerts . . . air attack . . . pings become echoes . . . classified submarine . . . rattlers sounding for action stations . . . ships blowing up in the night . . . always night . . . and those RNVR watchkeepers loose on the bridge . . . half-trained, half-baked louts . . . the ship's always in danger with them up there.'

Skape's sobbing, hysterical and seemingly endless tirade had then stopped for a moment. He had looked up, his face wet and twisted. 'They hate me, Number One . . . I know it, I can feel it . . . the whole setup's crazy . . . and it's driving me mad . . . I tell you, I can't stand it any longer, Number One . . . I just cannot.' Skape had begun to weep, all self-control gone.

Lawson, who'd listened patiently, had been deeply embarrassed. It had not been edifying to see the Captain, a man close to forty, reduced to an emotional wreck. He had not understood how a man could so lose control, but he'd realized that the best part of two years on Arctic convoys had imposed enormous strains upon Skape, a man whose unfortunate personality ensured the added burden of unpopularity.

'Stress affects all of us, sir,' he said, somewhat ambiguously. 'Too much of it can undermine the – the strongest nerves. I imagine that is what has happened to you.' Lawson felt that he might be exaggerating but he believed there was a good deal of truth in what he was saying. He had in mind, too, what Bailey had said to him the night before. Here, possibly, was an opportunity to do something, a way out of what had seemed an insoluble problem.

By the time he'd left the Captain's cabin he had convinced Skape that the most sensible thing he could do would be to go across to the flagship, see the Surgeon Commander, explain to him the situation. 'Say that after nearly two years of these convoys you are suffering from nervous exhaustion, that you simply cannot take any more. Not that you don't want to but that you cannot. That it's unfair to you, to the ship's company and to the ship.'

Lawson had expected a hostile reaction to that last bit, blurted out somewhat inadvertently, but Skape had just sat there sniffing, his head bowed.

'I'm sure', Lawson had continued, 'that you'll find him sympathetic and understanding, sir. He will give you a thorough check-up and report to the CSO. Between them they'll come to a sensible decision.'

He had paused then, uncertain how to finish. 'They will certainly see to it that you don't have to endure unnecessary suffering.'

When he'd arranged for Skape's possessions to be packed and transferred to *Launcher*'s motorboat, Lawson went back to his cabin. He sat down at the desk, covered his eyes with his hands and said a brief prayer of thanks to his God. He would not be telling Bailey or anyone else about the CSO's letter, nor about his conversation with Skape that morning. *Witherston*'s officers would already have seen the signal from the flagship.

The Vice-Admiral's chief staff officer could not have worded it more tactfully. Senior officers in the Royal Navy had a genius for doing the right thing – for caring for their own. What lay behind the signal was a very private matter.

There was a knock on the door and Kieran O'Donovan came in, a broad grin on his face. 'Captain, *sir.* The wardroom officers would be honoured indeed if you would join them for a drink.'